Books in this series:

The Dreamer ~ The Beginning (2016)

The Dreamer II ~ The Gathering (2017)

The Dreamer III ~ The People of the Wolves (2018)

The Dreamer IV ~ The Cave of Bones (2019)

The Dreamer V ~ The Blood-Red Skies (2020)

Much more to come!

Reader reviews from The Dreamer saga

The Dreamer- the Beginning is a captivating tale, giving a convincing and passionate voice to a young man from humankind's early history. It is well researched and based on scientific study, lending additional credence to a very creative story involving a time in our history that is very much shrouded in mystery and conjecture.~ N. I. Bourdeau

As an avid reader I am always excited to step out of the box and read something different, The Dreamer Series delivers! A delightful journey set during the last Ice Age brings to life a Neanderthal family; their lifestyle, daily struggles to survive, love and loss. The author delivers a story set in prehistoric times described so well, so vividly it leaves the reader wanting more! Write faster, we want more! Donna R. Fox

Fascinating saga of the times and life amid a Neanderthal family as seen from the perspective of a man with a special gift and a love of his family. It's just like being there; you become involved with their trials and joys. The dreams give you a glimpse of future dangers and events, leading you through an engrossing journey. ~ C. H. Beusee

This is not the usual type of book that I read but I was fascinated and could not put it down. The author did so much research that it felt like I was reading a true story of a family and how they lived during that time! I wish the author could write faster so I could get my hands on those next ones...keep them coming!~ L. B. Collins

This is a unique and interesting read. I couldn't put it down–almost missed my flight! ~ J. Simmons

Just like The Dreamer – The Beginning, once I started reading Dreamer II – The Gathering I could not put it down. It is so interesting with a great personal story line. And I love all the historical information. After reading the first two books of this series I cannot wait to get the third one! Keep it up! – Patti Stribling Lauer

I read this book and thoroughly enjoyed it...so exciting that you can't put it down. Kept me on the edge of my seat. Great writing. ~ J. Stuller

I've read the whole Clan of the Cave Bear series by Jean Auel, and I was bummed when it ended; you got the ancients going again in totally different happenings and people's! I will probably read all three again. Can't wait for book four! ~ John G. Smith

The Dreamer V

THE BLOOD-RED SKIES

The Dreamer Book Series

By E. A. Meigs

Dreamer Literary Productions, LLC

2020

For information regarding this novel or permissions to reproduction selections from this work, please visit

Dreamer Literary Productions at:

www.dreamerliteraryproductions.com

ISBN: 978-1-7350558-1-7

 First Edition 

Cover photo by my friend Paula Krugerud

www.PaulaKrugerudPhotography.com

I dedicate this book to my father

with love and gatitude

The Dreamer V

THE

BLOOD-RED SKIES

The Dreamer V ~ The Blood-Red Skies continues an ongoing saga that follows the life of a young Neanderthal man. The story takes place at a time in history when much of the world was experiencing brutal climatic changes and man's position within Nature's food chain was indeed perilous. *The Dreamer V* is written as a stand-alone novel, meaning it is not necessary to have read the preceding volumes to understand the plot. An updated version of the original Introduction is included for those who are new to this time period.

Introduction

This tale takes place approximately 40,000 BCE (Before Common Era), when the last Ice Age was well underway. At the peak of the Great Glacial Maximum, nearly one-third of the earth's surface was hidden beneath a thick layer of ice. A substantial percentage of the planet's moisture was frozen solid, causing the oceans to recede and coastlines to become greatly expanded. At that time the Eurasian landscape consisted of vast, wind-scoured tundra and small pockets of woodland populated by at least two groups of people: the Neanderthal and the Cro-Magnon. These populations probably coexisted in parts of Europe for only a relatively short period of time, geologically speaking. They lived a seasonally nomadic lifestyle; we can only guess at what their lives would have been like: their languages, their social behaviors, their spirituality.

Due to the passage of time and the impermanent nature of most materials they would have used in their day-to-day lives, there is little to tell us about their existence besides the tantalizing clues left by their remains, their tools, their art, their burials, and . . . their refuse.

Analyses of fossilized Neanderthal skeletons show that the males averaged five feet, five inches to five feet, six inches in height. The tallest Neanderthal men found to date were five feet, nine inches. The females were five feet to five feet, one inch. Their bones were about one-third stouter than ours. They were heavily muscled and had tremendous upper-body strength. The Neanderthal had the largest brain size of any known humans. Initial DNA testing showed that they likely had fair coloring: red to auburn hair, green or hazel eyes, and pale, probably freckled skin. Later genetic research on Neanderthal individuals found in different parts of Eurasia revealed that some had brown hair, brown eyes, and dusky skin. It is now considered likely that the Neanderthal had the same variety of skin tones, hair and eye coloring as do modern Eurasian people.

The Neanderthal roamed the earth for roughly 200,000 years before their trail went cold around 37,000 to 42,000 BCE. That said, the Neanderthal may have persisted to eke out a living for some time afterward. However, since most modern humans outside of sub-Saharan Africa share between one and four percent Neanderthal DNA, it would appear that the Neanderthal are still with us even now, albeit in diluted form.

The Cro-Magnon first appeared in the European fossil record around 42,000 to 47,000 BCE. They were named for the rock shelter in which they were discovered in the Dordogne Valley in France, in 1868. At one time, early anatomically modern humans in Europe were often referred to as Cro-Magnons, but that term has since fallen out of favor. However, since these novels take place almost entirely in ancient France, my Homo sapiens characters actually are Cro-Magnons.

Over a period of tens of thousands of years the predecessors of the Cro-Magnon migrated out of Africa, gradually making their way into Eurasia. The men averaged about five feet, nine inches in height, but it is thought that some taller individuals may have been upwards of six feet, five inches. Like the Neanderthal, their brains were also bigger than those of today's people. They are believed to have had dark coloring: dark brown to black hair, brown eyes, and tan or olive-toned skin. (Blond hair and blue eyes are a relatively new development in modern humans, having first appeared about 6,000 to 12,000 years ago, long after the pinnacle of the Ice Age, but possibly coinciding with the end of that last glacial period.)

* * *

It is my humble opinion that after so many years of existence in a world that often presented extreme challenges, these intelligent beings would have been at the top of their game in leveraging the available resources to ensure their own comfort and the continuation of their species. Some indications suggest that early man was potentially much more advanced than is generally credited, and it is my guess that we will continue to be surprised by what is revealed when ongoing and future anthropological studies peel back layers of time as we search for ourselves within the lives of our ancestors.

* * *

An animal index is presented at the end of this novel for the convenience of those unfamiliar with the animals of Ice Age Europe. It gives basic information about most of the creatures mentioned in this book. It might be useful to know, for example, that a wisent is a European bison, and that the animal to which North Americans refer as a moose is called an elk in Europe.

* * *

This is a work of fiction and it is not intended to hold up to scientific scrutiny. I merely seek to tell a story that is set amid this ancient backdrop. I have peopled it with those whose lives — when broken down to their most basic elements — would not have been so different from ours: sharing care and concern for loved ones, enduring all life's hardships, and reveling in serendipitous moments of love, beauty, and joy when they grace us with their presence.

Cave hyena

*(Read more about the Cave hyena in the
Author's Notes at the end of the book.)*

Chapter One

Howling fills the heavy air as though an unearthly beast has been loosed upon us. Swallowed by an ominous darkness, I am sightless in the pitch black and I feel a terror unlike anything I have ever known...

My mind muddled with sleep, I slowly came to realize that I was safe in bed. All the same, the horror of my Dream stayed with me for several moments. I snuggled closer to my mate, Morning Star, who dozed peacefully beside me. I was happy to see I had not disturbed her. She had given birth to our newest child only a little over two moons ago and now needed all the rest she could get. The baby was generally good-natured and not prone to undue fussing, but she had been born a tad early and thus required frequent feedings. Morning Star coped without complaint; in fact, we were both very pleased with our new daughter. Morning Star and I were delighted to see she was growing well in spite of the harsh season that had accompanied her arrival.

We were still deep in the throes of winter. This was made all the more apparent by a stray gust of wind as it found its way through all the defenses I had set up to thwart the cold. Every year I erected a windbreak outside the doorway of our earth-bermed home, and added several additional hide entryway coverings to keep out most of the drafts and drifting snow.

Just then, it seemed a storm was upon us. Fierce winds rustled the weighty doorway flaps and rushed down from the chimney hole, making the low flames in our fireplace dance and smoke. I knew I needed to arise to put wood on the fire, and also empty my bladder. I was not looking forward to leaving the warmth of our bed.

I wriggled out from under the fur blankets, careful not to awaken Morning Star. It took only a moment to poke the fire so as to concentrate the red coals in the center of the fireplace, before adding a few pieces of wood. Our dog Raena arose as well and followed my steps dutifully. Although naked and shivering, I then stopped to peer at my three children as they slept in their cubbyhole, well swaddled in thick pelts. First, our oldest, Fox, now a rambunctious, robust boy of two winters and some moons; then Pony, a daughter about eighteen moons old; and last, our new infant, Raven. They seemed contented, so I looked to making my way outdoors.

Raena saw me reach for my wisent-hide cloak and her tail began to wag in anticipation. She knew it meant I would be leaving the confines of our snug little home. While our dwelling kept us safe and warm, it could be rather crowded and restrictive, especially throughout the long winters, and Raena welcomed any opportunity to go out of doors.

I stuffed my feet into tall winter boots, which were pleasantly hot after having been hung near the fireplace last evening. As my toes found the inner extremity of the boot, they met with a foreign object. I extracted my foot and reached into the boot, there finding one of Fox's toys: a rattle in the shape of a bear cub's head that had been made for him by a friend from a visiting clan. The rattle's handle had long since snapped off, and now the object consisted of a cub's disembodied head. I placed the rattle to the side and once again stuck my foot into the boot. Not bothering to include the inner insulating layers of the boots or even to lash them to my lower legs, I simply wrapped my cloak around me and walked to the entryway, where I quickly parted the curtain and slipped into the windbreak, with Raena close at my heels.

As we exited the shaking structure, a shock of cold air struck immediately, causing me to involuntarily draw in my breath. Raena and I wasted no time in finding a spot to urinate as the biting, wind-driven snow found places where the cloak did not cover adequately and stung my flesh.

As I looked around, I saw only darkness. The storm hid the moon and stars. I found our doorway only by listening for the noise of the outer entryway hides flapping in the gale and following the sound home.

Still, even if the wind had not offered that auditory clue, I knew I needed only hang onto Raena to be guided in the right direction.

Once inside the windbreak, Raena and I shook to rid ourselves of the dustings of snow and I stamped my feet. Moments later, my boots rehung by the fire and cloak returned to its hook, I clambered back into bed and once again nestled up to my sleeping mate.

I heard Morning Star suddenly gasp.

"Tris!" she exclaimed quietly, careful not to rouse our children. "You must have gone outside! Your skin is freezing cold! And you still have snow in your hair and beard!"

"I did go outside. I am sorry to awaken you," I told her.

"Your feet are like ice!" Morning Star added, but she turned to me and wrapped her arms around me, rubbing the chilled flesh. "I do not know why you will not use the storage area at this time of year," she chided gently.

During the warmer seasons, we usually made the short trek to the far reaches of our family compound to relieve ourselves. This effectively marked our borders and had kept larger predators at bay for generations. But during the winter we kept an upturned skull of a large animal in the corner of a storage room, which Morning

Star — and the children, to the best of their ability — used at night and in inclement weather. The skull could be rinsed and reused or discarded in favor of a newer version, but it provided a serviceable receptacle for the purpose.

"Because I would fill up the skull's cavity too quickly, and then I would still need to go outside to empty it," I said. "Besides, it is so much more pleasant to come indoors and be warmed up in this way."

Morning Star giggled at my last words.

"I supposed that is true," she admitted.

Even in the dim light, Morning Star looked enchanting as the warm glow from the fire highlighted her lustrous skin. She peered seductively through stray tresses of dark hair. I kissed her long and deeply.

"Nothing could be as nice as this," I murmured to Morning Star.

"Indeed," Morning Star agreed, eagerly returning my kisses.

* * *

The new day dawned with sluggish gray skies, but mercifully, the storm had abated. A fire was now ablaze at the hearth, banishing all but the most persistent drafts. I had attempted to keep Fox in my lap in an effort to keep him out of Morning Star's way as she dealt with our two youngest children, but in a moment of inattention he had managed to break from my grasp. While Fox ran about with glee, Raena came to take his place.

"Good girl," I said to Raena, stroking her head as she tried to arrange her large furry body across my legs.

Just then, Morning Star's mother, Little Fawn, and her sister, Petal, ducked through our entryway, hallooing as they came in. Both of Morning Star's parents were exceedingly tall, as was her next youngest sister, Petal. Morning Star herself was actually quite petite, and she had to crane her neck as she looked up to greet her relatives.

"Pleasant day to you both," Morning Star said with a smile.

"A chilly but pleasant day," Little Fawn replied, looking at me quizzically, since it was not usual to cuddle a dog on your lap as you would a child. "Tris, you spoil that dog!"

Raena lifted her head at this, almost as though she had understood.

"I am sure I do spoil her," I answered. "But I depend on Raena for many things. She looks out for us and I do not doubt she would lay down her life for us. For that, I feel a little spoiling is in order."

Little Fawn shook her head, but she smiled at my lighthearted response.

"You have always doted upon dogs!"

Little Fawn and Petal were too tall to stand completely upright in our home, so they were soon seated, each holding one of our daughters and chatting with Morning Star. This was a typical morning for us. Our families lived on a small compound, hidden in a dense wood. My Puh, Tor, his new mate Ria, their son Mror, my youngest siblings, and great-grandmother all lived in one household, Morning Star's parents, Black

Wolf and Little Fawn, lived in another with her brothers and sisters, and my sister Ru and her mate, Bror, lived in yet another with their baby girl. The previous summer, Puh and Ria had also adopted two more people into their fold, a young woman named Aessa and a boy named Binty.

We resided only a short walk from one another, and each day Morning Star's mother, sometimes accompanied by Petal or one or two of her siblings, came up to see us. Usually, they did not stay long. I thought the visit was mostly to assure Little Fawn that all was well in her eldest daughter's home, and to spend some time with her only grandchildren. Little Fawn adored our babies; if she did not appear by late morning, I was sent out to be sure there had not been a mishap.

As I took in this domestic scene, I was ever grateful for my good fortune. Not so many years ago, Little Fawn had been actively trying to discourage any relationship between Morning Star and me. Not out of malevolence — I knew Little Fawn was genuinely fond of me — but because she did not believe we would be happy. Morning Star and I were of two different peoples. Morning Star's family came from one of The People from the East's tribes. They were a darkly good-looking folk of gracile build. My kin were Old Ones; we were generally somewhat shorter and stockier, and we were sometimes thought to be primitive compared with The People. And, in stark contrast, my clan tended to be red-haired and freckled. Mixed pairings were not unknown, but they were also not common. Little Fawn feared that we and any potential children from our union would be ostracized. She had had dreams of procuring for Morning Star an exceptional match. As a fellow parent, I can now empathize with wanting the best for one's children.

As luck would have it, however, fate intervened. Just when I had almost lost all hope we would ever be paired, I was visited by my first Dream. This fleeting vision showed that my Puh and uncle, then embarked on a hunting trip, were in grave danger. Morning Star's father, Black Wolf, was my Puh's closest friend, so I had spoken with him about going after them on a rescue mission. Black Wolf readily agreed. We had indeed managed to rescue my Puh, but much to our grief, we were too late to save my uncle. However, before we were through, Black Wolf found himself in mortal danger, and fortunately I was on hand to extricate him. Morning Star's father was profoundly grateful, and he then offered her to me. While Little Fawn was initially displeased, she soon came around to accept the match.

I continued to stroke Raena, absently listening to the conversation regarding Petal's future. Petal, now sixteen winters old and at the age when she would be expected to be paired, had not garnered much interest. I thought this was sad because Petal, although standing much taller than even the tallest of men — all but her father — and what could only be called exceedingly plain in appearance, was a good-hearted girl. She had a ready smile and she was as talented a homemaker as any man could wish for. The one man who had expressed a desire to be joined with her was an acquaintance of her father's. He was also well known to me, although I had not seen him in some years. His name was Fish Hawk, and I thought he would be considered a very good match for almost any woman. Fish Hawk was a congenial sort of fellow; tall, well made, a proficient hunter, and never one to shy from adventure. Petal seemed receptive to the idea despite the fact that she had never met the man, and that Fish Hawk was at least ten winters older than she.

"Tris," Morning Star started, "why do you not tell us about Fish Hawk? You have spent time with him, have you not?"

"Yes, I have," I replied. "He is a very fine man. Competent, but not too serious. He enjoys a good laugh."

"Da says he will go to the Village when the weather improves and bring Fish Hawk home to meet me," Petal said excitedly. "I have just turned sixteen winters old and I am still unpaired. I have been wondering if I would ever find a mate. . . . I do hope that Fish Hawk will not be disappointed when he finally sees me."

I hoped for Petal's sake that Fish Hawk would be charmed and impressed, as we all were.

"Only a great fool would not wish to have you in his home," I said to Petal, wanting to encourage her.

"Black Wolf has spoken of asking you and your Puh to accompany him to the Village," Little Fawn said. "Has he mentioned this to you yet?"

"He has on several occasions," I replied. "Of course, Puh and I will go with him whenever he decides to make the trek."

Little Fawn nodded and smiled. She and Black Wolf had coexisted in a state of perpetual discord for quite a few years now, but they were united in their desire to find a suitable mate for their daughter.

* * *

As it happened, the next day ushered in clear skies. Morning Star and I had expected that Black Wolf would come to collect me to begin this journey, and so he did. Like Little Fawn and Petal, Black Wolf was extraordinarily tall; in fact, he was much taller than his mate and daughter. He was a handsome man whose black hair and long beard were just beginning to show the first strands of white. Black Wolf had formerly prided himself on his thick, luxuriant mane, which he had worn in a series of stiff braids that stood out at odd angles from the sides of his head. However, last summer a severe head injury had required that his hair be shorn nearly to his scalp. Now, his bounteous crop had regrown to an awkward length, but nevertheless, it was good to see him looking a bit more like himself as he stood grinning and hunched over, with neck bent under ceilings so low that they barely cleared the top of my head.

"Your Puh is readying to leave as well," Black Wolf boomed cheerfully in his deep bass. "I hope to make the Village well before sundown. I am going to bring my snowshoes, but we should not need them. The snow will only be deep in the drifts, and we can wade through those."

I nodded in agreement as I savored the last few moments at home with my family. Morning Star helped me to put on my boots. She inserted the sole cutouts into the insulating fur liners, and then placed the liners into the outer boots. My feet were then seated into the now assembled footwear, and my leggings tucked into the boots before they were finally lashed to my lower legs.

"Many thanks, my sweet," I said to Morning Star, and I arose to put on an elk-skin tunic and then donned my coat. Last, I slipped a small water bag inside my coat, which was the only place where it would not freeze during our journey, and I stuck my arms through the straps of my pack.

As I finished dressing, Black Wolf knelt on the floor matting and turned his attention to my son, as Fox showed him a bird's skull he had found.

"That must have belonged to a crow," Black Wolf told Fox.

"A crow! *Caw! Caw! Caw!*" Fox sang out, flapping imaginary wings with great animation, his red-gold curls jouncing with each movement.

"That is right!" Black Wolf laughed heartily, "That is exactly the sound a crow makes!"

Pony, pretty, dainty, and black-haired like her mother, tottered up to Black Wolf, holding her arms out to him. Black Wolf obliged and he easily lifted her into his embrace.

"G'Puh!" Pony cried out, leaning forward to give her grandfather a somewhat slobbery toddler kiss.

"Yes, my darling little mite," Black Wolf began. "Have you come to give me a kiss goodbye? We will return in a few days with your future uncle! Are you ready to depart, Tris?"

"I am, as soon as I take my leave of my family and take up my spear," I answered, thinking that I would need to get outdoors very soon before I started to sweat under all that cumbersome clothing.

Black Wolf and I both took turns hugging and kissing the children and Morning Star, but I saved my beautiful mate for last. I held her tightly.

"I will miss you so," I said to Morning Star, kissing her face.

"I will miss you as well, but I am glad to know that you are only going to the Village and back," Morning Star responded. "Please take care on the trail! Keep your feet dry!"

"I will," I promised her. "You take care, too. I love you. My thoughts will be with you, always."

"And mine with you. I love you," Morning Star returned.

After one last kiss, I was ready to leave.

Raena was watching me intently, her wagging tail demonstrating her hopes of being invited to accompany us. But it was not to be. I caressed her head and ears as I passed her by on my way to the door.

"Stay," I said to her in a low but firm voice. She sat down. "Good girl, Raena."

* * *

Black Wolf and I walked down the hill to the center of the family compound.

"I welcome this opportunity to get out for a while," Black Wolf stated. "I was starting to feel as though I could not stand one more moment in my house!"

"It is good to see the sun and breathe fresh air," I acknowledged.

"Little Fawn has been somewhat easier to live with since I had a talk with her last fall, yet it is still not a pleasant situation," Black Wolf divulged with regret. "I have come to realize that I have treated her badly; she is a good woman and she deserved better from me. She has come to grudgingly accept that my heart now resides elsewhere, and in fact finds some comfort that at least my illicit relationship is with Willow . . . being that she is the Head Elder and all. But – *ack* – there is little I do that meets with her approval."

I could only listen helplessly and make sympathetic noises at the appropriate times. Monogamy was rare. Life was dangerous and fleeting, and although I was raised in a clan that valued faithfulness, most did not pass up a chance to lie with a potential lover. Black Wolf had embraced this notion wholeheartedly up until recently. It was only after his relationship with Little Fawn had soured that he finally found a woman who inspired in him a desire to be bound only to one person. He still lived with Little Fawn and their younger children out of a sense of obligation to take care of his family, but he and Little Fawn were now merely housemates who did not much like each other. On the other hand, his true love, Willow Woman, and their small son, Black Oak, were often living at a distant place, and thus Black Wolf was able to be with them for only short periods a few times a year. I did not know how he endured those long separations.

"Never mind my gloomy ramblings," Black Wolf said, changing the subject. "What a wonderful morning! When I first came up the hill to see you, the sun was still rising and the sky was a vivid red! I do not know if I have ever seen it to be such a bright hue." We had now reached Puh's home and Black Wolf called out to announce our arrival. "*Halloo! Halloo!*"

We then ducked under the flap that covered the entrance to the windbreak that Puh had built outside his dwelling, and made our way through the multiple flaps that helped to seal the inner compartments. As always, I was struck by the smallness of my boyhood home. The chambers that had seemed amply spacious when I lived in this place — and indeed were considerably larger than those of my own house — had somehow shrunken in the intervening years since I had stayed there.

The familiar sights and smells were still comforting, however, and I smiled to see my younger siblings as they gathered around us in greeting. All but my younger brother Ty, who at fifteen winters had attained manhood this past season. This meant that he was free to choose a mate, and I was amused to see that he and Aessa, the young woman who had been adopted into our family last year, were sitting, heads together, fully engrossed in conversation.

My youngest sister, Mi, approached me for hug. She was in her fourth winter, but she was a large child; rather tall, as our mother had been, and she also shared our Muh's dark red hair. As I held and snuggled Mi, her hands ruffled the reindeer fur exterior of my coat. It was quite soft, and I could imagine that it felt much like petting a dog.

"I like your coat, Tris," Mi told me in her clear, piping voice.

"Morning Star made a new coat for me this year. It is very nice, is it not?" I said to her.

Puh came to stand next to me, grinning at this exchange.

"My coat looks a little shabby in comparison," Puh observed.

"Just a bit weathered and battered, is all," Puh's mate, Ria, chimed in.

"Same as its owner," Black Wolf laughed.

As life-long friends, Puh and Black Wolf indulged in a lot of good-natured ribbing. But it was true that Puh had the look of a man who had endured a hard existence. He was of average height, powerfully built, and lean, and scarred. He and I owned the same light red hair and pale green eyes. In fact, I looked much like a younger version of my father, except that I, having inherited my height from Muh's kin, was at least half a head taller and slightly more robust in build.

Great Gran approached to get in a quick word with me before we left.

"What are your Dreams of late?" Gran asked. It was said that I had inherited my ability to Dream through her, and we sometimes discussed our visions.

"I had a very confusing Dream a few nights ago," I said quietly so as not to alarm the others. "It was dark and I could just hear unearthly sounds — almost like howling, but not like that from any animal I have ever heard."

Gran nodded gravely.

"That is quite odd. If the Dream returns I would like to hear of it." She paused a moment before continuing. "But you leave on a happy errand. I have high hopes that Fish Hawk will be pleased with Petal. She is a sweet girl and I would like to see her happy. I know she is eager to start her own family."

"Yes," Black Wolf said, having overheard Gran's last remark, "Petal yearns to start a new life with a mate, like her older sister — and her best friend, Ru, too."

Puh was now shouldering his pack and reaching for his spear.

"Let us take our leave and begin our trek," Puh said, but he smiled broadly at Black Wolf's words. He was quite pleased with my relationship with Morning Star and my sister Ru's pairing with Bror.

I was sweltering inside all my layers of clothing, so I was more than ready to leave. We quickly said our farewells, though Puh lingered an extra moment or two with Ria before we exited into the frigid morning air.

* * *

The previous night's strong winds had in some places scoured the ground bare of snow, and in others, piled it into deep drifts. The winds were now light, but the temperatures were quite cold. We trudged down the path with our hoods drawn up around our heads. Our hands were enveloped in thick mittens made of wisent calfskin, the woolly fur turned to the inside for extra warmth. I was grateful that this was to be a short journey. Sometimes our treks took us away from home for a half moon or more, and I hated to be away from my loved ones for so long. It was not only a matter of missing them, but I also worried for their safety.

"You two are very quiet this morning," Black Wolf observed, his words accompanied by foggy little clouds as his breath hit the icy air. "But then, it is rather cold for talking."

Puh and I nodded at this. It was late in the season: we were currently experiencing slightly moderating conditions, but we still considered it prudent to breathe only through the nose and keep conversation to a minimum. Nevertheless, this was by far the most pleasant weather we had seen in some moons. Spring was still a long way off, but I was encouraged to see the first sign of winter's abating.

The sun had not yet reached its pinnacle when we made a stop at what had been Black Wolf's former homestead. Just a few years ago, Little Fawn had asked Black Wolf to move the family closer to where Morning Star was living after she and I had been paired. Black

Wolf's old home was at about the halfway point to the Village, and it was a convenient place to rest. Black Wolf looked around the outside of the dwelling, noting the tracks of several sizable bears.

"They may have been awakened from their hibernation to go for a quick wander in this agreeable weather," Puh remarked.

"The tracks lead away from the entryway of the house. It would appear that my previous abode has new occupants," Black Wolf said. "Let us leave."

Although we were curious to see how the home had fared, none of us cared to meet with these bruins, which had evidentially decided that the structure built under a rock overhang made a handy retreat for the winter. We retraced our steps back to the main trail and recommenced our journey.

The sun was midway through its decline to the horizon when we reached the Village. Temperatures were falling sharply. We could smell the burning refuse that marked the location of the settlement, long before we saw it. I had not been here in nearly four years and I was shocked to see that it looked more dilapidated than ever. The log walls that surrounded its perimeter were falling down in some sections, and most of the houses seemed to be abandoned. I had heard that many of the Village's occupants had moved away, but I had not envisioned anything this dismal. As we walked by the Challenge Circle, an important landmark that was marked by the roughly circular enclosure built of mammoth tusks, I could see that many of the tusks had fallen from place and now lay on the ground. I had won my mate here. I was deeply saddened to see the site in such a state of disrepair.

Black Wolf led us to Fish Hawk's home, one of the few that looked to be reasonably well kept. It was small and its frame was made up of mammoth bones. Like the Challenge Circle, mammoth tusks were part of the foundation too. The outside was covered with many layers of animal hides to keep the weather out. Fish Hawk had recessed the floor into the ground almost to the permafrost and then placed various mattings and hides over the floor to create a comfortable place to live. A cheerful fire was alight at the hearth, and I could see that Fish Hawk's belongings were packed and neatly stowed near the entryway to the dwelling.

"Halloo, Fish Hawk," Black Wolf greeted him fondly.

"Black Wolf!" Fish Hawk responded, grasping him by the forearms in the traditional way of The People. "How good it is to see you! I am so glad you made it here safely!"

"I am glad to be here, as well! And so pleased to be on such a happy mission!" Black Wolf replied with enthusiasm.

Black Wolf then lowered the hood of his coat, exposing cropped hair that barely reached his ears. I could see that Fish Hawk was startled at the sight. Most men of The People had hair long enough to wear in braids, and we Old Ones, who have always believed that our hair gives us a heightened sensitivity to the world around us, never cut off any significant length. Short hair just was not seen. But Fish Hawk soon recovered and he turned to me.

"Tris! It has been too long since we last met! Take off your gear . . . settle down by the fire," he invited.

"Many thanks, Fish Hawk. Yes, it has been too long," I agreed, leaning my spear against a wall and beginning to take off my pack and coat.

"Tor, welcome!" Fish Hawk now greeted Puh the same as he had Black Wolf and me. "I hope you are hungry. I have some fresh venison; I managed to get out with a few other hunters yesterday morning and we brought down a deer. I am afraid this little doe was rather thin, but the meat will be a nice change from my dried stores."

"Many thanks, Fish Hawk. I am indeed hungry," Puh admitted. "Did you have to go far to find the deer?"

"Not too far," Fish Hawk began. "We have discovered that if we leave out some of last year's grain, the deer — which of course are starving by late winter — are drawn to it and will come much closer to the Village than they have in previous years."

"Clever!" Black Wolf exclaimed.

Fish Hawk now moved to the hearth, where one by one he turned spits of roasting meat. I then had a moment to observe that he had not changed much in the years since I had seen him. His hair was still as black as night and worn in two long braids at each ear, plus one longer braid that hung down his back to his waist. His beard was long and neat, but not nearly as intricately braided as many men of The People's beards were. He may have reached twenty-seven or twenty-eight winters at this time, but his skin was still relatively unlined except for a few laugh lines around his mouth and his dark, deep-set eyes.

"I am not much of a cook," Fish Hawk admitted. "My mate was quite a good cook, and she taught me a few things. I wish I had learned more. If only I had known. . . " Fish Hawk trailed off.

I had heard that Fish Hawk's mate, like my Muh, had perished during a miscarriage. Fish Hawk had lost his mate and their only child in one devastating event. It had taken him a long time to consider searching out a new pairing, and fortunately, right about at that time, Black Wolf had begun to inquire about prospective matches for Petal.

"You will be happy to know that Petal is an excellent cook," Black Wolf spoke up. "If you still wish to learn more, I am sure she would be pleased to teach you."

Fish Hawk smiled at this.

"I do hope she will like me. I hope she will not think I am too old," he said.

"Old? *Ack!* You are still a young man," Black Wolf assured him.

"You do me a great honor, Black Wolf, in considering me for your daughter," Fish Hawk went on. "I will do my best to be sure you will never regret it."

Black Wolf turned to Fish Hawk and smiled at him warmly.

"That is exactly why I give you this honor. Petal may not be the pretty, lissome mate that many men would desire, but she is pleasant and good-hearted, and there is no nubile young female who is more handy around the house," Black Wolf said.

Fish Hawk nodded eagerly in response. Puh, Black Wolf, and I sat with dripping beards as the heat from the fire and warmth of the room melted the frost on our whiskers. Fish Hawk suddenly looked our way and then bent to retrieve a stack of gourd cups.

"You must be thirsty after a long trek in the dry air," Fish Hawk said, offering us each a cup of water.

"Many thanks," I replied, accepting gratefully. We had only sipped sparingly at our water bags, and I was quite parched.

Black Wolf and Puh uttered their gratitude as well.

I thought Fish Hawk seemed a trifle anxious, and very eager to please his guests. I wondered if he was lonesome for company or simply trying to make a good impression on Black Wolf as a prospective mate for Petal. Or perhaps both.

"Tor, how goes it with you and Ria? I have not seen you since you were first paired," Fish Hawk said as he again adjusted the sizzling meat.

"We have been very well," Puh informed him. "We have a young son now." This was one of the few topics that Puh was often loquacious about, but I could see that he had abruptly ended his sentence. Puh knew the angst of losing a mate in childbirth, and I guessed he did not want to speak too much of his good fortune to one who had suffered such a grievous loss.

Fish Hawk's back was to us as he faced the fireplace, but he then turned toward us, smiling resolutely.

"That is good news," Fish Hawk said. "And you, Tris? You and Morning Star have been well, too? Any little ones running about?"

I almost wished he had not asked, as I felt also guilty about my comparative good fortune, but I felt obliged to answer.

"It is good of you to ask. Yes, we are most happy. We have three children: a son and two daughters."

"Has it been so long that you could have three offspring already?" Fish Hawk mused. "You are still a young man!"

"I turned twenty winters old this winter, but my Muh had always told me that I was born in the spring, so the twenty-first anniversary of my birth will happen in a few moons," I informed him. "But yes, the children did come quickly. The two eldest are just under a year apart in age."

"How interesting to know the season of your birth!" Fish Hawk said, seeming thoughtful. "My mother never told me when I was born. Like everyone else, we just measured our years by how many winters we had survived."

"Tris's mother, Awna, was a very exacting woman," Black Wolf said, laughing at his statement. "She was the most thorough housekeeper I have ever known. Everything was clean, nothing odiferous was allowed in the home, and the children were scrubbed daily. It is no surprise to me that she also kept track of the time of year when each of her children was born."

Puh's face bore a bittersweet expression. "She was an amazing woman. I do love Ria with all my being, but I miss Awna every day. After nearly twenty years of life together it is difficult to . . . well, they were happy times. And I most earnestly wish the same happiness for you, Fish Hawk."

"Thank you, Tor," Fish Hawk said appreciatively. "It is my hope as well."

The scent of roasting meat seemed to have traveled from my nose to my stomach, which now growled hungrily. The venison's juices occasionally dripped amongst the red-hot coals and sent tantalizing bursts of smoky aroma into the air.

"I am sure you soon will," Black Wolf said to Fish Hawk, interrupting my reverie as I anticipated our coming repast.

"And you, Black Wolf? How goes it with you?" Fish Hawk inquired.

"Not as well as I would like. I miss Willow and our boy, Black Oak, terribly," Black Wolf responded. "My other children, of course, keep me busy. My boys are thirteen and eleven now; old enough to want to accompany us on hunts, but – *ack* – they scarcely have the sense that resides in a rabbit. I am afraid that they will wound one of us instead of our prey."

"*Willow?* Willow Woman the Head Elder? You two have formed a real attachment, then?" Fish Hawk pursued. I could understand his surprise. Even Black Wolf had been somewhat cowed by Willow Woman when he had first met her. She was covered with tattoos, the first such decorations we had ever seen at that time. She was very tall for a woman — about my height — and she was probably equal to the weight of any two men. Willow Woman also had an intimidating presence. Her voice thundered like none I had ever heard before — except possibly Black Wolf's — and she owned a strikingly forceful personality. When she spoke, even the bravest of men — men who would fearlessly engage even the most dangerous prey — cowered like frightened children. But as time went by, we came to realize that despite her unusual outward appearance and manner, she was a wise ruler and a very kind and generous woman. Willow Woman and Black Wolf were deeply in love and completely devoted to each other.

"Ah, yes!" Black Wolf exclaimed. "A very happy attachment. She is a wonder. . . . I only wish we had more time together. I have not seen Willow and Oak since The People's annual Gathering last fall. My only comfort is that I know Willow's household staff and her healer are taking very good care of them."

"Ah. Was it a good Gathering? I have not been to one since the one we attended together several years ago," Fish Hawk said, shaking his head. "I spend all fall stocking my larder lately. Food has been scarce."

"Yes, it was quite good," Black Wolf replied. "That was where I heard that you were finally seeking to become paired again. You have waited a long while. How lucky that Petal came of age at just the right time."

"Very lucky," Fish Hawk agreed. "Hmmm, I do believe the meat is ready to eat."

Fish Hawk grabbed the spits of meat, handing one to each of us. The venison was still quite hot, but it was eagerly consumed. Our sup was accompanied by friendly chatter now and then, but mostly we simply concentrated on chewing the meat and the handfuls of dried stores that Fish Hawk offered to us. It was a thoroughly satisfying meal. This lulled us into a state of drowsiness.

I only became aware that I had fallen asleep when later I was awakened by Black Wolf's vociferous snorts, rattles, and rumbles. I opened my eyes to see that both Puh and Fish Hawk had cracked their eyelids as well. They were glancing at Black Wolf's contentedly sleeping form as he lay on his back, mouth slung open and issuing noises that would have given a charging bear pause. I thought that Fish Hawk appeared a little unsettled, and it occurred to me he might be hoping that Petal did not share her father's habit of snoring.

 **Chapter Two** 

It is hot. The sky is a brilliant blood-red, except near the horizon, where the color gradually dissolves into a deep, vibrant purple. Not a bird flutters by, not an insect's hum disturbs the lifeless air. It is as though a cataclysmic event has brought a deathly stillness to our world.

My Dream woke me from a sound sleep. Unlike the warmth I had felt during that startling vision, I was chilled through and through. The fire had died down to a few weak tongues of flame that lazily licked at the cold air. I roused myself and reached for the tinder Fish Hawk kept nearby, and then returned to the fireplace, where I carefully placed the slender sticks of wood in a loose tripod around the flames so as not to smother them. As the new fuel caught, I gradually added more wood until a healthy fire chased the chill air from Fish Hawk's little abode.

The others soon awoke as well. A quick check out the doorway flaps showed that a pale moon was still visible, hovering defiantly in the slowly brightening firmament. Meanwhile, off to the east, a scarlet sun had just appeared, creating a blazing pink band at the horizon.

"I think we will have good weather for our journey homeward," Black Wolf announced. "Fish Hawk, we can help you to pack your sled, if you would like."

"Thank you, but it will only take a moment," Fish Hawk said. "The leftovers from last night will be dry and chewy, but please help yourselves while I load up."

Fish Hawk took one of the now overcooked chunks of venison and began to gnaw it as he dressed. We all followed suit. It did not take long for Fish Hawk to place his belongings on the sled and lash them down securely: a few items of clothing, an assortment of tools, his large household water bag — which he emptied into the smaller bags we all carried, since the contents would otherwise freeze solid on the journey — a little dried food, his bedding, a collection of miscellaneous household things, his cloak, snowshoes, axe, and his extra spears. Men carry spears that are longer than they are tall in an effort to avoid being impaled on their own weapons should they lose their footing and fall; Fish Hawk was quite a bit taller than average, and his long spears hung awkwardly off the end of the sled, but there was not much to be done about that.

The sun was still low in the sky when we were ready to depart. Fish Hawk took a final lingering look at his dwelling.

"This has become a sad place for me," Fish Hawk mused aloud. "Both because my mate has passed, taking our child with her, and because the Village has become a mere shadow of what it once was. During my boyhood it was a cheerful, bustling place. Now I just see falling-down homes, piles of long-discarded refuse, and the few remaining inhabitants who are struggling to eke out a living."

"It is a forlorn site these days," Black Wolf agreed.

I wondered if Black Wolf would expound on the thought, but he did not. Black Wolf's cousin Eagle Owl had once lived here as well, a fact that unfortunately complicated his relationship with Fish Hawk. Eagle Owl was violently cut down at my pairing ceremony in a raid led by Fish Hawk's older brothers when they abducted Morning Star. Fish Hawk's eldest brother, Snow Leopard, had wished to have Morning Star for himself, and I had had to meet him in The People's Challenge Circle to win her. And win her I did. But Snow Leopard had not been satisfied to abide by the results of the Challenge Circle, and he and a band of cronies had decided to capture her at our pairing festivities. There, they had stayed in hiding until Puh and I left to show Black Wolf the home that Morning Star and I would soon occupy, which left Eagle Owl as the only adult male on the main compound.

It was then the men descended upon our families. Eagle Owl was mortally wounded as he tried to protect my new mate. Black Wolf had been devastated by the loss of his beloved cousin, but he did not blame Fish Hawk for the actions of his kin. When Fish Hawk had learned what had taken place he was appalled, and he had taken pains to seek us out to let us know that his allegiance was firmly rooted with Black Wolf. Fish Hawk also apologized to me for his brothers' behavior and — quite unusual for many men of The People who did not often socialize with Old Ones — said he hoped that he and I could be friends.

More than three years had passed since that time, but a telling moment of grief fleetingly crossed Black Wolf's face. Puh noted this as well.

"Come, old friend," Puh said as he touched Black Wolf's arm. "I think we are ready to make our way home, are we not?"

"I am quite ready," Fish Hawk said with a grin.

"Me, as well," I agreed.

"Yes, let us go then," Black Wolf said, smiling too. "We will be there in plenty of time to eat the evening meal with everyone."

* * *

Years ago, visitors and inhabitants of the Village were forced to come and go via one of its several gates. Nowadays, we were able to find the nearest exit through one of the many gaps in the shabby wall that surrounded the community. I was glad to leave this depressing place behind and to go home to my family.

The sky was gradually losing its rosy tones as the sun climbed higher. I thought today's weather seemed slightly warmer than the previous day's.

"Fish Hawk, let me assist you with your sled," I volunteered.

We generally used travois sleds, but Fish Hawk had altered his small sled so that the load was supported over a couple of branches that acted to help slide the load over the snowy trail. It was loaded to capacity and would soon become a tiresome burden.

"Thank you, but no," Fish Hawk said, determinedly pulling against the weight of his gear.

I edged my way closer and moved to take hold of one of the sled's handles.

"Let me help," I persisted gently. "We have a long walk ahead of us. If you drag this sled by yourself for the entire distance, you will be exhausted by the time you finally meet Petal."

Fish Hawk's eyes widened at the thought. He had already expressed concern about seeming old to her. I could guess that he wanted to appear as young and vigorous as possible to his soon-to-be mate.

"Thank you, Tris," Fish Hawk said with a start. "I had not thought of that."

Fish Hawk made room for me to join him at the head of the sled, where I adjusted my grip and began to pull in earnest. This also had the advantage of allowing us to move at a slightly faster pace.

We stopped late morning to rest briefly and consume a small amount of dried meat. After a few sips of water to wash it down, we recommenced our journey.

"Switch sides?" I suggested to Fish Hawk, indicating the sled.

"Yes," Fish Hawk readily agreed. "Good idea! My left shoulder was becoming sore."

Fish Hawk had a harness that was slung around his left shoulder and he had been pulling from his left side since I had joined him. We exchanged positions, but Fish Hawk still kept the harness, although now on his right shoulder, so that he still bore the brunt of the load, whereas I was simply pulling by hand.

As we approached Black Wolf's former home, I looked for signs of the bears. It did not take long to spot several sets of tracks coursing through the area. Just then Puh stopped walking and pointed to a large, torn-up, rotten log near the side of the path. Numerous bear tracks marked the spot, as did the pieces of log, part of which was still frozen to the ground while the other parts were ripped into sizable chunks. The sight demonstrated the immense power of the beast that had laid waste to the huge fallen tree trunk. We paused just long enough to note the bear's tufts of winter wool caught in the nearby brush, and to view the frozen slime left by the animal's maw as it had devoured the overwintering insects and larvae that had resided within the rotted wood.

"That could not have been much of a meal," Puh observed.

"Yes," Black Wolf chimed in. "I am sure the brute is still very hungry. Look at these tracks," Black Wolf said, pointing to the ground and placing his own very large foot next to one of the hind paw prints. "This must be an old boar bear. And look! His feet are as big as mine!"

"It is the claws that make them seem longer," Puh began with a smile. "Your feet are actually bigger."

Puh was teasing Black Wolf, but I could see that it was true. As enormous as the bear's tracks were, Black Wolf's feet were larger.

"Speaking of feet, mine are hurting me terribly," Black Wolf announced. "Let us continue our trek so we can get home and I can put them up by the fire."

"Is it the cold that bothers your feet?" Fish Hawk asked.

"No," Black Wolf replied. "Well, it does not help, but they just hurt most of the time."

Black Wolf was too polite to mention that this ailment had started back when Fish Hawk's brothers and their band of miscreants had taken Morning Star, and Puh, Black Wolf, and I had gone after them to rescue her. We had been forced to run for over a day to catch up with them, and Black Wolf's feet had never completely recovered.

"Yes, and it will not do to linger here, given that at least one hungry bear is roaming the area," Puh added.

"The bear is bound to be in a vile temper," Black Wolf said. "The warmer weather has roused him, but there is nothing much for him to eat yet. It is possible that as many as five moons have passed since he filled his stomach."

We had not gone far when suddenly Puh held up a mittened hand, stopping us in place. Just visible through the trees, we saw what had caught Puh's attention. A very large bear was shuffling around a spot just off the trail, often pawing at the snow as though to find sustenance under the crusty white coating. We immediately began to walk backward down the trail, Fish Hawk and I now pushing the sled instead of pulling it. We dare not take our eyes off the bear, except to quickly look behind us to be sure we would not trip over some obstacle. When we had retreated out of sight of the bear, we exchanged glances.

"Now what do we do?" Black Wolf said in frustration. "We are toting a veritable feast of dried foods between our packs and Fish Hawk's sled. That brute surely will not shy away from a potential meal, even if it means a rash attack on four men. We cannot afford to delay our trek."

"We can leave the pathway and walk around him," Puh suggested.

Our heads swiveled as we took in the tangled woodland surrounding the trail. It was obvious that Fish Hawk's sled could not be pulled through that landscape.

"We will have to carry Fish Hawk's sled," Black Wolf stated. "Come, let us each take a corner. We will need to make good time in order to still make it home before dark."

"Oh, but . . ." Fish Hawk started to object.

"Do not even think of leaving your belongings behind," Black Wolf told him. "It will not be so heavy if all of us carry it."

Black Wolf and Fish Hawk, although unequal in height, were the tallest of us, and they took up a corner at the back end of the sled. Puh and I toted the front of the vehicle. We were also unequal in height, so it was a bit awkward, what with each of us trying to find a comfortable grip on our share of the load. We were then forced to push our way through the thick brush. The footing was not always secure. I hoped we would be able to circumvent the bear's last known location and get back to the trail as quickly as possible.

"Have a care with those branches!" Black Wolf exclaimed as Puh and I pressed on through yet another thicket.

"Sorry, old friend," Puh said over his shoulder. "I was hoping the sled would catch the backlash instead of you and Fish Hawk."

"Not only are the limbs striking me, but they also fling their burden of snow at me!" Black Wolf sputtered. "I believe we can head back to the path now. I have had enough of this!"

"What if the bear has also made a detour?" I asked.

"We can only hope that we have made enough noise to frighten him off," Puh said. "But failing that, the sight of the four of us carrying the sled just might appear to be some strange, very large animal . . . it is possible we might look just odd enough to make him turn tail."

"Not if he smells our food." Black Wolf grumbled darkly.

We made our way back toward the path, still slogging through an inhospitable terrain. I thought we were yet a little way from the trail when we suddenly found ourselves within ten paces of the bear. He was to the left of us and stood up on his hind legs upon spying the spectacle we presented. The bear stared at us as though in disbelief. We were close enough that we could hear his jaws popping, a sure sign that he was agitated. The bear went down on all fours, and he roared as he came at us.

It all happened so quickly, that we involuntarily held up the bulk of the sled before us as to absorb the creature's wrath. The bear slammed into the sled, easily knocking us aside. I was sent sprawling into a snowdrift that had accumulated at the lower boughs of a fir tree. I struggled to my feet, clearing the snow from my eyes, and hurriedly searched for my spear. I feared that the bear would concentrate his attention on one of us, and certainly an animal of that size would make short work of a mere human. But the beast appeared focused on Fish Hawk's sled, now in shambles after the collision. It seemed that Fish Hawk's dried stores had indeed caught the attention of the bear's sensitive nose.

I gazed around me and saw that Black Wolf, Puh, and Fish Hawk had also picked themselves up, and by now each of us had found our spears. I knew that we could probably withdraw and leave the bear to pillage Fish Hawk's sled, but everything he owned was on it. Without speaking, we were all of one mind. We nodded silently to one another and quickly approached the bear, spears poised. It was imperative that we make good on our first strikes. There would be no second chances.

The bear wheeled as he heard our crunching footsteps, and he again rose on his hind legs to his full height. This was our opportunity. Without hesitation we thrust our spears into his heart and lungs, giving him no time to react before the spearheads found their targets. I drove my spear into his chest with all my might, habitually twisting the spear's shaft so as to incur the most damage to his breast. I was immediately buffeted to the side once again, this time against a tree trunk, and all at once I felt something hot running down the side of my face. My spear was still embedded in the bear's torso, so now I drew my only remaining weapon, my knife. But the bear was already passing from life.

We stood motionless for a moment, but then I grasped my spear and wrenched it from the bear's body. The others followed suit. The boar's hind legs and one forepaw twitched, but otherwise the beast was still.

"Well, Fish Hawk, we can skin this bruin so that you have a pairing gift for Petal, and then we can take some choice cuts of meat for the ceremony feast," Black Wolf said, grinning.

"*My gift!*" Fish Hawk cried out.

Fish Hawk stepped over the bear's still-trembling hind legs and then knelt by his destroyed sled, frantically searching for something.

"What is it?" I questioned, then realizing that the contents of my pack had been flung in all directions when the bear had twice tossed me aside.

Fish Hawk looked up at me, mouth hanging open.

"Your face!" he gasped.

Puh was already coming toward me with a handful of clean snow.

"You are bleeding, Tris," Puh pointed out, reaching up to gently place the snow against my cheek. "It is not too bad, but this will help to clean the wound."

"Many thanks, Puh," I said to him, "I thought I felt something running down my face."

Fish Hawk too came to my aid with a scrap of cured hide.

"Take this and hold it over the cut," he offered. "It will help to stem the flow."

Black Wolf was already starting to cut the skin off the bear, causing its steaming body heat to vent out into the cold air.

"I will need help to roll him over when I have finished this side," he called out.

"We will help you," Puh assured him. "But first, I will pick up all the things that have been scattered from our packs and the sled."

"You stepped on my foot," Black Wolf suddenly said in an accusatory tone. "I will be limping all the way home," he muttered.

We turned to Black Wolf in unison, wondering whom he was addressing, but then saw that he was speaking to the dead bear. Black Wolf then glanced over toward us and continued. "The bear's teeth are rather worn," he noted out loud as he worked on the carcass. "It must be quite an old boar. While he is still a fine-looking specimen, he would have been a magnificent animal when he was in his prime."

"I must find my gift," Fish Hawk said as he returned to sorting through his belongings.

One hand holding the piece of hide to my cheek and the other re-storing my things into my pack, I cast a glance at Fish Hawk.

"Let me look, too. What am I looking for?" Now that my pack was properly re-stowed, I began to pile Fish Hawk's things in a heap. The spears he had lying across the length of the sled were shattered into two or three sections. His bedding and clothing were still rolled in a tight wad and seemed intact. I found a few gourd cups, one of which was cracked. His bag of dried stores was broken into, the contents almost entirely consumed by the bear. Under the bag, almost obscured by the snow, was a smooth white stone with a zigzagging line of contrasting black running through it, and it was strung on twine. I held it up, peering at it curiously.

"I made a present for Petal," Fish Hawk said, absently digging through the remains of his now broken snowshoes and then inspecting his axe, which seemed to have survived the attack. Fish Hawk glanced up at me. "You have found it!"

I placed the necklace in Fish Hawk's extended hand.

"It is a very nice gift," I said to him. "You must have worked on that for a long time. It would take a great while to drill a hole in stone."

"It did indeed," Fish Hawk said with a nod. He placed the pendant around his own neck for safe keeping as he continued to gather up anything that could be salvaged from the wreckage of his sled. "I have never attempted to drill a hole in rock before, and I am afraid my work was not as neat as I had hoped, but with the twine looped through the hole, it hides my rough work."

"Yes, it does," I told him. "I think it is a very beautiful pendant. Petal will like it."

"Well, you can give her the bearskin, too," Black Wolf suggested. "He was molting some of his winter coat already, but it is still quite a nice pelt."

"Thank you, Black Wolf," Fish Hawk said earnestly. "Perhaps we can use it to help transport my belongings to my new home. I will cut some saplings to make a new frame and then we can fold the skin over the frame and lash my things over top of it."

I let go of the scrap of hide that I held to my cheek and removed my own hatchet from the top of my pack and followed Fish Hawk to a stand of saplings. We began to chop at the thin trees, and once they were separated from their lower trunks, limbed them until they were just single stems.

"It is not going to be much of a sled," Fish Hawk admitted. "I dare not spend much time on it, but at least it will adequately do the job."

Fish Hawk and I finished the construction of his sled even before Black Wolf and Puh had finished skinning the bear and harvesting the choicest pieces of meat. We were sorry to leave so much valuable meat behind, but there was far too much to be able to transport home. Our only comfort was that many animals would feed off the bear, and it was entirely possible that this boon would be enough to get them through the remainder of the winter, when they might not have else survived.

* * *

We made it home just as darkness was falling. We usually gathered our families together to eat the evening meal at the end of the day, and this night, our repast was being prepared at the dwelling of Black Wolf and Little Fawn. This was probably wise, since introducing Petal to Fish Hawk in any of the other homes would only highlight the fact that Petal was too tall to stand upright in the average house. Black Wolf's many dogs barked their greeting to us as we entered his abode. I stroked a few of the furry heads as I walked past, but I went straight to my mate.

As always, Morning Star looked at me anxiously as soon as we entered.

"Your face!" she exclaimed. "What happened to you?"

"I fell into a tree . . . there may have been a jagged branch or something," I explained. "It happened so fast that I really do not know."

Morning Star put her arms around my neck and drew me close as I bent down to kiss her lips.

"We were starting to worry; we expected you men to return earlier in the day," Morning Star whispered into my ear. "The blood has dried and matted your beard on one side. And it dripped onto your new coat, as well."

"I know; I am sorry. And I am sorry you were worried," I apologized. "We had to take a longer route than was originally planned."

"I am just glad to know you all are safe," Morning Star said, then pausing as she saw Fish Hawk being welcomed. "This is Petal's suitor? He is quite handsome."

"Yes, that is Fish Hawk," I replied, removing my pack and leaning my spear against a nearby wall.

I grinned to see Fish Hawk being presented to Petal, who was carefully primped to show her at her best. Her long black hair was usually plaited, but today, it hung loose and glossy down the length of her back. She blushed and smiled demurely at Fish Hawk, but could not seem to bring herself to speak. At that moment, Petal actually looked pretty. Fish Hawk smiled back and gently took her hand.

"I am so happy to finally meet you, Petal," Fish Hawk said quietly, but warmly.

Petal nodded, still smiling.

"I am glad, too," she finally said.

Little Fawn appeared overjoyed as she observed this scene closely. She had done an excellent job of making her home comfortable and well stocked with everything needed to maintain a family. Little Fawn was eager to put on a good show for our guest, and I could smell the wonderful aromas of the cooking food. In my state of hunger, I was looking forward to this meal immensely.

"Mama, what do you think?" Morning Star said in an aside to her mother.

"I think he looks like a fine man," Little Fawn gushed. "And Petal seems to like him. He seems to like her, too."

I had to remind myself that this was the typical way pairings took place. I had loved Morning Star for years before we were joined; she was the only woman I had ever wanted. But most pairings were not bonded by love. It was just hoped that the couple would like each other and go on to raise a successful family. As in Black Wolf's case, the couples did not always find happiness together; but as I knew Petal and Fish Hawk to be two very amicable people, I was optimistic that they would indeed live contented lives.

After we were welcomed by our families, we returned outdoors to retrieve Fish Hawk's belongings off the makeshift sled before complete darkness descended upon us. Black Wolf, Puh, Bror, and I had constructed an annex to Black Wolf's home last fall in anticipation that Petal would soon find a mate so that they would have a place to live, at least until they could build their own home. Fish Hawk's things were deposited in the annex, which was dark except for a fire in the fireplace.

Then, at last, we could remove our outer clothing and find places to sit. Fox and Pony soon came to me and settled onto my lap. I could see that one of my younger sisters, eleven-winters-old Twie, was carrying little Raven while Morning Star helped to complete the meal preparations. Fox looked into my face with concern.

"Puh-Puh, you broke your face!" he said.

"Yes, but just a little," I told him. "It will soon fix itself."

Our dinner was very pleasant, except that Morning Star noticeably stiffened and gave me a displeased sideways glance when her father regaled everyone with the story about our confrontation with the bear.

"Are you sure it was a tree branch that cut your face?" she asked skeptically.

"I believe so," I answered honestly. "Only because I think the bear would have left much more than just a little gash on my cheek."

But when Black Wolf came to the part where the bear's skin would be a present from Fish Hawk to Petal, and that we would have bear meat at their pairing ceremony feast, Morning Star smiled broadly.

"Oh, that will give them something memorable for their special day," she beamed. "I am so pleased for dear Petal. She has the sweetest, gentlest heart, and I so want her to be happy."

* * *

It was only a formality, but once it was determined that the couple still wanted to be paired after having met, it was decided that they would be joined on the morrow at midday. Fortunately, the good weather held, but since it was still too cold to hold the ceremony outdoors as we often do, the event would take place inside the home of Black Wolf and Little Fawn. As with the previous night's sup, this was the only place where most of the principal attendees could stand fully upright.

* * *

Petal wore a new gown, beautifully assembled from the impeccably cured skins of several does and trimmed with otter fur. Her hair was attractively arranged in a way that left most of it hanging free, but pulled softly back from her face. Fish Hawk was also dressed in his best clothing; over his loincloth and leggings he had donned a deerskin tunic that was carefully tailored to fit him well. Not to be outdone, Black Wolf's suit of clothing was impressive indeed. Willow Woman had it especially made for him, and it not only fit his long, lean frame, but also featured such things as fringes, shell embellishments, and contrasting dyed panels. It was by far the most well constructed and artfully designed items of clothing I had ever seen, and Black Wolf wore them proudly.

When all were present and silently awaiting the start of the ceremony Black Wolf nodded to Petal and Fish Hawk as they stood before him. They each returned his nod. Black Wolf grasped Petal's hand with his right and Fish Hawk's hand with his left and then he spoke the traditional words.

"Fish Hawk, son of Eagle Eye, I give you my daughter, Petal." Black Wolf spoke as he placed Petal's hand in Fish Hawk's. "May she bring you much happiness and many children, and may you enjoy long and fruitful lives together."

"Thank you, Black Wolf," Fish Hawk responded. "I am very pleased to accept Petal, and I am very sure that your wishes for us will be well met."

Fish Hawk then stepped closer to Petal and embraced her gently. Petal scrunched down a bit until she could lower her head to his shoulder, wearing a blissfully contented smile.

"Thank you, Petal," Fish Hawk said to her. "Thank you for accepting me. I vow to do everything humanly possible to be sure that you will never want for anything."

"And I thank you, Fish Hawk, for your kind words," Petal began shyly. "I also promise to do my best to be a good mate."

Fish Hawk then reached into his tunic and drew out the pendant he had made for her. He lifted it from around his neck and placed it around Petal's, taking care to rearrange her long silky tresses after disturbing them.

Petal gasped with pleasure when she saw her gift.

"Thank you, Fish Hawk," she said softly, "I think this is the most beautiful thing I have ever seen! I will treasure it always!"

Fish Hawk beamed at Petal's reaction to his present, and he impulsively bussed her cheek, causing Petal to redden.

The couple was then mobbed by well-wishers, and gladly received the numerous hugs, kisses, and congratulatory words. I stood by Morning Star, holding Fox and Pony while she carried Raven, and I noted Morning Star's glowing smile.

"Does this remind you of our pairing day?" Morning Star asked me.

"Yes, a little," I replied. "Our pairing took place outdoors and it was spring, but the happiness, the joy of Petal and Fish Hawk . . . it does bring back many memories. And, of course, the fact that you are wearing the same garment you wore at our pairing."

"It is the only thing I own that is not stained from being splashed with our children's bodily fluids, or from kneeling and sitting on the ground," Morning Star noted with a grin.

"You still look just as lovely in the dress as you did on that day," I told her. In truth, the gown fit her more closely now than it did when we were paired, and I thought that Morning Star looked absolutely breathtaking in it. She had always been the most beautiful woman I had ever known.

Morning Star tiptoed up to kiss my cheek.

"Thank you, my dear Tris," she said. Morning Star's eyes met mine for a long moment, saying much more than her words ever could. I bent down to kiss her lips.

The pairing ceremony meal soon followed. This was the most festive and happiest occasion in which I had ever taken part. I included even my own pairing in this, since it had been considerably marred by Morning Star's abduction.

Even Morning Star's younger brothers Swift River and Hawk seemed to sense their father's good humor.

"Da," Swift River said, staring up at his father, "Will you take us on a hunt this spring? Hawk and I are big enough to go, now."

"Yes, Da," Hawk added. "We need to learn how to take down game if we are to grow to be men."

Black Wolf frowned.

"Now is not the time to discuss this," he replied, suddenly irritable. "You two must first prove to me that you are mature enough to be hunters before I will take you on any excursions."

The brothers appeared downcast, but only momentarily. Then Hawk picked up a toy spear and he sharply poked Swift River in the side with it.

"Ho ho!" Hawk laughed. "I have killed a hare!"

"I am not a hare!" Swift River retorted indignantly. "I am a buck, a buck at the very least! A ten-pointer! A hare, indeed!"

"I do not see any antlers on your head!" Hawk giggled. "So, you must be a hare, or a squirrel . . . or are you a new fawn who has not yet sprouted his antler buds?"

Swift River reacted by swinging at Hawk, who shrieked with laughter as he darted away.

"There will be none of that, now!" Black Wolf roared after them. "This is to be a solemn and dignified event!"

"Oh, Da!" Morning Star said. "Let them play!"

"They are so eager to be men, but they still behave like children," Black Wolf answered, shaking his head. "How can I take them hunting when they will be so noisy and unsettled that they will surely scare away any game, or worse, attract predators that will try to drag them off?"

"I know, Da. But this is a happy day. Try not to think about it for now," Morning Star advised.

"Yes," Black Wolf conceded, smiling at her words. "This is a very auspicious occasion. I should not let those two imps distract me."

"And besides," Morning Star carried on, "you are looking so handsome in your grand clothing."

"I still feel rather naked with this short hair," Black Wolf admitted. "And because it is so short, I cannot yet braid it, so it often hangs in front of my eyes. Maybe by this fall I will be able to plait my hair once again."

Morning Star reached up to push her father's hair back from his face.

"It will grow back before you know it. In another year or so, your hair will be as long as it ever was." Morning Star paused a moment. "In the meantime, at least you are recovered from your head wound and you are still with us."

"For which I am very glad," Black Wolf said with a grin.

From across the sea of people in the room, I could see that Swift River and Hawk had stopped chasing each other and were speaking with Fish Hawk about his hunting adventures. I could catch a few words of their conversation now and then. It seemed that they hoped he would take them with him. Fish Hawk seemed to weigh their request.

"But that will be up to your father," Fish Hawk told the disappointed duo in a firm voice, just loud enough for me to hear. "Maybe if you practice being still for long periods of time, learn about stalking game, learn to make your own weapons, build up your endurance and strength, and learn where to hit game to make a lethal strike . . . maybe then your father will take you." Fish Hawk then noticed their downcast expressions. "Keep heart. I will help you."

The boys then grinned widely and thanked Fish Hawk profusely. I knew that Black Wolf had tried to educate his sons, but the boys had simply not taken their studies seriously. They preferred to play and subject each other to their never-ending pranks. But perhaps Fish Hawk would have better luck making an impression on the young lads.

As the afternoon wound down, I could hear the wind rising. Everyone was still thoroughly enjoying the post-ceremonial meal, but I sensed that the weather was quickly deteriorating. I ventured to the entryway, stepped over the many dogs that were sheltering in the windbreak outside the door to escape the heat of the inner rooms, and saw that the skies were indeed darkening and that snow was falling thickly.

I went back indoors and approached Morning Star.

"I think a storm will soon be upon us. We should get the children home," I said quietly.

Morning Star nodded.

"Yes. Let us say our farewells, then, and spread the word so that everyone can go to their homes before things get too bad."

 **Chapter Three** 

At long last winter's blustery days seemed to come to an end, and a cold wet spring took its place. Snow still clung to the shadows where the sun's rays could not reach, but otherwise, the ground was largely a muddy quagmire. There had been little successful hunting, primarily because of the weather conditions and a general lack of prey. Several years ago a wildfire had destroyed much of the forest just a short distance away from our family compound and had driven off or killed much of the local game. While both the woodland and its former inhabitants were making a slow recovery, it still left us with a quandary. How long could we continue to survive here?

We were now living off of dried stores occasionally supplemented with fresh meat. Thankfully, spring's annual fowl migrations were adding much-needed variety to our dreary diets. Puh's mate, Ria, had brought a new weapon to our arsenal when she joined our clan. We had never seen a bow, nor the tiny spears called arrows that it propelled through the air. Her little bow was not big enough to take down large game, but it could slay modest prey such as small deer, or some of the many ducks, swans, and geese that were darkening the skies as they winged their way northward to their warm-weather haunts.

My brother Ty, our best woodworker, was striving to recreate Ria's bow and had made several different versions, including a bow of great size that I had been practicing with. I was still learning to shoot as fluidly as Ria. She was able to send numerous arrows into the air within a matter of moments, all the while hardly seeming to take aim. I could hit fairly consistently if I was able to focus carefully and my target was stationary, but I was still far more proficient at hunting with my spear.

Morning Star's younger brothers seemed to take Fish Hawk in earnest. It brought to mind the time we were visited by a group of young men who called themselves The People of the Wolves. They were adventurous, fun-loving, and, above all, skilled huntsmen. Swift River and Hawk had done their best to emulate their new heroes, but those men had left us some time ago, and now the boys seemed to have chosen Fish Hawk in their stead. Unless he managed to evade his admirers, they dogged his every step. Fish Hawk dealt with them with a remarkable patience that did him credit.

I met with Fish Hawk on one misty morning as we each gathered up armloads of firewood from our communal wood cache.

"Pleasant day to you, Fish Hawk," I said to him as I looked for the driest pieces of wood, speaking over the din of twittering birds that chirped in alarm at our proximity.

"Pleasant day to you, Tris," Fish Hawk responded; he was wearing a grin despite the cold wet conditions, as moisture dripped steadily from the still leafless trees and brush around us.

"You are alone this morning," I noted.

"Well, a man must bear being away from his beloved for a few moments now and then," Fish Hawk replied lightly.

I smiled at his answer.

"Yes, that is true. But I meant that the boys have left you to your chores without their attendance. I seldom see you without them."

"I invited them to help me bring in firewood, but they declined," Fish Hawk said with a laugh. "But no matter. They are good boys. Mischievous, but there is no harm in them. I was the youngest in my family and my kin put up with me, so I suppose I can now repay that debt. Besides, I find that I like to be the one who is the mentor, for a change."

"I am glad to see you are so happy," I remarked. "And you are a great help to Black Wolf and Little Fawn, both with the boys and the household chores."

"I am very happy," Fish Hawk admitted. "Petal is a wonderful girl. I am very lucky. I am also pleased to be able to assist where I can. Little Fawn complains of terrible pains in her back; she should not be doing heavy work. But I hope that we might be able to get away from our more mundane tasks soon. Black Wolf spoke of going on a hunt, perhaps on the morrow."

"Yes, he spoke of it to me and Puh, as well," I said, wiping the dampness from my face. "It would be good to get out for the day. My legs could use a good hike."

"I suppose the boys will want to join us, but I doubt Black Wolf will be willing to bring them." Fish Hawk shook his head. "Although in this case, I understand his reasoning. It is too important that we bring in game. I think Swift River and Hawk have come a long way in the past few moons, but they are not reliable enough to restrain themselves so that they will not spook potential prey. I have told them to be patient and not to pester their father. To wait to be invited."

"That is wise counsel," I agreed. "How did they take it?"

"I am sure they would have preferred other words from me, but they promised me they would not badger Black Wolf on the subject."

* * *

We met under gray but dry skies early the next morning. The sun had not yet fully risen; but the drab color of the firmament held no promise of that bright orb for some while. It was still cool enough that our words came out in puffy little clouds. Black Wolf, Fish Hawk, Puh, and I discussed our options as Puh's mate Ria stood at his side, carrying their young son. Puh's arm was casually draped around Ria's shoulders as he looked at her fondly. Each time she happened to glance up at him, her eyes too were full of love.

"Are you not willing to leave your little boy with Twie again today so that you might accompany us and bring down more fat geese?" Black Wolf teased Ria gently.

Even though Great Gran and Aessa would be on hand to supervise, Twie, at eleven winters old, was the oldest remaining sister in the household, and she very often looked after her younger siblings, including her half-brother, Mror, Puh and Ria's two-winters-old son. For the first year or so of little Mror's life, Ria steadfastly had refused to leave him with another caretaker. She had waited for thirty-six years to finally bear a child, and she seldom let him out of her sight. The tot had accompanied us on hunts, usually snoozing in a sling at his mother's back while she trekked along or made use of her bow and arrows. But then we were charged by a bear last summer. At first the creature was interested only in the deer we had killed, but then it was incited to attack by Mror's cries of alarm. Ria soon realized she could not continue to bring him.

"Not this day," Ria replied, smiling up at Black Wolf cheerfully. "Anyway, are you not tired of eating fowl, yet? Last time we ventured out, we saw lots of churned-up ground east of the creek. Would it not be wonderful to enjoy the fresh meat of a sow for a change?"

"It would, indeed," Black Wolf agreed. "Shall we bring a few dogs?"

I could see that Swift River and Hawk were peering longingly from behind the hide-covered doorway to their home. They dared not appear too eager to join the hunting party, but neither did they want to be forgotten.

Black Wolf's dogs also seemed to sense that something was afoot. They were alert and their tails wagged with happy anticipation. Like Hawk and Swift River, they looked from face to face as though to gauge the chances that they might be included in this outing. The dogs would be helpful if we wanted to go after boars, for they kept the sharp-tusked animals occupied and at a distance until we could slay them. On the other hand, the dogs often frightened other game into panicked flight before we could get anywhere near them.

"We are as likely to get a sow or two as any other creature," Puh mused. "I leave it up to the rest of you to decide."

Puh did not volunteer to bring his young dog, Ochs, nor did I mention Raena. Our dogs were valued members of our households, but they were not hunting dogs. Although Black Wolf's canines were a friendly lot, they could act in concert with one another to corner and worry a beast — and they bore the scars to prove it.

"We need only to find where the sounders nest," Fish Hawk pointed out. "They will likely be asleep for the day by the time we catch up with them."

"That would be ideal, but I have found them to be light sleepers," Puh said with a droll smile. We had all been treed by rampaging boars in the past. It was not easy to sneak up on them, and it would be even harder when accompanied by a pack of noisy dogs.

My cousin Bror, my sister Ru's mate, then joined us. Bror had been smitten with Ru and patiently wooed her for several years before finally triumphing over her indifference. At that time we were enjoying the visit of the men from The People of the Wolves, whose leader, Karno, also strove to win Ru's affections. Karno was brave and an excellent provider, but he was a graceless suitor. He had been aghast at Ru's final choice. In his clan, cousins did not pair. Our people did not especially seek out a cousin, but if one's heart desired a cousin, or if a cousin was the only other person available for pairing, it was not prohibited, either.

"You are a little late to the gathering," Black Wolf noted, smiling down at Bror.

"Yes," Bror agreed simply, returning Black Wolf's smile and adjusting one of the shoulder straps of his pack. Bror knew that Black Wolf liked to jest, and he often chose to respond by not responding.

While most Old Ones were sturdy in build, Bror owned an exceptionally robust physique. He was of average height, but he was built like an aurochs. There are very few men I would hesitate to take on, but Bror was one of those few. That said, Bror owned a placid and pleasant demeanor; he was methodical and conscientious in both his thoughts and the completion of his tasks. Bror was a few winters older than I, but besides being my cousin, he was also one of my closest friends. His father had been a Keeper of Stories, and after his passing Bror had stepped into the role without really meaning to take it on, simply because he knew his father's tales by rote.

It was not long before we decided to seek out the boars and set off with four of Black Wolf's dogs. We hiked swiftly, without speaking. The muddy soil pulled at our booted feet with each squishing step. We needed to track the boars to their nests and then let the dogs single out a beast or two. It was still midmorning when we paused at the site of a well-scavenged bear carcass.

"Many of the bones are broken to little bits," Puh said as he knelt by the remains.

"This was a very old bear; it seems he survived the winter but met his end in the spring," Black Wolf stated. "He was a big one, though. Perhaps even larger than the one that broke Fish Hawk's sled."

"I would not think that even a wolf could break the bones like this," I remarked. "Even the heavy bones of the skull are shattered. The animals scavenging off this carcass must have been very determined to eat the bear's brain to go through so much trouble to get at it."

"Yes," agreed Puh. "I have not seen anything like this since I was a boy, when my father took us on a long journey to the east. There we saw strange creatures he called hyenas. They can grow to be as large as the biggest wolf, but they are heavier, and their jaws are immensely powerful. I would not like to think that hyenas have settled onto our lands."

"What do these hyenas look like?" Bror asked.

"You might say they look like a cross between a wolf and a bear," Puh began. "They have the paws and muzzle of a canine, but the shoulder hump and sloping back of a bear. The muzzle is short and broad, and their ears are rounded. Their coats are coarse and spotted. They make most peculiar sounds . . . they whoop and cackle."

We were silent as we each tried to imagine this unlikely creature.

"The paw prints are nearly erased by recent rains," Bror said, pointing at the faint tracks. "But it looks as though there were a number of these beasts."

"They hunt in packs," Puh said as he nodded to Bror. "We had best keep moving."

Black Wolf's dogs were busily sniffing the bear's scant remains and the area around the broken bones, with their hackles raised and lips upturned. We returned to our hike, and Black Wolf clacked his tongue at the dogs to call them to him as we strode down the trail. His lead dog once again took up his position ahead of us, as the others bounded up and down the path, sharp eyes and ears gathering from our surroundings information that was beyond our ken.

* * *

The sun was still climbing through the treetops when we found an area where the earth was furrowed here and there, and piled into clumps of dirt and leaves. These were not freshly churned patches, but it was likely that the sounder was not too distant. Black Wolf again clucked to his dogs and they obediently approached and sat at his feet, staring up at him expectantly for further instruction.

We looked for hoof prints, and like those of the suspected hyenas, the tracks we found were not fresh, but they were probably not more than a day old. We moved ahead slowly, Black Wolf keeping his dogs close by.

At last, we came upon fresh tracks and droppings, and numerous places where the boars must have plowed up the soil during the previous night. We continued on, following the signs, taking care to step quietly and not to speak.

I noted that Puh kept looking behind us. He seemed uneasy. I did not want to break our silence to ask him what was wrong, but it was enough to cause me to come to a state of heightened alertness as well.

Suddenly, the dogs halted in place, hackles bristling. We stopped, too. Black Wolf clucked to the canines once and they dashed into the brush, barking furiously. A cacophony of raucous grunts and shrieks met our ears as a small herd of panicked boars burst from their nests in the underbrush. Last year's shoats, now good-sized youngsters, and sturdy sows, some bloated and nearing the end of their gestation, all trotted forth with nary a backward glance as the dogs sought to detain some of the beasts until we could lance them. However, we were doing our best to dodge the frightened and irate animals, which were not at all pleased by our presence.

One of the dogs succeeded in latching onto the hind leg of a yearling, so we immediately darted in with our spears in an attempt to strike it low, behind a foreleg, where we could hope to hit the heart or lungs, or both. Puh and I, one on each side of the sow, found our targets, and we were in the midst of subduing the thrashing and squealing creature, just as our companions were seeking to do the same with another victim, when we heard a scream. It was a distinctly human sound.

Puh and I stood over our young sow, spears still deeply embedded in its side, as the others looked up from their prey, as it was just passing from life.

"What was that?" Fish Hawk asked anxiously.

"Or *who* was that?" Puh responded. "I have felt that we were being followed."

"Followed?" Black Wolf echoed.

"At a distance," Puh began. "I cannot even say what it was I sensed, but I could not shake the feeling that something was coming up the trail behind us." Another cry rent the air. The dogs seemed to have forgotten the boars, and they started to whine. The remaining members of the sounder had disappeared from sight, having vanished into the surrounding woodlands. The whimpering dogs moved hesitantly toward the sounds.

"I will take my dogs and see who has found themselves in distress," Black Wolf said. "That is, if you will stay here with our sows."

"I will go with you," Fish Hawk volunteered.

All at once, the dogs perked up, their tails wagging. They yipped excitedly as we heard the sounds of a breathless approach.

Swift River and Hawk almost collapsed at our feet, lying by the bodies of the dead swine. Black Wolf's visage went dark with rage.

"*You two!*" he thundered. "*You rascals!*"

I did not think I had ever seen Black Wolf so furious. He grasped each boy by the arm and hauled him to his feet, which allowed us to see that they wore a considerable amount of blood on their hands, arms, and down the fronts of their clothing. They were also liberally bedecked with dirt and bits of dried grasses, leaves, and moss, as though they had been rolling on the ground.

"B-but Da!" Swift River stammered. "We were careful! We were quiet! We did not disturb your hunt!"

Black Wolf's ire softened at the sight of their red-stained limbs and clothes.

"All right, yes, you did not disturb our hunt. But what happened to you boys?"

"We followed your tracks. Everything was going so well . . ." Swift River said.

"Except that we forgot to bring any food or water," Hawk interrupted. "We were able to drink from a stream where we found a little watercress to eat. But we are still hungry!"

Puh immediately dug into his pack for some dried meat, which he gave to the boys. They quickly uttered their thanks as they gnawed at the hard slabs with enthusiasm. Black Wolf prompted them to continue.

"What about the blood? Where are you bleeding from? And where are your weapons? You did not leave home unarmed, did you?" Black Wolf's tone started to rise again as his ire got the better of him.

"We brought our spears and our knives," Swift River said as he resumed his tale, removing his bloodied knife from his belt and displaying it to us.

"But we lost our spears when the boars ran at us!" Hawk exclaimed.

"Yes," Swift River nodded vigorously, "we stabbed at a small boar that came toward us, but it ran off . . . and took our spears with it!"

"Did the boar cut you up?" Black Wolf inquired with some alarm.

"I am not cut. Are you cut?" Swift River questioned his younger brother.

"No," Hawk replied, shaking his head. Then he turned to us and said, "Why did that boar not fall after we struck him? We tried to hold onto him and he dragged us a little way into the forest, but he would not stop running!"

We all listened incredulously, imagining the two boys lancing and determinedly trying to tackle the young boar. Black Wolf began to examine his sons more closely to reassure himself that they were truly uninjured.

"Your hand has a small gash," Black Wolf noted, speaking to Hawk. "You are lucky not to be hurt worse!"

"We — we just wanted to prove to you that we are not as useless as you would think," Swift River said quietly. "We just want to learn to be men."

Black Wolf kneeled and gathered both boys to his chest in a heartfelt hug. They embraced him as well as he kissed their begrimed foreheads.

"Let us go in search of your prey. We should be able to follow its blood trail. If it has lost as much blood as you two are wearing, it could not have gone far." He then paused before going on in a more serious note, "Your mother will be frantic by now. You must promise me you will never do anything like this again. Do you promise? Both of you?"

Hawk and Swift River guiltily exchanged glances.

"Mama . . ." Hawk said with widened eyes, "I never thought that Mama would be worried. Yes, I promise."

"I promise, too," Swift River echoed.

"Good," Black Wolf said, rising to his feet once again. "I will make a promise to you as well. I will take you both out hunting soon. If you heed everything you are taught you will learn to be fine hunters and fine men."

He grinned down at his boys, and likewise, they grinned up at him.

Whilst this discussion had been going on, the rest of us had gutted our two sows and trussed their crossed ankles to hastily lopped-off and limbed saplings so that we could carry our prizes home. Puh and Bror shouldered one sow and Fish Hawk and I, the other.

We set off down the trail, following the many hoof prints that signaled where the sounder had taken flight toward Black Wolf's errant sons. I counted my strides until we found the place where the animals had made contact with Hawk and Swift River. I had walked ninety-one steps. The site showed signs of the scuffle and was marked with bright splashes of blood.

"Here," Swift River said, pointing. "Here was where he dragged us into the woods. I tried to hold on and dig in my heels, but he was too strong for us!"

"There is nothing like terror to give an animal strength," Bror noted.

"Indeed," Black Wolf agreed.

The dogs led the way a short distance into the brush, where we located the now deceased creature. The spears of Swift River and Hawk still jutted out from his sides. He was clumsily hit, but it appeared he had eventually bled out. He was still warm to the touch. Black Wolf instructed his sons on how to gut the little boar, while he cut down an appropriately sized sapling and prepared it for toting the beast home. Other than tending to the sapling, he made the boys do all the remaining work, including carrying their prey all the way to our family compound.

* * *

We arrived just as the sun disappeared into clouds near the horizon. As Black Wolf had predicted, Little Fawn was beside herself with worry. She had correctly guessed that her sons had snuck away to follow their father, and she had had all day to speculate on what fate might have befallen them. Little Fawn was both relieved and angry; she did not know whether to punish them or smother them with hugs and kisses.

However, taking note how exhausted the two boys were from the trials of their long day, she held her tongue. Little Fawn looked to Black Wolf for confirmation that all was well and she merely put an arm around each boy to give him a squeeze, and then told them to wash prior to our nightly sup.

Chapter Four

The days gradually lengthened. Puddles of snow melted and mud dissipated as the season of warm weather settled over the woodlands. At long last, after a three-year hiatus, we were planning the journey to the coast. Those outside of my immediate family had never been there — excluding my children, who all had been born since our last trip to the beach.

As it turned out, not all of us would make the trek. Fish Hawk and Petal opted to stay behind with Great Gran and Ty, who usually remained at our homestead while the rest of us made our annual migration to the shore. If Fish Hawk and Petal hoped to finally have some privacy, their hopes were dashed when Little Fawn announced that she and the children would not be going either, despite Black Wolf's steadfast insistence that nothing would keep him from making the trip.

"Petal and I need to finish outfitting our new home," Fish Hawk pointed out to Little Fawn as we congregated for the evening meal the eve before our departure. "There is really no reason you should miss an opportunity to see the ocean."

It was true that Petal and Fish Hawk's newly constructed dwelling was still a little rough, and Fish Hawk was working tirelessly to make it comfortable for his new mate. Petal, too, was busily feathering her nest with all the things they would need to live independently of her parents. Plus, they were hopeful that they might be expanding their family in the not-too-distant future. Petal showed no outward signs of pregnancy, but Morning Star had kept me apprised of her sister's wishes to have an infant of her own as soon as possible.

Curiously, Aessa had no interest in seeing the ocean. She disliked large bodies of water. I could not say that I blamed her. Several years ago, I had almost drowned in river rapids, and I was wary anytime I was near roiling waters. However, the sea, although it might have big waves during our summertime visits, was usually far more predictable and less perilous than the raging torrent that had almost swept me away. The tide ebbed and flowed a little a few times a day. Sometimes the ocean's surface was calm with barely a ripple and at other times, the rising winds brought in foaming combers that washed the shore with an awe-inspiring fury. But for the most part there was no danger. I suspected that what she really wished was to stay near my brother Ty. She and Ty were nearly always together, and in fact, they had already departed from our gathering around the fire and had gone into the house.

This left only Binty, the small boy who had come to us at the same time as Aessa. He was completely deaf and although he could communicate with us through hand signals, no one could figure out how to tell him about the sea and ask him if he would like to come along. Aessa was like a mother to him, and I thought it was most likely that he would choose to stay near her.

After all had consumed their fill, we sat comfortably by the outdoor hearth. We usually cooked over coals, but when the food preparations were complete, the fire was built up once more to bring a circle of light to our gathering. We watched the flames dance as we contentedly enjoyed the pleasant evening air and the company of our loved ones.

I sat at Morning Star's side, holding our tired and droopy toddlers on my lap. Morning Star held Raven, who was slumbering peacefully in her mother's arms. I looked up past the gently swaying tree limbs to the star-filled nighttime sky and thought on how happy we had been.

It pained me to think that it was unlikely we could continue to stay here. My clan had been incredibly fortunate to have been able to reside at this convenient location for generations untold. Here, we could make a trek out to the plains to pursue game during the spring, venture to the coast at summer for the fruit, fish, and seal we found there, and then pursue deer and elk each fall during the rut. Perhaps best of all, it provided a safe and warm place to hunker down each winter to wait out the long days of darkness, the biting cold, and frigid winds that blew relentlessly until spring. Additionally, a nearby stream brought us potable water. Now, having been joined by Black Wolf and his family, Ria, Aessa, Binty, and finally Fish Hawk, we had a cozy encampment of close friends to share in this wonderful place. If not for the wildfire that had devastated so much of the adjacent lands, we probably could have remained here for as long as we wished.

A pair of owls calling back and forth to each other brought me back from my somber thoughts of leaving our beloved home. My six-winters-old sister Saree approached Bror and commenced begging him for a story.

"A story, my Little One?" Bror said, his mouth wearing a hint of a smile.

"Oh, yes!" Saree piped, nodding vigorously. "An exciting story! A story I have never heard before! I know you think some stories will frighten me and keep me from sleeping, but I am ever so much bigger now. Stories do not scare me."

I could see that Bror was deep in thought. An exciting story was one thing, but a story that Saree had never heard before? That would be a challenge.

"But what of the younger children?" Bror asked.

"Why, they are all asleep . . . or nearly so!" Saree pointed out.

"Ah, I see." Bror paused before going on. "Very well. I will tell the story of The Villains."

"Who are The Villains?" Twie questioned.

I was somewhat drowsy after eating a prodigious meal, but I curious about this myself. I had not heard of The Villains.

"Oh, they were a group of very bad men," Bror started.

This group of bad men belonged to a clan of Old Ones who lived on a far-off land. It was a land of swamps and swarming insects: an evil place. Although there was game aplenty, The Villains decided that they would become eaters of man-flesh!

My drowsiness fled and I sat up straighter as Bror continued.

The men used magic darts to sting their victims, and make them fall asleep so they could drag them back to their cave . . . a cave filled with the bones of both men and animals. They used these cowardly hunting tactics on their human prey until one day they captured three strangers: two men of the Old Ones and one man of The People. These men might have been eaten just the same as all the earlier victims, if not for the bravery of the two youngsters who were being kept with the bad men against their will. They released the captives from their bindings, and the first to be released, a very large Old One, battled one of the evil men. This evil man was terrible, in both looks and smell! He had little close-set eyes that would not have been out of place on one of the boars that was brought home today. He wore his hair in long greasy strings and his clothing reeked of filth and refuse. His smell alone was a powerful weapon. But the very large man of the Old Ones was able to triumph over the stinky bad man, which allowed the three former captives and the youngsters to escape.

The eaters of man-flesh wanted to recapture them, of course, and they chased them high and low. Finally, the small boy, showed the escapees a special hiding place in a beaver dam. There, they hid until the bad men passed them by and eventually lost their trail.

Then, the hunters became the hunted. The former captives tracked the evil men, but The Villains managed to sneak up on them and attacked. The men and the youngsters fought valiantly, but all of the sudden they were aided by a cow mammoth. The matriarch of the herd saw their trouble and saw that they were outnumbered. She came to their aid and stomped the life from the evil man . . .

I was so transfixed by Bror's story that I had forgotten that it had happened to Black Wolf, Puh, and me, and that Aessa and Binty were the two young people who had released us from our bindings and had escaped with us.

"*Oh! Oh!*" cried Twie. "The mammoth squished the bad man? Did she squish any of the others, too? Did she know not to crush the good people?"

Saree held up her doll Hork to her face.

"Did you hear that, Hork? You must always behave around mammoths, or they might crush you under their enormous feet! You would not like that at all!"

Puh pulled Saree onto his lap and enveloped her into a hug.

"Perhaps we shall leave the rest of the story for another night." Puh then looked pointedly at Bror. "I seem to recall a story about a fish that liked to stare at the sun and the clouds through the surface of the water and longed to live on the land," he said. "His friend Frog used to tell him many happy tales about all the beautiful things he had seen when he ventured away from the pond. Perhaps we could hear that story."

"That is a one of my favorites," Bror said, launching into this new yarn.

* * *

The day of our departure was soon upon us. Normally our travois sled was light on the outward trek, carrying just a selection of household items, tools, and such. But this time, since we could not be sure that the cached hides used to cover our beach shelters and the ropes used to secure them would not be moldy and rotted by now, we had piled the sled with many hide tarpaulins and newly braided ropes. Most of us were also carrying packs as well, so we could tote our personal items.

Before we left, I looked on as Puh took Ty and Fish Hawk aside to tell them more about the mysterious hyenas. Puh used a stick to draw the creature in the dirt. First, he sketched a blocky head, with large round ears and a strong jaw. Then he drew the hump at their shoulders, which sloped downward to smaller hindquarters. Shortish legs and a stubby tail finished off the animal.

"It is a poor rendition," Puh admitted. "But you will certainly know them by their cries. They sometimes sound more bird-like than like any canine I have ever heard. They do not howl like a wolf, or sing like a coyote. They have a sharp, high-pitched cackle that is never forgotten once heard."

"What color is their coat?" Fish Hawk asked.

"Black and russet, mostly," Puh answered. "They also wear spots. I seem to recall that they prefer to scavenge their meals, but they are quite capable of bringing down prey. The pack harasses its victims until one or two of them manages to latch onto the victim's flank or a leg, and then they wrestle the creature to the ground. They are able to take down a sizable animal this way. My father claimed he had even seen a pack of hyenas kill a lion."

This was startling news. Ty seemed disturbed at the thought of meeting these beasts.

"But we have not actually seen or heard any hyenas," Ty began. "Are you sure they are in the area?"

"Sure?" Puh repeated. "No, nothing is ever sure. But it would be prudent to remain watchful."

"Even if it was hyenas that demolished that bear carcass, perhaps they were only passing through," Fish Hawk said.

"Yes," Puh agreed, "we can hope that is so."

* * *

The morning of our departure found us assembled at the center of the family compound, dressed in our usual summer attire in preparation for a long trek under sunny skies. We men were dressed only in loincloths, and the women were dressed in midthigh-length garments made up of a rectangle of cured hide with a neck-hole at the center of its length, which was draped down, front and back, and belted securely at the waist.

We were all barefoot. Those who were not accompanying us to the coast stood by to see us off and exchange farewells. Black Wolf was pleased to be embarking on an adventure, but he seemed grieved to leave his family behind.

"You take good care of yourself," he admonished Petal gently as he embraced her and kissed her cheek.

"Yes, Da," Petal said, returning his kiss. "And you take good care of yourself, too. Especially around that big water. Do not catch a fish so huge that it drags you away," she teased.

"That would have to be a very big fish," Black Wolf said with a laugh.

I smiled to myself at the thought. Black Wolf had seen large salmon, but he had never seen some of the enormous fish that lived in the ocean, nor the seals that could easily outweigh a man. The idea might not be as far-fetched as Black Wolf supposed.

"I leave my daughter in your hands," Black Wolf said to Fish Hawk, each grasping the other's forearms in the way of The People.

"As always, I am honored to have that privilege," Fish Hawk replied. "Safe journey to you all."

"Thank you," Black Wolf responded. "I ask you, as well, to watch over Little Fawn and our younger children. Especially my two boys. You know their propensity for finding trouble!"

"I do, indeed," Fish Hawk said, chuckling at this. "Have no fear, I will do my best."

Black Wolf nodded and then hugged and kissed his

younger children goodbye, and even stooped to pet his many dogs, since they would also be staying at home. Black Wolf made sure to strongly caution his boys to mind their mother while he was absent from them. If they were somewhat abashed at this, they perked up when he told them that he was counting on them to be men while he was away and help their mother take care of the household and family. Lastly, Black Wolf came to Little Fawn. She had not betrayed any expectations that she would receive a heartfelt farewell, nor did she get one.

"Be well," Black Wolf said as he stood opposite her. "I will return in a few moons with a load of foodstuffs and maybe some seal hides, if an opportunity arises to hunt the creatures."

"Be well, yourself," Little Fawn responded. "I will be here. Waiting. As ever."

Black Wolf only nodded before turning away toward his sled. He stepped between its wooden handles and placed the thick leather strap over his head until it lay across his chest. Puh and I were already fastened to our larger sled.

When all had said their parting words, we entered the trail heading west, Puh and I at the lead, taking care with our spears not to accidentally jab each other as we trekked along, and little Fox riding on top of our load, cheerfully waving goodbye to those staying behind. Raena and Ochs canvassed the path ahead of us for potential threats. We were followed by Morning Star, who carried Pony in a sling at her back and Raven in her arms, and by Ria, who also carried Mror in a sling and was armed with her bow and arrows. Then came my sister Ru, with her little daughter, herding my younger sisters, Twie, Saree, and Mi, followed by Black Wolf pulling his sled and toting his spear. Finally, Bror brought up the rear, where he could guard the back end of our procession.

It was a happy excursion. We were on a well-worn trail and not moving at a fast pace, since we were all loaded down in one way or another. Black Wolf, despite being burdened by his sled, sang most of the time. The song would be broadcast somewhat breathlessly whenever he came to an upward slope, but Black Wolf tackled both song and hill with gusto. The youngest children frequently clambered onto one of the sleds when they tired of walking, and sometimes even napped there. We stopped now and then for a swig of water or perhaps a nibble of some of our dried rations. Even considering our leisurely pace, we still managed to reach our first destination, the home of my Aunt Vee, Bror's mother, and his brothers Dor and Lor, by the time the sun had settled halfway between its midday peak and the horizon.

The family's dogs met us first, barking vociferously at our arrival. Aunt Vee greeted us joyously. She was especially pleased to see Bror and to meet her first grandchild, Bror and Ru's infant, Hona. A surprise awaited us, as well. I was pleasantly taken aback to find Sere residing there. I had initially made his acquaintance when I met my mother's older brothers; Sere was kin to a woman paired with one of those uncles. His mate had perished, as had Vee's mate. Now that I thought on it, I remembered that Sere and Aunt Vee had been introduced the summer before last. They must have enjoyed one another's company, because now they were paired and they seemed quite pleased to be together.

Bror took only a moment to recover from his initial shock.

"Awna's oldest brother Inlee was kind enough to officiate at our pairing ceremony, since I had no one who could give me to Sere," Aunt Vee explained excitedly. "But never mind about all that. We can speak of it later! Let me hold my grandbaby! And oh, I am so glad you are all here! I had hoped that nothing would prevent you from making your annual sojourn to the coast as has happened the past few years; I have been so eager to see my Bror and assure myself that he is well! I have waited for this full moon, knowing that if you were going to attempt the journey, it would be about now."

"Yes, Muh, all is indeed well," Bror said with a broad smile. "It is so good to see you and my brothers, too. I am glad to see you so happy. I have been fortunate to be able to spend some time with Sere and I know he is a good man."

Aunt Vee and Sere glowed at Bror's remarks. Although Aunt Vee had never previously taken to Puh's new mate Ria, she now spoke to her warmly, admiring their toddler, who was named for her late mate, Mror.

"And I believe you have put on a little weight,"

Aunt Vee said to Ria, who had always owned a lithe, wiry frame. It was true that while she was still lean, she did look a bit more filled-out. Aunt Vee had ever been a very small woman herself, but at this time she also appeared to be more than adequately nourished. "Life with Tor's family must agree with you."

"I no longer hunt as often as I used to, and I am certainly well fed these days," Ria admitted. "I am not surprised to know that I am not the frightfully bony woman I used to be."

"You are just right," Puh told Ria, putting an arm around her and squeezing her shoulders.

"Tor, you and Ria are still like a newly paired couple," Sere said to Puh. "I hope that Vee and I will enjoy the same happiness as you two have found."

"I hope the same for you, as well," Puh said with a nod to Sere, seeming a little embarrassed that his loving relationship had been so noted.

We eventually all settled around the outdoor hearth, everyone catching up all the things that had happened in the intervening time since we had last seen one another. Black Wolf sat by Morning Star and me and our children. He knew everyone present, but perhaps he felt he should sit with his closest relative, given that the rest of his family had not made the trip. I thought that Black Wolf seemed somewhat introspective as he listened to the ongoing chatter. He said little until the topic turned to hunting.

"Have you seen any signs of a strange creature in the vicinity?" Black Wolf inquired of the assemblage.

"What sort of strange creature?" Sere asked. "I saw a buck with some very odd antlers last fall, but other than that there has been nothing terribly out of the ordinary." Sere rose from his seat. "I will show you the antlers. I saved them."

Black Wolf waited for Sere to return before responding, "Yes, it is a curious pair of antlers — more tines than I believe I have ever seen on one animal! But I mean a predatory beast. Sort of a wolfish animal. I will tell you more of it, later."

Puh sat a little way from me, but he and I traded glances, knowing that Black Wolf was speaking of the hyenas. Sere nodded calmly in acknowledgment, but Bror's youngest brothers, Dor and Lor, still seemed interested to know more.

"We saw a few funny animals — sort of like wolves — a few moons ago. But they were way off in the distance, so we did not get a good look at them. The only other strange wolfish creatures that we have seen were those Wolf-men who stayed with you a few years ago," Dor said with a laugh. "They were entertaining fellows — huntsman such as I have never seen! Running up to that woolly rhino as though it were no more than a small boar!"

"Several of their party were also grievous injured in that hunt," Black Wolf pointed out.

"It is all well and good to be brave," Sere began, "but the whole idea is to survive each day so you can continue to go after game and feed your family. Those who act rashly and become injured, or worse, are killed, do not help their clan."

"That is true," Dor acknowledged.

"But it does not make for very good stories," Lor chimed in.

Black Wolf became silent again as the light chatter resumed. It was only later as we were all shown to our chambers in Aunt Vee's sizable home, which had once housed a great number of her clan, that I realized Black Wolf might have been missing Willow Woman and their son, Black Oak. We were all with our families, but he had not seen them since the previous fall's Gathering of The People, and it was likely he would not see them again until the upcoming Gathering. It was true that the Gathering lasted an entire moon, which he had managed to stretch out half as much again, but it was still a lengthy separation for a man who so desperately missed his loved ones. Little Oak would be old enough to be trotting to and fro by now, and beginning to speak in short sentences. As before, I could not imagine how he managed to bear such long absences from them.

* * *

The next day brought mild and sunny weather. We enjoyed a satisfying meal, the conversation flowing as easily as it had the previous evening. Aunt Vee insisted on holding her grandchild as much as possible. She loved children, especially babies, and now that she had a grandchild to spoil, Aunt Vee was thrilled. Little Hona was a sweet-natured, robust baby who owned the same light red hair as did most of my Puh's side of the family. Her skin was pale, but her rosy cheeks and pink lips made her look almost too perfect. Aunt Vee did not want to miss a moment with this little one, and she seemed earnestly heartbroken to give the baby back to her mother before we hit the trail. However, at least she had the comfort of knowing that she would see her grandchild again when we stopped over on our way home in a few moons.

Before leaving, we took turns keeping watch over the more vulnerable members of our family as they washed at the stream. While I had a quiet moment with Black Wolf I asked if he had indeed spoken with Sere and the others about the hyenas.

"Yes," Black Wolf replied. "I do not want to alarm anyone unnecessarily, particularly the children, so I have taken care not to mention them to anyone but the adults. If those beasts are expanding into our territories, everyone should know."

"I agree," I told him. "I have talked to Morning Star about them, and I have also given her a description of the animals. I can only hope that we can consider it a good sign that there have not been any additional sightings of their tracks, or any more discoveries of heavily gnawed carcasses."

"Yes," Black Wolf said again. "Just the fact that Tor speaks of them so gravely is enough to make me hope that we never encounter a pack of those brutes."

My dog Raena had gone down to the water's edge to slake her thirst, but she now came to my side and looked up at me, mouth still dripping. I smiled and reached down to stroke her head.

"I hope the same," I agreed again.

* * *

Our procession trudged along in the same order as it had the day before. I could feel my skin heating up from so much exposure to full sun, despite our efforts to stay under the canopy of the trees. Those of us with fair, freckled skin had to be on guard to keep from becoming badly sunburned. We stopped only once to let everyone rest and break for a bite to eat and drink water, but soon resumed our hike.

"Fox, stay close by," Morning Star called after him.

Fox was capering with high spirits along the path, darting amongst his fellow travelers.

"Yes, Muh-Muh," he answered, tripping over a root as he looked back at his mother.

"Have a care, Fox," Morning Star called out again.

"Yes, Muh-Muh," Fox said again. Then he went on, "Puh-Puh, why Rae-na so far up?"

He pointed up the trail, where we could just see Raena and Ochs in the distance as they sniffed out the identities of any animals or people that might be in the area.

"She is working," I told him, trying to glance over at Fox while I addressed him, without tripping myself up as Puh and I pulled the sled along. "Dogs have a very serious job to do. Raena's job is to protect us from anything that might do us harm."

"She find bear?" Fox asked, trotting to keep up with Puh and me.

"Probably not," I replied. "At least, I hope not. We

are making far too much noise to surprise a bear. Most bears will run away as soon as they hear such a commotion coming near."

"She find bee?"

"Find what?" I was momentarily confused.

"*Bee!*" Fox repeated, pointing to the spot where a bee had stung him on the knee some days ago. The bee had lost its life in the attack, and between the pain of the sting and his fascination with the lifeless body of the small insect; it had made quite an impression on him.

"I suppose she might find a bee, but that is not the type of danger she is looking for," I said. "And as long as we are making so much noise — what with your Grandpa Black Wolf singing so loudly — it is unlikely that she and Ochs will come across any predators."

Puh gave me a sidelong gaze. We both knew that lions would probably not be deterred by our noise; and then there were also potential two-legged threats, but that went unspoken.

Fox seemed to be deep in thought.

"I will be dog, too!" he suddenly announced, and like Raena and Ochs, he ran up the path and broke through a line of brush.

Fox was out of sight in an instant.

"Fox, come back here!" I shouted, dropping my grasp on the sled and stepping out of the sled's harness.

"Tris, go after him!" Morning Star cried out, her voice tinged with panic.

Puh quickly joined me. As always, we were both armed with our spears. Many bushes and saplings were interspersed amongst the trees, and they completely hid Fox from view, but we could hear him as he pushed through the undergrowth.

"Fox, come to me!" I tried again, feeling a fear that gripped my chest.

"Fox!" Puh yelled out as he moved a short distance from me, so we could cover more ground. "Fox! Fox!"

We continually called his name, stopping to listen for any sign of him, and eyes shifting as we searched for signs that he had passed this way. But other than a few broken twigs and shifted leaf litter, to our utter frustration and terror, we neither heard nor saw him. Our dogs had broken off their foray and now joined us.

"Fox! Fox, answer me!" I shouted as loudly as I could.

"Fox!" Puh echoed.

We stood in place, ears straining and looking all around us.

"*Puh-Puh!*" I was relieved to hear his faint cry.

We dashed forward.

"Stay where you are, Fox," Puh instructed.

"We will be right there!" I added.

"Puh-Puh," Fox said, a little louder this time.

Puh and I soon found him. Fox was stopped at a long-dead carcass. I was palpably relieved to know he had found a deceased animal and not a live one. The dogs sniffed the well-scattered remains tentatively. "Deer," Fox said, pointing at the assorted bones calmly. He had identified the beast by its antlers, which lay broken into pieces on opposite ends of the site. Fox held one of the broken tines in his hand.

Puh and I knelt by the deer's remains. As with the bear we had discovered the previous spring, the deer's bones had been shattered into small fragments so that every last bit of nourishment could be extracted from the marrow and the brains within the skull. We would speak of this later.

"Come, Fox," I said, lifting him into my arms. "Let us go back to the others. You are *never* to run off like that again."

"But I found something," he insisted.

"You will find lots of things during your life," I replied, "but for now you will wait until I am with you before you go looking."

"Yes, Puh-Puh," Fox said with resignation.

Black Wolf, Ria, and Bror had hung back to guard everyone who was left standing on the trail while Puh and I went after Fox. Morning Star was almost in tears by the time we returned, and she hugged and kissed Fox until he squirmed and protested.

"Oh, my little Fox! You will *never* do that again!" Morning Star admonished him, still squeezing him tightly.

"Puh-Puh say that too," Fox said unhappily. "Muh-Muh, *too tight! Too tight!* Fox *down!*"

"Well, your Puh-Puh is right! You will ride on Puh-Puh's sled for now. No more running around for you!" Morning Star had gone from being frightened to being angry.

Fox recognized that tone, and he knew better than

to argue. He obediently climbed onto the sled and sat with considerable dignity, I thought, for an almost three-winters-old child who had just been thoroughly chastised.

* * *

The sun was midway through its decline when I sensed a change. The breeze had picked up, and it felt distinctly cooler.   The air had a different smell; somehow, it was tangier than the inland air we were accustomed to breathing. Black Wolf had been regaling us with song as usual, but he broke off and shouted up to Puh and me, who were still at the head of the line.

"I think I can smell the sea!" he cried out, his deep bass clearly heard over the distance.

"Soon, you will feel it through the earth, as well," Puh replied.

"Through the earth? How?" Black Wolf shouted to us again.

"There is a strong wind coming off the ocean. It will be driving big waves before it and soon we will be able to hear them and feel them as they crash on the shore," Puh informed him.

"That will be a sight to behold!" Black Wolf stated.

I could appreciate his excitement. Even those of us who had gone to the beach nearly every summer of our lives were all grinning with anticipation at being back on the coast once more. Black Wolf, Bror, and Ria had heard a great deal about all the wonders they would find there, and they were eager to finally experience them for themselves.

"The trees are stunted and twisted," Bror observed, speaking louder than usual so we could hear him from his position at the rear of our procession. "Is it the storms that so deform the trees?"

"It is," Ru answered him. "Every year when we return, we see that great tempests must have thrashed the shore during our absence. That is why we must bury the materials we use to build our homes — to protect them from the elements and keep them from being washed or blown away."

As we cleared the forest's edge and hiked the short distance across the grassy plain that lead to the dunes, the scene that met our eyes showed that our beloved spot had suffered some erosion, but was otherwise unchanged. All evidence of our previous occupations was completely erased by wind and water.

But now there was much work to do. We had to erect our homes as quickly as possible so that we would be sheltered from both sun and inclement weather.

Puh and I showed Black Wolf and Bror where we had buried our building materials, and we immediately began to dig. In the meantime, the others unlashed all our supplies from the sleds and began to sort through everything. Morning Star, Ria, and Ru worked to set up a temporary lean-to so that there would be at least one place where we could get out of the sun — most especially the children, whose tender skin would quickly burn under the harsh rays.

As expected, we found that many of the sealskin hides had started to rot. The rope was hopelessly fragile, too. Fortunately, many of the poles were still in good condition. We carried the best of the poles to the crest of the dunes and looked for convenient hollows where we could begin to construct frameworks. Most of us would reside in the large round domicile where Muh and Puh and my siblings had always lived. Last time we had ventured here, Morning Star and I had just been paired, and we lived a little distance away, in our own lean-to. We planned to do the same this time, though it would have to be a bit more substantial, as it would now also house our three children and our dog. Likewise, Bror, Ru, and Hona would have their own domicile. And now that Puh's family had also changed, it would be Puh, Ria, Mror, and my younger sisters and Black Wolf staying in the largest dwelling.

Black Wolf and Bror caught on to our building methods with very little instruction. Black Wolf's great height was a wonderful asset; he could easily reach even the topmost bindings without the need to stand on his toes. He often looked out to sea and smiled broadly, seeming completely awed by the enormous expanse of bright blue water. As Puh had said, the wind-driven waves washed the sands at regular intervals, each one landing with a resounding roar and a great rush of water as it came foaming up the beach and then retreated again.

When our rudimentary households were in place, the sun was nearing the horizon and we were all famished. A fire of driftwood was alight, and although we would sup on dried foods, I was content to know that we would soon enjoy succulent fresh fish and all the other comestibles that were typically gathered during our stay.

Now that most of the day's work was done, we all went to the water's edge and let the waves engulf our lower legs. I grinned at the tickling sensation as outgoing waves sucked the sand from under my feet. Each time, the loss of ground caused me to sink slightly, and I had to step out of the hole I had sunk into. The children ran about, picking up shells and seaweed and splashing one another, enjoying their games immensely.

"The movement of the water is so strong it pulls the sand out from underneath me!" Black Wolf exclaimed. "If I were to stand here for a very long time, I wonder how far down I would sink?"

"If wind is lays down and the bugs come out," Puh said to Black Wolf, "you will not want to stay here long enough to find out."

"Hmmm," Black Wolf uttered. "Ah, but look at the sunset over the ocean! Thinking back, I would say it started last spring — since then we have been treated to such amazing colors when the sun is low in the sky, especially at sunrise. Nearly every day I think I have never seen such a brilliant hue, and then the next day, the color is deeper and stronger than ever!"

Morning Star and Ru took the children back up to the dunes where our homes were situated to prepare them for bed, leaving Black Wolf, Puh, me, and Ria holding Mror, standing by the surf.

"When Fox ran away he found a deer carcass," Puh said quietly. "It was broken up much like that bear we came upon last spring."

"The old bear with the gnawed bones you told me about?" Ria questioned.

Puh nodded.

"Was it a fresh kill?" Black Wolf inquired, suddenly serious.

Puh shook his head.

"No, it was at least as old as the bear. Possibly older. It was a buck, and he still had his antlers, so it may have been brought down early last winter."

"But you think it was those hyena things that killed it?" Black Wolf persisted.

"They may not have actually caused its demise, but they certainly left their mark on the scene," Puh stated.

Chapter Five

It is dark and wet. The fearsome howling sometimes comes in low moans, other times rises to piercing shrieks. I am caught in an unending barrage of cold water that threatens to overwhelm me.

"Oh, you are so pink!" Morning Star said, shaking her head as she looked at me. "Is it painful?"

"Only a little." I was indeed sore, but after a lifetime of dealing with sunburns, I was used to coping with it. The worst part would come later, when the peeling skin began to itch.

Fox and Pony were still asleep. Only Raven was awake just now, hungrily nursing at her mother's breast. "Do you recall that I told you about the hyena animals Puh thinks were scavenging off that carcass?"

Morning Star looked up at me sharply.

"Were you Dreaming about them last night?" she asked. "You were restless in your sleep. You kept pushing at something."

"I did?" It was not surprising to learn that I had been restless, but I was unaware that I had been shoving at anything.

"Yes, you were moving one of your arms in a little sweeping motion, as though to sweep something away," Morning Star said. "It was not for very long, though. Just a moment or two."

"I do not think I was Dreaming of the hyenas, but I wish I would so I might see what they look like." I paused as I reflected on the best way to tell her of Fox's discovery, so as not to alarm her about the incident any more than she already was. "When Fox broke away yesterday, he found another carcass. It was a deer. Puh and I think the hyenas had killed it, or at least eaten the remains of it, most likely sometime last winter."

"You mean it was a buck with antlers?" Morning Star correctly surmised. This year's bucks were still growing their antlers and a doe's remains would not have provide that obvious clue.

"Yes," I said with a nod.

"I see," Morning Star responded. Her words were calm, but she appeared unsettled.

"I thought you should know." I wrapped an arm around Morning Star and kissed her cheek. "Let us hope that the hyenas were stopping in this area temporarily and have long since moved on."

"If there is a good thing about that wildfire that burned out so much of the forest near our homes, it is that it also did not leave much behind for predators and scavengers to eat, either," Morning Star pointed out.

Then she sighed as she looked over at our sleeping tots, "They are exhausted after the excitement of the journey and their first day at the beach. I do not believe I have ever seen them sleep so long."

"Well," I said with a grin, "that has also allowed us a wonderfully quiet morning to ourselves . . . mostly to ourselves."

Morning Star smiled too.

"It has. I suppose you must go now to continue with your work."

"I am afraid I must," I said, pausing to heft our water bag. "I will fetch more water later, when we break around midday." I leaned down to kiss her in parting.

"You are leaving? You have not had very much to eat."

"I will take this with me." I reached into one of our bags of dried and smoked foods and withdrew a hunk of desiccated freshwater fish from last year's catch. I then kissed her once more and exited our little shelter.

This would be another day of much work. We were all still dehydrated from our long trek and from setting up housekeeping. By midday it was necessary to retrace our steps up the trail to the place where Puh had dug down many years ago to locate a spring. It was potable, if slightly brackish. Most summers the rain provided us with enough water to satisfy our thirst, but either way, we would need to refill our water bags frequently.

Today we would complete the final touches to our homes and then, while waiting for low tide, build fish traps. These traps would become completely submerged at high tide, leaving the fish trapped in the base of the devices when the tide once again receded. Each year we had to make new traps, so it took some days to finally get the proper number in place. We would gorge on the delicious sweet flesh until we could not possibly hold anymore, and by then, our drying racks would be ready to receive the bulk of our catches, thus preserving the meat for later consumption.

Seals were another prime source of food. The meat was not as delicate in flavor as the fish, but it was extremely fatty and did much to keep both us and our oil lamps fueled. We did not expect to hunt any seals for at least a few days. This usually happened when one of the ungainly creatures would smell our catches drying on the racks and, hunger overcoming discretion, would heave itself up onto the shore. There, it would floppingly propel itself over the sand to investigate, and instead would meet up with our sharp spearheads. Despite their size and mouthfuls of impressive teeth, their awkwardness on land put them at a distinct disadvantage. They might try to bolt for the relative safety of the ocean, but they almost never made good on their escape.

"This is like living in another world," Black Wolf noted as we lounged in the shade of the main dwelling, over which we had just finished adding more hide tarpaulins to the exterior and partitioning off the interior into three sections. Puh and Ria had a small space to themselves, as did Black Wolf, so he could find some peace and privacy from a household that included many children. The largest portion was used for daily activities and as sleeping quarters for the little ones.

"It is indeed," Bror agreed. "I could never have imagined a place like this. Everything is so different. The plants and trees are different, many of the birds are different; the sand is soft and nearly white."

"In full sun, the sand almost looks like snow," Black Wolf added. "Only it becomes hot! It feels so good on my sore feet! Perhaps my feet will no longer ail me by the time we must leave for home."

"What shall we tackle next?" I questioned.

"Bror, shall we complete your home now?" Puh suggested.

"Either mine or Tris's," Bror replied with a good-natured grin.

The sun was not yet fully arisen, so we did not tarry long in the shade of the main house, and we promptly went to where Bror and Ru had chosen to set up their small hut. Ru was pleased to see our approach. She came out to greet us, holding little Hona in her arms.

"Pleasant day to you all," Ru said cheerfully.

I thought that both her pairing with Bror and motherhood agreed with her. Formerly, Ru had not been a particularly jolly person. I was somewhat startled every time I saw her broad smile, half expecting it to dissolve into a frown or sharp words at some perceived slight. Now, the old Ru seemed but a memory and the new Ru was infinitely preferable.

We returned Ru's welcome and then she went on, "Our little home was very comfortable last night. Hardly any insects came in through the gaps in the hides. I believe that just a few more ropes to fasten everything tightly will put the house to rights."

The entry flap to their home was held up with a section of slender pole to keep the doorway open, exposing a view of a tidy little room. Another section of hide was similarly propped open on the opposite wall to allow a cross-breeze to enter. Ru had covered the floor with woven reed mats, which were in turn covered with a combination of hides and pelts. Their belongings were neatly stashed alongside one wall and their water bag was suspended from one of the larger poles that supported the structure. We quickly added the requested lashings and then moved on to my dwelling.

Both Fox and Raven were awake by this time. They had breakfasted and now Morning Star had her hands full, considering how intrigued the children were with their new surroundings. It required all her vigilance to keep them from scampering off either to investigate the nearby dunes or running to the sea. Fortunately, Raena was on hand to assist. She would deftly round up each child and, leaning her body against the stray, steer it back home like a cow wisent keeping her errant calf from wandering away.

Like Bror and Ru's abode, our place consisted of just one room. We adjusted the hide tarpaulins and tightened the ropes, taking care to be sure that the whole assemblage was well staked to the sandy ground. This meant pounding long wooden stakes into the earth at a steep angle, and even so, I would not count on them to hold against anything more than a moderate wind.

Now that our homes were as secure as we could make them, we collected our water bags for refilling. The spring was located near the edge of the woodlands, and it needed to be dug out a little before we could access the water. The digging process caused the water to cloud with silt, so we sat in the shade of the trees as we waited for the sediment to settle.

"What do you suppose winters are like here?" Black Wolf asked of no one in particular. "It is so pleasant just now that it is hard to imagine this place to be any different."

"It is very nice," Bror said, looking around at the peaceful setting. "I have seen no signs of predators. Although I did note some deer droppings. Do you hunt deer when you are not hunting fish?"

Puh shook his head.

"We have plenty of other meat to pursue," Puh replied. "We eat deer most of the year, so it is agreeable to consume something else instead."

"There appear to be quite a few varieties of fruit, as well," Black Wolf said.

"Yes, we will be eating fresh fruit before we leave, and also drying much of it to add to our winter stores," Puh told him.

"The low bushes we passed on the way here have small purple fruit," I said, my mouth salivating at the mere thought. "They are my favorite. We call them sea plums. The flavor is so tangy and yet sweet; you cannot imagine."

When we returned with our replenished water bags, we were pleased to find that our families had gone out foraging and raided a number of gull nests. They had also harvested a variety of shellfish. The eggs were now standing upright, tops pierced, at the edge of the fire, where the coals were cooking the eggs within their shells. The mussels and clams were also nestled amongst the coals, their shells now agape, giving us a glimpse of the tender meat inside. I ate three eggs, four mussels, and two large clams; and in fact, could have eaten much more, but that was my allotted ration. All the same, this delicious treat was a most welcome respite from the preserved foods we had brought with us on this excursion.

Black Wolf suddenly cried out.

"*Ack!* I believe I have broken a tooth on this curious turtle thing!" he exclaimed.

"It is a clam," Puh told him.

"Whatever it is, my tooth did not like it," Black Wolf said, holding out a whitish object that was approximately tooth-sized.

"Are you sure that is your tooth?" I questioned.

Puh took it from Black Wolf and smiled.

"That is a pearl," Puh said simply, and gave it back to Black Wolf.

"A *what?*" Black Wolf asked. "It has a glossy surface like a tooth."

"A pearl. They are found in shellfish, sometimes,"

Puh replied.

"Well, you might have said something about that before now," Black Wolf said, studying the lumpy pearl. "But it does have a nice sheen. *Pearl.* Hmmm. Maybe I can collect a few and make an ornament for Willow. She would like that."

"Yes, she would," Ria agreed. "The gift of an ornament proves that you are remembered."

"She is indeed," Black Wolf responded, his visage bearing a singularly poignant expression.

* * *

After our midday meal, it was time to harvest the materials needed to make new fish traps. This meant walking back to the forest and cutting slender bush stalks about as long as a man was tall, stripping off the smaller branches, and carrying the bundles of twigs back to the main shelter. There we would twist the fibrous stalks until they broke into stands and begin to create the many traps it would take to keep our drying and smoking racks stocked with fish fillets throughout the summer. Our families generally assisted us with this labor-intensive chore.

"If we can get some of the traps in the water this afternoon, perhaps we may be able to have fresh fish for supper," Twie said hopefully.

"Perhaps, but I would not count on it, just yet," Puh spoke as he rapidly worked the twisted fibers into shape.

The finished traps resembled loosely woven baskets, portioned into two sections, with an opening near the top. The bottoms were weighted with rocks so they did not float and the tidal currents would not sweep them away. The gaps in the baskets were large enough to allow small fish to escape, but once a bigger fish ventured in after the bait that was secured near the bottom level of the trap, it often was unable to free itself, and thus was trapped but kept alive until we removed it from its prison.

It was near evening and not quite low tide when we carried the first baited and weighted traps out into the relatively quiet waters of a nearby inlet and placed our woven creations in their proper positions in the thigh-deep water.

"The water is so warm here," Bror marveled. "It seems so much colder in the open ocean by our homes."

"This shallow inlet has been absorbing warmth from the sun all day," Puh remarked. "It is a decided benefit when it comes to checking the traps, not only because the water is at a more comfortable temperature, but because the shallow depth makes it easier to set and check the traps. And the shallower waters are also less apt to be visited by some of the larger predator fish."

"What kind of larger fish?" Black Wolf asked.

"Most particularly, sharks. Seals inhabit the shores a short distance from here, and they are a great favorite of the sharks," Puh explained. "Sometimes we find a dead shark washed up on the beach and we can see that they are indeed fearsome creatures — big jagged teeth and a huge maw that would do a lion proud — but I have never seen one this close to the shore. At least not in this inlet."

Black Wolf and Bror both looked around us, carefully scanning the surrounding waters for any sign of the killer fish, but as Puh had said, there were none to be seen. Sometimes I had noted them swimming in the ocean near our homes; a few times I had even witnessed a shark attacking a seal. It was sobering to see them grab up the seal and watch the blood gush into the sea in great red torrents. Mature seals were much larger than men. If a shark could do that to a seal, I could only imagine what would happen if a man found its way into its jaws.

* * *

Our evening meal was made up of more foraged foods to supplement the dried and smoked goods we had brought from home. Black Wolf chewed with care, hoping to find another pearl, but his various shellfish contained nothing but sweet meat.

"Another spectacular sunset," Black Wolf spoke as the sun disappeared into the sea and the last crying gulls winged their way home overhead.

We all nodded in agreement. It was true that the skies had shown us amazing colors for some moons, but by now, the novelty was wearing off.

"We will make more traps tomorrow?" Bror asked of me.

"Yes," I answered, "we will continue to make more traps until that little bay is well dotted with our handiwork."

"Then we will set up drying racks," Puh added.

"Do you smoke any of the fish?" Black Wolf inquired.

"Some," Puh replied, "but most is dried in the sun. The hot air over the sand dries the fish very quickly. Seal meat takes a little longer. It has more fat in it."

I was hungrily looking forward to these harvests. Fresh fish cooked over a bed of hot coals was a far cry from the dried fish fillets we struggled to gnaw during the cold-weather seasons. Fish just taken from the sea was mild in flavor, almost delicate; and it was so tender that it broke into small flakes in one's fingers.

Seal meat, on the other hand, was very dark, with a rather strong flavor, but it made for a fortifying meal, and it was plentiful. Plus, the copious seal blubber rendered down into valuable fuel for our lamps. During the long, dark winters, little shell or clay bowls filled with the fat and fitted out with a plant-fiber wick were all that lighted our homes, except for the bright blaze cast by the flames within the fireplace.

If ever there came a time when we were permanently unable to make our annual treks to the beach for all the supplies on which we so depended, we would be decidedly hard-pressed to find suitable replacements elsewhere. This was yet another aspect of the dread I felt at having to find a new, likely distant home, at some point in the future.

"The fire has many colors," Black Wolf mused. "Why is that?"

"It is only a guess, of course," Puh started, "but the driftwood we burn has spent much time in the ocean and it has absorbed a considerable amount of salt while in the water. In daylight, you can see that it glistens with tiny salt crystals. I believe it is that which makes the fire appear to have occasional flames of blue and green."

"It looks like magic fire," Ria noted. "I have never seen fire like this before."

"This is a magical place," Bror agreed.

"Were it not for the winter storms and this being such an open and vulnerable spot, it would be an ideal location to resettle," Black Wolf said.

"I think so too," Bror agreed. "There is much food to be gathered, and it is near my family. I have seen no signs of the usual predators such as wolves and lions. Perhaps a deeper spring might need to be dug, but there is much to recommend it."

Puh and I traded glances. We knew how tempting it was to want to extend these golden days forever. Here, it was warm and food was readily available. But even if we chose to brave the winters in this windswept locale, I tended to think that we would soon overtax the area's resources. There might be fish and seals aplenty, but repeated harvesting of gull eggs would eventually bring about the annihilation of those birds. The nearby trees were small, gnarled things that would not provide much firewood or suitable building materials for our households, so we would be forced to haul wood over distances to cook food and construct and heat our homes.

Additionally, as Bror had pointed out, our spring yielded only brackish water. It would do when we had no rainwater, but no one would want to drink that slightly saline liquid indefinitely. A deeper well or an alternate source of water would be needed.

And lastly, I thought that if there was a permanent base camp established here, large predators would eventually be drawn to our homes. Our stays were too brief to attract much attention, but eventually the smells emanating from our drying and smoking racks would surely advertise the presence of fresh meat to their keen noses — theirs for the taking if they were brazen enough.

Puh and I said nothing. We knew that they were cognizant of the reasons we could not relocate here. But for now, I was content to enjoy the balmy sea air and the soft rumblings of the waves as they rolled up on the beach.

"Puh-Puh, look!" Fox exclaimed. He was sitting on my lap and he suddenly extended an arm as he pointed skyward.

"What do you see?" I inquired.

"The first star of the night!" Fox said excitedly.

The sky was so open here that we could easily see the whole firmament from our seats by the fire. Although there was still a rosy glow off to the west, the eastern sky had gone dark and the nearly full moon lent a gentle luminescence to the scene.

"I like the way the moonlight glimmers on the ocean," Saree said dreamily. "Sometimes the moon appears to rise right out of the forest. Is that where the moon lives, Puh-Puh?" She asked.

"I suppose it might," Puh said, pausing to consider for a moment. "But then again, both the sun and the moon set in the sea. Perhaps that is where they make their homes."

* * *

The new moon had just passed and our drying and smoking racks were heavily laden with fillets. We were catching and eating as many fish as our stomachs and our racks could hold. We would have a substantial amount of meat to bring home.

The weather was decidedly hot now, and although those of us with fair skin still burned on a daily basis, these sunburns just brought a warmth and pink glow to our complexions, instead of the bright red we sported following the first exposures at the beginning of the summer.

One afternoon we were gathered, as usual, in the shade of the largest dwelling, eating a leisurely midday meal of fresh fish, crabs, and meager handfuls of ripened early berries.

"I think I will take a nap," Black Wolf announced. "My belly is pleasantly full and I am starting to feel drowsy."

"A diet of fresh fish has done wonders for you," Ria told him. "You have been so thin ever since I have met you, but now you are looking positively robust!"

Black Wolf grinned widely at this news. It was true that he had at last seemed to recover from the trials of recent years and had once again regained his formerly strapping physique.

"Thank you for noticing," Black Wolf said to Ria, standing to retire to his chamber. "I feel better than I have felt in a long time. I believe you are right. It must be the fish. After all, when bears prepare to hibernate for the winter, do they not feast on fish? Within a few moons their coats are thick and glossy and they are sporting a considerable layer of fat."

Puh looked at Black Wolf, "You may not yet wear a considerable layer of fat, but your coat is indeed thick and glossy."

Black Wolf laughed, in spite of himself.

"I know you speak of my copious body hair, but actually, it seems that the hair on my head has grown noticeably while we have been here," he said. "It may finally be long enough to braid again by the end of fall. Or at least pull it back out of my face." Black Wolf extended his arms and looked down their lengths and sighed. "Between my sun-darkened skin and the hair on my arms, my beautiful tattoos are almost completely obscured. I am hoping to have a lower leg done to match my arms the next time I am with Willow. Eventually I will be covered the same as she is, but what with all this fur, it does not have quite the same effect."

"The only thing that matters is that you are happy with the tattoos," Puh told him. "Enjoy your nap."

Black Wolf then took his leave of us, disappearing behind the partition where he had kept his bed. Ere long, we heard his contented snores drifting out from behind the wall.

We resumed our quiet conversation, chatting about

our plans for the day, when all at once, both Raena and Ochs came alert. They stood in unison, hackles up, ears straining forward, and eyes intent. They suddenly barked and ran from the structure, racing toward the beach where our drying racks held our catches.

Puh, Bror, and I snatched up our spears and followed the dogs down to the shore. Black Wolf, armed and nap forgotten, quickly exited his room as well, and he soon caught up with us.

There we saw the reason for the dogs' excitement. A large seal had hauled itself out of the ocean and was eyeing our bounty with interest. The racks were just a bit too high for him to reach, but the seal looked as though he were trying to devise a way to hoist himself up high enough to pilfer a meal.

The dogs approached the marauding animal, snarling and growling. They kept the seal occupied until we could get there, and we positioned ourselves on either side of the beast. The seal was now on the defensive as he barked back at the dogs, his bark sounding like a prolonged, loud burp, interspersed with opened-mouthed hisses. This male was longer than I was tall — possibly even longer than Black Wolf's great height, but at least twice if not three times my weight. Although he looked impressive and was doing his best to intimidate us, Puh and I knew that he was nearly defenseless. He tried charging first the dogs and then us a few times, but his bulk weighed him down too much to effectively defend himself.

Puh and I darted in with our spears; while Bror

and Black Wolf, taking their cues from us, did the same on their side. We struck the beast low on his chest, near his flippers. He was mortally wounded, but he still strove to drive us off, turning this way and that to make halfhearted charges until exhaustion and blood loss made him sink down onto the sand, where he finally collapsed and soon expired.

Black Wolf and Bror now examined the dead seal curiously.

"What a creature!" Bror marveled. "He looks like a huge otter that has grown incredibly fat, but with odd fin-like things instead of paws and a tail."

"His fur is different from an otter's," Black Wolf noted. "And his teeth are certainly larger than an otter's. Those teeth would not be out of place in the mouth of a wolf."

"We had best get to work on this animal," Puh suggested. "He is not going to age well under the hot sun."

We returned to our homes to retrieve our butchering tools and then set out to process his valuable meat, organs, blubber and hide.

"How often does one of those seals present itself on the beach?" Bror asked.

"Usually, there are a few throughout our stay here," I replied. "Sometimes as many as five or six in a good year."

"After eating so much of your dried seal meat over the years, I will be eager to try some fresh seal this evening," Black Wolf said. "This looks like very good meat. Dark and firm. I will get fatter, yet!"

Puh laughed silently, as we Old Ones do. "You may put on a little more flesh on your bones before we return to our woodland homes, but I doubt you will have much fat."

"Yes," Bror agreed, laughing too. "We may eat a lot while we are here, but we also work hard. No time to get fat. Unless, we are very lucky and our women become very round about nine moons from now," Bror added with a grin.

* * *

It was fortunate most of the fish that was drying and smoking on the racks was now sufficiently processed that we could free enough space to begin curing the seal meat. Our families came down to the beach to help us pack the fish into the first of the many sacks we would take home to add to our winter stores.

As always, the children were fascinated with the seal. When wet, the seals' speckled bodies could appear dark gray or even black, but as the salt ocean water evaporated from the dense coat, we could better see the mottled markings on the soft fur.

The large pelt was now rolled up into a long bundle and placed to the side while we worked. Saree, Mi, Fox, and Pony knelt by the newly harvested skin, stroking it as one would pet a dog.

"See?" Saree said to the younger children, "It is nice to touch. But only touch a dead seal, never a live one. Live ones can bite!"

"Bite like bee?" Fox asked.

"No, silly," Saree replied. "Bees sting! Animals bite!" Saree pantomimed a biting motion with her own mouth for Fox's benefit.

Fox looked as though he had had an epiphany.

"Nee bite me last moon!" Fox nodded with understanding, speaking of his sister Pony. "Muh-Muh tell Nee *must not bite*!"

"Yes, we only bite food," Saree instructed solemnly. She held up her doll Hork to address her and said, "*Never* bite people!"

Mi stuck her finger into the permanent smile that had been carved into Hork's face and then quickly drew it away.

"Oh!" cried Mi. "Hork bite me!" Mi began to giggle at her joke. Fox seemed to think that looked like fun and he wanted Hork to bite him too.

"Me too!" Fox said, holding out his finger to Hork.

Saree held Hork to her chest.

"No biting," Saree said firmly.

Fox seemed disappointed, but he was soon distracted as he watched a few curious gulls fly in and land near the seal's carcass.

"Big birds!" Fox announced, trotting toward them.

The gulls withdrew a short distance, but they were brave birds and they soon began to come closer, step by step. Even though we had taken all we wanted from the carcass, Raena and Ochs still saw it as their duty to guard the seal's body from any and all who might want to help themselves to its pitiful remains, and they faithfully chased away the persistent birds.

Morning Star noted this too. "Perhaps they wish to gnaw on the poor beast's flippers themselves."

"Perhaps," I said with a shrug. "But in any case, chasing the gulls makes them feel as though they are doing their job. They like to have something to do."

"I have always thought that dogs were lucky in that sense," Morning Star said, still watching them.

"How so?" I inquired.

"They are the only members of the family — other than the youngest children — who are not required to work most of their waking moments," she replied. "The dogs are able to spend most of their days taking their ease, only rising to occasionally do what we require of them."

"I suppose that is true," I began, "but they are also willing workers and able to defend us at any time. And besides, when I leave Raena at home with you and the children, I know that she will guard you all with her life. That gives me much comfort."

"Me, as well," Morning Star said with a smile.

* * *

Our evening meal consisted largely of fresh roasted seal. I had always found the flavor to be somewhat strong, but there was no doubt that the meat was extremely nourishing. While we ate, the smell of seal blubber wafted through the air as it was being rendered into oil.

The constantly eroding shore often broke open to display a new deposit of clay, which we fashioned into various objects. Depending on the quality of the freshly exposed clay, we might be able to make some small bowl-shaped items, but the clay was often too sandy to make anything that did not soon crumble. This year, the clay was particularly fine, and it was perfect for being pushed and pinched into pots for small lamps. It also encased many a gutted fish so that it could be laid upon the hot coals and roasted and steamed within the clay until the fish's meat reached the point of tender perfection. Additionally, it also allowed us to create a large bowl that we used to render the seal fat. The bowl was formed and then hardened amongst red coals, and then cooled. For the rendering process, we created a depression in the sand large enough to contain a bed of coals, into which we fitted the bowl, and then heated enough to cause the fat to melt. The resulting liquid was ladled off into various receptacles, including finished lamps, where it would solidify again until it was ready for use.

Here at the beach, we did not need to use lamps. The summer days were long, and at night we had the light of our fires to see by. The lamps would be set aside until the inevitable shorter days of autumn set in. But for now, fall only loomed far off in the distance.

Chapter Six

We are running through a shadowy landscape. Ominous clouds pelt us with stinging wind-driven rain as a dark sky rages above us.

This Dream was like many of late. I was vaguely aware that I had been shifting in my sleep, but Morning Star was nestled in my embrace and she had managed to doze through my movements and subsequent waking. Now I lay still, listening to the waves gently lapping the shore as they provided an ever-present backdrop of sound. I wriggled out of bed and stood and stretched as well as I could in the confines of the shelter. Even though it was too dim to see very much, I peered at my children. I could just discern their huddled forms, Fox and Pony were cuddled together under a blanket, and Raven was well swaddled against the cool night air.

Raena was awake now too. I could see the glint of her eyes as they followed me around the hut. I then lifted the door flap and looked outside. Unlike the wild maelstrom of my Dream, the scene was utterly peaceful. Only the gentle cadence of the ocean and an occasional crying gull disturbed the silence. The moon had waxed full and it was now gradually waning, but it was still bright enough to lend a soft glow to the silvery-white sand dunes outside our little home.

Raena accompanied me outdoors, and we walked a short distance until we found a place to relieve our bladders. We then strolled through the dunes to the beach and looked out over the great expanse of sea. The moon was low in the sky, almost touching the horizon. Its pale reflection glimmered on the surface of the ocean, creating a path of shimmering light that seemed to lead to shore, almost as though to invite us to follow it across the sea. A few clouds floated across the field of bright stars; as we watched, a shooting star arced across the firmament. I smiled to see this fleeting spectacle. I reached down to stroke Raena's head and her tail wagged in response. She leaned against my leg and gazed up at me, as if to ask what we were going to do next. A chill raised bumps on my skin; nevertheless, I paused to savor the many scents in the air: the smell of the salt sea, the sweet aroma of the beach roses, and when an occasional gust blew from the east, the earthy, woodsy scent of land.

"Let us return home now," I said to her. "Well, to our shelter, anyway. But we will be going home again soon enough. It will be time to prepare for winter and there will be much work to do."

I petted her head one more time and we retraced our steps to the little hut.   I crawled back into bed with Morning Star. As I wrapped myself around her and settled in, I heard Morning Star sigh and say *Mmmm* as she felt me press up against her. An arm drew me closer and she nuzzled her face into my neck. My Dream and brief venture out to the beach were quickly forgotten.

* * *

The new day was ushered in by a rising sun that painted the skies in vibrant shades ranging from violet to fiery red to pink. The winds were so light as to barely move the grasses that crested the dunes. As usual, we set to work early, before the sun gained too much strength. First we refilled our water bags while we waited for the tide to recede a little more, and then we checked the condition of the fish on the racks. The smoking racks were empty, although we might smoke a little more fish later on with today's catch. The drying racks did not hold much at this time, and most of what it held was seal meat.

We had killed four seals this summer, leaving us with an abundance of meat and oil, and four large seal hides. We had twelve bags of dried or smoked fish, the same of seal, and several small bags of dried berries and rose hips. There was also a collection of clay items. All these things would be divvied up after our return home, although some would be traded with Aunt Vee's family, too, in exchange for the dried reindeer meat they usually stowed away after the spring and fall migrations.

"When will we check the traps for the last time?" Black Wolf asked Puh.

Puh was looking up at the sky, his sharp eyes taking in every detail, but he then turned to Black Wolf.

"We have about as much as we can tote home," Puh began. "I would think that after today, it would be pointless to harvest any more fish."

"Yes," Bror agreed. "There is no point in taking more than we can carry back."

"I would like to dig for shellfish and maybe gather crabs one more time before we leave," Black Wolf stated. "I have been hoping to find more pearls ever since I found that first one, but I have not had any luck."

"That is a good idea," Puh said, nodding thoughtfully. "We can enjoy shellfish over the next few days while the last of the fish cures."

"It is too bad there are not more mussels. I believe we have eaten them all," Black Wolf said, shaking his head ruefully. "I did so like those mussels!"

"There may be more mussels over by the cave," I pointed out. "In years past I have seen great clusters of mussels living on the rocks in that area."

"What cave?" Black Wolf questioned. "I have not seen any caves since we have been here."

"It is not a very hospitable cave," Puh told Black Wolf. "It is very damp inside. It is not a place where you would want to spend much time."

"We will have to walk in that direction to check our traps," I said. "It is not much farther to the cave. Why not go there now while we wait for the tide?"

My companions liked this idea, so we walked down the beach, passing the area where our traps waited. Some distance beyond,   we saw the waves splashing up against the rocks that were scattered all over this section of coastline. The tide was receding bit by bit. We waded out to the nearest rocks in search of mussels.

"Here! I have found some!" Bror announced.

"And there are more over here," Puh chimed in.

Black Wolf waded out a little deeper.

"And more here! This is plenty for a feast!" he said excitedly.

"What is that dull booming sound I hear?" Bror questioned.

"That is the noise the waves make when they hit the inner walls of the cave," I informed him. "The sound can be very loud during high winds that drive big waves into shore."

"I would like to see this cave," Bror said.

As a group, we waded back to the beach and continued on until we reached the cavern. As Puh had said, it was wet. The rocky mouth of the cave yawned open to the sea, and within it harbored many chambers. The first chambers that diverted from the main tunnel were shallow in nature. It was those rooms that produced the hollow booms that Bror had remarked on. As we entered, the swirling water rushed in and out around our legs. The cavern floor gradually sloped uphill, seeming to follow the contours of the coast, rising as it proceeded inland. The sandy ground was still damp, but eventually we had progressed past the many odd little nooks, irregularly shaped pillars and lumps of bare rock to the rear of the cave, where the floor was at last dry. But there was not much light in this part of the cave. Looking back at the entrance, it was just a bright shape against the darkness. Black Wolf had to use his hands to feel his way around.

"There seems to be a rock ledge," Black Wolf said. "Part of it is covered with sand, though. How does the sand get all the way back here?"

"The wind blows it in, I suppose," Puh mused.

"How high does the tide rise up in here?" Bror inquired.

"I do not know," I answered. I turned to Puh as I awaited his response.

"I have not seen it come more than perhaps a quarter of the way in, even at the peak of a very high tide, but I have not spent much time in this cave," Puh replied. "Our families are more apt to be able to tell us. They frequently come this way when they are looking for gulls' nests. There is a thriving gull colony not far from this spot."

"Well, it is no matter," Bror said with a shrug. "I was simply curious. I did not see any signs of shellfish except for a few dead crabs and broken shells near the entrance, so I wondered if perhaps there was not enough water for them to live in here."

* * *

The tide finally receded to the point where we could access our traps. After checking them, we emptied the stone weights out onto the beach and carried the traps, fish and all, up the coast to where the racks awaited their last loads. The fish were gutted and filleted, tails left still attached. Each fillet was held up to the sun and inspected for worms. If a worm or two was found inhabiting the flesh, it was lifted out at the tip of a knife and cast away. Then the fish was slung over the racks to dry or be smoked. This was all accomplished well before midday. I was just beginning to feel my skin heating up with yet another sunburn when we returned to the main household to rejoin our families for a meal and some water.

I greeted Morning Star with a hug and a kiss.

"I am famished," I told her.

Morning Star grinned.

"What a surprise!" she teased. "As luck would have it, I have anticipated your hunger and we have prepared a meal of cooked eggs, tubers, and lots of fresh berries. Even those round purple berries you so like."

"That sounds wonderful," I said, giving her another kiss.

"Enjoy those eggs," Ru advised. "I do not believe there will be many more. It is too late in the season and we do not want to take them all, or eventually there will be no more gulls."

"While I would miss their eggs, I would not miss their thieving ways," I said. "They are constantly stealing fish from our racks."

"Since we steal their eggs, I guess that is only fair," Morning Star said thoughtfully.

As we sat down to eat, Saree settled by Puh, who was holding two-winters-old Mror in his lap and sharing his food with the tot.

"Puh-Puh," Saree said, "we have not yet cut our hair this summer."

"That is true," Puh said, nodding as he offered a few bits of fish to Mror.

"Will we cut our hair soon?" Saree persisted.

"Ah, is it time for the annual trimming of the locks?" Black Wolf said with a laugh. The People from the East did not believe, as we Old Ones did, that our hair gave us an innate second sense; they cut their hair whenever the whim presented itself while we trimmed ours only sparingly each summer.

"I have made two new clay dolls," Saree went on. "I want them to have hair like my Hork does. They must have hair, Puh-Puh, or how will they know things? And how will I get hair for them unless we have our hair cut?"

Puh smiled at Saree with understanding.

"All right, my Little One," he said to her. "We will cut our hair this afternoon and I will help you affix it to your dolls' heads."

"Many thanks, Puh-Puh," Saree leaned over to Puh and hugged him. She then put down her shell bowl and reached behind her to show us her new dolls. Like Hork, they were made of oblong blobs of clay. They were limbless and currently bald, but they shared Hork's deep-set finger-poke eyes and wide leering grin. "These are my new babies," she announced proudly.

"Very nice, Saree," Puh told her.

"Yes, they are very nice," Ria joined in. Ria had just then finished eating, so she reached for Mror to take him from Puh, so Puh could finish his meal in peace. "What will you call your babies?"

"This one, the smaller one, I will call *Snork*," Saree announced, then she looked thoughtfully at the other doll. "This one I will name *Zork*."

After a brief pause, Puh again said, "Very nice, Saree."

Black Wolf chuckled. "Tor, it was your parents who started this when they gave you and your brothers rhyming names."

"I was hoping it would end with us as well." Puh then noted Saree's suddenly downcast expression and hugged her. "But that does not include dolls. Dolls can have any name you like."

My littlest sister, Mi, then approached Puh and held out her doll. Mi had also produced a doll of clay, and while it was a little lumpy in texture, otherwise it resembled Hork and her siblings, with finger-poke eyes and a broad smile.

"Puh-Puh, hair for my baby, too?" Mi asked.

"Yes, Mi," Puh said, pulling her close for a kiss. "We will put a head of hair on your baby, too."

After our meal was finished, Ru brought out her sharpest cutting blades while Twie went to choose a large piece of driftwood from our pile of scavenged wood. We each waited our turn to have a hand's breadth of length cut from our hair. First came Puh.

"My hair is still wet from checking the fish traps and then bringing them to shore," Puh said apologetically to Ru.

"No matter, Puh," Ru assured him. She unbound his long coiled tresses until she held just the tail end of them, which she then placed across the piece of driftwood. Ru used a quick sawing motion to neatly slice off a short section of hair.

I was next. Like Puh, the ends of my hair were still wet. Then came Bror, with another wet head of hair. But there was one good thing about having our damp hair unbound for cutting — at least now that it was loose it would dry much faster. Everyone else, except Black Wolf, who was still trying to grow out his hair, and the youngest children, whose hair was not yet long enough to cut, all had a bit of hair shorn. Saree waited patiently at Ru's side, eagerly grabbing all the cast-off hair before it could blow away on the gentle breeze.

Puh later melted some pine pitch glue on a slab of stone in our fire pit, which was still heated by the fire after the cooking our midday meal. Both Snork and Zork and Mi's nameless doll had their naked heads slathered with the melted glue, and then Puh applied generous amounts of the lopped hair to their pates. The multicolored strands looked a little odd, especially when one considered that Morning Star had graciously submitted to having her hair cut, too. Her silky black locks mixed in with our various shades of red created quite an unusual effect. It was of no matter to Saree or

Mi, however; they were delighted with their newly coiffured babies.

"What will we do with the fish traps now that we have finished with them?" Bror asked.

"We usually flatten the traps and burn them, since even if we return next summer, they would not hold up well over the winter," I replied. "But we do save the wood used to create the racks from year to year."

"I suppose we will leave in a day or so," Black Wolf said sadly. "I will not like to leave. I can see why you so enjoy coming here for a moon or two every summer. I will miss the warm beach, although I must say, I will not miss trying to rid myself of all the sand that accumulates in my fur. It is just as well that Little Fawn did not come here; she would be having fits to see how much sand I carry in with me every day."

"Well, it is the beach, Da," Morning Star said to her father. "One must expect a little sand in just about everything."

"Yes, my old friend," Puh affirmed, "we will leave soon. I will hate to go, as well."

"This has been a most unusual summer," Ria stated. "I did not know that a place such as this existed. It makes me wonder what else it out there that is unknown to us."

"We may find out if we keep searching for a new home," I pointed out.

"We might, at that," Black Wolf agreed.

* * *

The rest of the day consisted of preparing to cook our shellfish dinner, which would be steam-baked in a pit. We began by digging a large hole in the sand on the beach, roughly hip-deep and about one and a half paces across. This we lined with stones and then piled with deadwood, carried from the nearby forest so we would not deplete what little driftwood we had left. The wood was very dry, since we had not had much rain recently, and we needed very little tinder to make our blaze. Once a healthy fire was going, we left our families to keep it fueled until the rocks were hot enough to cook over and then turned to our next chore.

Our last catch still needed to be bagged; first the smoked fish, since that was the first to cure, and by the end of the day, the dried fish. We carried these bags to the place where we cached our dried and smoked foods until we were ready to bring it all home. The cache consisted of an excavated chamber that was lined with rocks and then mortared with clay. We covered our stores with sealskins, then layers of stripped tree limbs, bulrushes, and finally stones. It was a chore to open and close this cache each time we accessed it, but it kept our food safe and cool and dry until we were ready to leave. We kept watch for signs of that animals might help themselves to our stash. Fortunately, just as they guarded our drying racks, our dogs kept these potential pilferers at bay, as well.

After that was done, we returned to the rocky waters near the cave, where we harvested great clumps of mussels and seaweed. These were deposited into large baskets, which were set in the water near the edge, although we often had to move these baskets to keep them from being knocked over or carried away by the waves on the incoming tide. Even so, the tide was still low enough to look for tiny holes on the wet sands that could indicate a clam in residence. If when walking near the hole we saw a stream of water shoot up from it, we then knew that a clam was just under the surface. We had to quickly drop to our knees and scoop away the sand as fast as we could, because clams are also proficient diggers, and they would try to escape by out-digging us. Fortunately, most times we managed to catch up with the clam before it could get away.

Splashing around in the tidal pools also led us to discover a number of good-sized crabs and as many handfuls of large snails as we cared to collect. When we thought we had garnered enough to feed our families, we stood over the six baskets: one of clams, two of mussels, one a combination of crabs and snails, and two heaped with wet seaweed.

"I have not noted any smoke rising from around the bend," Puh started. "So I would guess that the fire must have burned down to coals by now."

"I was just thinking that very thing," I agreed.

"Then our timing is perfect," Bror said. "And besides, I am ready to get out of this sun. My skin has had about as much as it can take before it will be badly burned again."

Black Wolf looked at us each in turn; he alone was not sporting a bright pink complexion. Our freckles had long since begun to meld together, the bridge of our noses had been blistered so many times that no skin grew there, and we had patches on our shoulders, backs, and chests that were scorched raw and peeling from numerous sunburns.

"Your skin does look rather uncomfortable!" Black Wolf said.

"It is not as bad as it seems," Puh assured him. "And it will surely be forgotten by the time we are feasting on all this seafood tonight."

As Puh had predicted, once the layers of hide tarpaulin, seaweed, and shellfish were removed, not a one of us had another thought. Our families had also gathered a variety of tubers, roots, and leeks to add to the pit, plus, a big basket of fresh greens and another of assorted berries.

"This is a fitting meal to end our season at the shore," Ria stated, while prying apart yet another mussel.

"Yes, it surely is," Bror agreed. "Even if it is not quite the end of our stay."

"When will we leave, Puh-Puh?" Twie asked Puh.

"Perhaps the day after tomorrow," Puh answered. "We still need to disassemble the drying and smoking racks and get the sleds ready to go."

Mi's doll was at her side, and Saree was eating with her three dolls lined up in front of her so she could admire them while she supped. Poor Hork looked as if she had been on the trail for many moons, what with her thoroughly disheveled hair and stained visage, but she still smiled gamely.

"I do not want to leave," Saree said sadly. "Why can we not stay?"

"You ask the same question every year," Ru reminded her. "The answer does not change."

"I still do not want to leave," Saree said again, sulkily.

"Me, too," Mi chimed in. "No go home."

Mi was close enough to Puh for him to reach over and pull her onto his lap, "This has been a pleasant summer, has it not?" Puh said to her. "When the snow is blowing and it is cold next winter, think back on these warm happy days. It will help to take away the chill. If we are lucky, we may be able to return again next year."

I knew it was likely that we would have to spend at least part of next summer looking for a new place to move our families, somewhere that had ample sources of game, potable water, and wood. But we could hope for at least a short excursion to the coast.

"I will miss lying on the hot sands," Black Wolf announced. "I may have baked myself like a wisent calf on a spit, but between the sun and the warm sand, it has done much to cure the many things that have pained me these past several years. I feel as though much time has been lifted from my body — I have not felt this well in ages."

"I will not miss the relentless sun, but I will miss the seafood," Bror said. "And I am eager to see my family on the return trip and tell them about how we hunt clams! Wait until they hear how they squirt us and then how we have to dig like badgers!"

"They do not always announce their presence with a stream of water, but it definitely makes it easier to know which hole to excavate," Black Wolf spoke as he helped himself to another clam. "It has occurred to me how helpful it would be if all our prey sent up some sort of signal as we approached. It would save so much time and fruitless searching."

"But, Da! Where is the fun in that?" Morning Star teased her father. "You know you love the hunt."

Black Wolf appeared to think on that for a moment, "Maybe when I was younger. Now that I am closing in on forty winters of life I just want to bring home enough for my loved ones to eat."

"Oh, Da," Morning Star began, "do not talk in such a way. You have many more winters ahead of you."

* * *

Water slams into me. It is cold. It is heavier and more forceful than anything I could have ever imagined. I struggle to keep from swallowing and breathing in the salty blasts. How much longer can I hold on?

The slanting rays of morning sun filtered through tiny gaps in our shelter, temporarily painting sections of the hide tarpaulins with wavering slivers of red. Morning Star noted this as well as she nursed Raven.

"Look at the red lines on the wall," Morning Star said, pointing at the stripes that undulated across the inside of the tarpaulins as the gentle breezes made them flutter.

"Yes, I saw that too," I told her.

I stood to raise the door flap and tied it open to let in the light of day. Now I could see the reason for this phenomenon. The sun was just cresting the horizon; it was a bright scarlet orb, and the sky was deep red, the deepest I had ever seen. It reminded me of the dark blood that poured from a game animal when we have made a strike to its heart.

"The sky is blood-red," I continued, "and there is hardly a cloud."

"Hear the surf!" Morning Star said, looking out the door opening, too. While we were seated, our view of the sea was obscured by the dunes, but the incoming combers were heard clearly as they thundered against the shore.

"It is good that we removed our traps from the water yesterday," I said. "I would not like to be out in those waves today."

"Yes, that is good," Morning Star responded with a nod. "I would worry for you if you were out in waters such as these."

There would not be as much work to do this day. We would finish our preparations to leave our summer homes so that all we had to do tomorrow was to disassemble our shelters and leave their various pieces safely buried in the ditch at the edge of the forest and then pack the sleds. After that, it would be a long and onerous haul to bring all our foodstuffs back to the family compound.

Fox and Pony soon awoke, so we took them over to the main shelter to join the rest of our families for breakfast. When we arrived, Puh was standing at the cusp of the dunes, looking out to sea.

"Pleasant day to you," Morning Star and I wished him.

"Pleasant day . . . I hope so," Puh replied.

Fox was pleased to see his grandfather and clung to Puh's leg while jabbering about a shell he had collected on the way over. Fox displayed his prize to Puh. Puh stooped to pick up Fox and admire his find while Morning Star continued on with our girls to join the others. I stopped next to Puh and also focused my gaze toward the ocean. The waves were laced with foaming white as they rolled in on the beach.

"The air feels different," Puh said.

"I guess it does," I agreed. "It is rather more humid than usual."

"It is," Puh nodded. After a moment he went on, "The sea has churned so much that it has darkened the waves with sand. I do not like the looks of this. Let us tend to our chores as quickly as possible after we break our fast."

Despite that Puh seemed to be trying to keep his conversational tone light, I sensed that he was worried.

"Do you think we should leave today instead of tomorrow — as soon as we pack the last of the fish and our homes?" I inquired.

"No," Puh said, shaking his head. "If the wind that is driving those waves onto shore makes its way here, the forest will be full of falling trees and tree limbs. It will not be safe there."

I then remembered all the twisted and fallen trees we passed by when we came and went from the beach, and realized that we did not want to be amongst those battered trees when a storm hit.

"What should we do?" I asked.

"For now, just do as we planned. It is possible that I am needlessly concerned." Puh gave me a sheepish grin. "At least, I hope I am."

Over breakfast Puh began to speak to the assemblage. "I am noticing signs that the weather might be deteriorating. *Might be*," Puh took care to emphasize those last two words. "After we finish eating, we should pack the last of the fish and take down our homes and racks as quickly as possible. At that point we can assess the weather once more and make a decision. If the conditions seem stable, we can leave as planned, but a day early. If the weather begins to worsen, I believe we should plan on sheltering in that cave down the coast and riding out the storm there."

A stray gust of wind rattled the frame of Puh's house and sent any loose hides flapping noisily for a brief instant. The crashing waves were a constant reminder of what might be lurking just offshore. Small flocks of gulls were winging their way home from their feeding forays. But one of the surest signs of an impending storm was the demeanors of Raena and

Ochs. Both dogs appeared wary and nervous. They stayed near at hand and watched us closely. Perhaps it was only the rough surf that sent vibrations through the ground that upset them, but I thought it was something more than that. Dogs always seemed to sense what we could not.

All the same, I had hoped that we would find our fears were unfounded. However, as we worked to take up and stash the drying and smoking racks, and then finish packing up and carrying the various parts of our shelters to the storage pit, the skies turned gray and the winds were picking up. We left our sleds inverted over our food cache to help divert any rain from our food stores.

We kept some of the shelters' tarpaulin hides to carry to the cave, along with a few lamps, as it would be nearly pitch black at the back of the cave. We also brought blankets and some food and water. We hoped we would not have to stay there for very long.

It was still midmorning by the time we were ready to evacuate to the cave. All of the adults were toting a pack or child on their back and carrying spears, armloads of stores, and belongings. By now the dark skies were spitting rain and the hard-driving wind blew stinging sand and little bits of debris at us. We did our best to shield the children and our eyes from the assault. The babies and smallest children were bundled in blankets to save them from the blasts, but for the rest of us, our scanty summer attire did not offer much protection against the elements.

We were relieved to arrive at the sanctuary of the cave just as we heard the first rumbles of thunder. The combers now slammed into the first chambers harder than ever and sounded with impressive booms that had the children covering their ears. The storm was piling up the waves against the shore and the dogs balked at swimming through the rough surf at the mouth of the cave. But neither did the dogs care to be left behind, so they braved the roiling waters and dutifully followed us. Carrying the younger children, we had to wade through water that sometimes came up to chest or shoulder height on all but Black Wolf. Despite that, as we timed our entry to coincide with an incoming wave, it was all we could do to maintain our footing in the turbulent waters. Once inside the cavernous opening, we wended our way past the numerous rock formations within to finally reach to the dry area at the rear of the cave.

We stood, huddled and dripping in the dark as the wind howled through the cave's many passageways while Puh and Black Wolf worked to light a little tinder so we could use our lamps. Morning Star and our children clung to me, shivering with cold and damp, as we watched the feeble sparks from the flint and iron pyrite fly with each crack of the stones. At last, the tinder caught and I could hear someone gently blow to breathe the flames to life.

There was a collective sigh of relief and a few ohs as the fire grew in strength, carefully fueled and nurtured, stick by stick.

"The lamps!" Morning Star said suddenly.

She and Ru brought forth a several lamps, which were lighted and placed on rocky outcrops within the cave. We now had a little light with which to inspect our surroundings. The ledge Black Wolf had noted during our last visit spanned nearly the entirety of the back of the cave. It was about two strides wide, with a low ceiling perhaps just high enough to sit under, and had a depth of about one and a half strides. Black Wolf could access it quite easily, but it was a stretch for anyone of average height to see over the ledge. Its rocky surface was somewhat rough until one reached the sands that had come to rest on the latter half of the shelf. We decided to place most of our belongings on this ledge to keep from stumbling over them on the cave's floor.

Except for the eerie keening from the wild winds, the sounds of the storm were muted here, and only the distant crashes of the waves and loudest cracks of thunder were heard. Our little fire would not last long, nor did we want it to, since there was no chimney to draw away the smoke. Once the few sticks burned out, we let it be.

I worried that our families would be frightened, but once they warmed from their immersion in the chill ocean, the children began to play and our mates set up housekeeping. Ria began to unroll a woven reed mat on the sand floor and placed a large pelt over it. She settled Mror on the mat, where he and Fox sprawled out on their stomachs and fought their toy animals against one another. My littlest sisters and Pony were entertaining themselves with the dolls, under Twie's watchful eyes, while lounging on matting and blankets prepared by Morning Star and Ru, as each held her baby in one arm. The dogs, too, had settled in, even though both still looked somewhat wild-eyed.

"I have wondered how our loved ones would adjust to a new home after we are forced to relocate," Puh said to me. "But now I can see they will make themselves at home anywhere."

"They are stronger than we credit them," Bror said, having overheard.

"Yes. They are coping, but I am not sure they like this much," Puh responded.

Black Wolf had been rearranging our belongings on the shelf, retrieving what was needed as the rear chamber of the cave was made more comfortable, but he now returned to our sides.

"Any notion on how long we will have to stay here?" he asked.

"Until it is safe to go out onto the beach again," Puh responded.

"Thank you for that astute answer," Black Wolf said dryly.

"It is difficult to say how long a storm will last," Puh said with a shrug. "We can only hope it will pass quickly. We have enough food and water for a few days. And enough rendered seal oil to keep lamps going for several days, at least, if we are careful not to burn through it too quickly. We can dig a few holes in that chamber over there to use to relieve ourselves. Beyond that, we just have to wait it out."

"I saw some large clam shells we can use to dig with," I said. "They were close to the mouth of the cave."

"Let us go find them before the waves wash them away . . . if they have not already done so," Puh replied, walking toward Ria. "Ria, my love, we are going back toward the entrance to find some shells so we can dig a few toilet holes in that chamber," Puh said, indicating a nook off the main cavern. "We will return shortly."

"All right, my love," Ria said with a nod, rising on her toes to give Puh a kiss.

Likewise, I spoke to Morning Star.

"I will go with Puh," I said, kissing her as well.

"Be careful in those big waves," Morning Star said, looking concerned.

"We will not need to go out in the big waves," I assured her.

When we reached the water's edge within the cave, I found that I had been a little overly optimistic. The waves were now washing an area that had formerly been dry, but nevertheless, we were still able to collect a few handfuls of sizable shells without having to go too deeply into the water. The booming within those first chambers was now powerful indeed.

"The water has come up a bit," Puh said to me. "And the tide is just turning."

I looked toward the cave entrance, some ten or twelve strides away, and at the blustering conditions outside, and then back into the shadowy recesses where I could just see the dim flickering of our lamps.

"I hope the water does not rise too much," I said, feeling a pang of fear.

"It will continue to rise. But the floor of the cave slopes uphill. And we have quite a way before the sea will reach us." Puh sounded as though he were trying to convince himself as much as he was me.

"Yes," I answered, trying to smile encouragingly. "We have that to keep us safe."

We did not linger there, but retraced our steps to the rear of the cave, and soon set to work with Bror and Black Wolf digging out a series of holes in the other room.

"If we leave a pile of loose sand by each hole, we can scoop a little into each hole as it is used to help keep the odor down," Puh suggested.

"Yes, let us do that," Black Wolf agreed. "Good thinking, Tor."

"While I am grateful to have a place to get out of the weather," Bror began, "I hope we will not be forced to stay here long enough to fill up any of these holes."

"There are twelve of us — if you do not count the dogs — and there are four holes. Let us hope that will not be a problem," Black Wolf responded.

When this chore was completed, we left the shell shovels by the piles of sand and took up the lamps we had borrowed from the main cavern to return them to their former places.

"Ru-Ru, I am hungry," Mi said to her eldest sister.

Ru looked to Puh, "Should we conserve our food? It is a little early to eat our midday meal."

"That is all right," Puh replied, "let her eat — and anyone else who is hungry. We have plenty of food for now."

Black Wolf and I were called upon to reach the food stores on the shelf, and after a lengthy discussion on which parcels of food they wanted, a meal of smoked fish and some of our limited stock of fresh berries was doled out.

Then we settled on the mats and talked quietly while we waited out the storm. We extinguished all but two lamps to help extend our supply of seal oil. From the back of the cave the entrance was hardly visible, but I thought it seemed as though the bright opening was becoming darker and darker, until finally it was barely discernible from the surrounding cave walls. Without the sun, it was hard to tell how much time had passed.

Usually, Bror would not tell a story unless asked, but while we sat in the semi-darkness Bror broke the silence. "Perhaps I could tell a story."

"Oh, yes, please do!" Ru said brightly.

"Yes! Yes!" piped my younger sisters in unison.

Bror began his tale,

There once was an aged giant deer stag who ruled his territory by virtue of his courage and his strength. Many younger bucks tried to unseat him and steal his harem, but the cagey old stag could not be defeated. After each battle, the great expanses of wood and meadow rang with his victorious bellows . . .

Bror's stories kept the children spellbound as his low soothing voice spun yarn after yarn. I was glad to have this distraction from our precarious situation.

Every so often, I noticed that Puh glanced toward the entrance of the cave. He was trying to pretend that all was well, but each adult was quite aware that the ocean was gradually making headway farther into the cave.

The little ones nibbled at food and eventually nodded off while listening to Bror. I was relieved to see that they were relaxed enough to sleep. Morning Star sat at my side, clutching my hand tightly while holding Raven in her other arm. Raena, too, lay close enough that her chin rested on my thigh, but she remained awake. We talked amongst ourselves, our conversation regularly punctuated by the immense poundings of the waves as they smashed into the outer chambers of the cave. Although the ocean continued its creep across the sand, it seemed to have slowed somewhat and I wondered if the tide had finally reached its peak.

At one point, a bright beam of light shot into the cave and we noted that the sun, now nearing the horizon, had come out from behind the clouds and small bits of pale sky peeked through the gray. The waves continued to hammer the shore mercilessly, so we dared not to exit our shelter just yet.

"Perhaps it is over now," Morning Star said hopefully.

"I wonder how long it will take for the waves to calm down so we can leave," Bror mused aloud.

"I wonder how much damage the storm has left behind," Black Wolf added.

We could only wait and see. But then the heavy gray skies soon obliterated the sun, and the storm continued as though it had never abated. Now, however, the wind seemed to have shifted direction and it roared into the cave, whistling and howling as though a living thing were running amok within the cave's numerous chambers.

"Is this another storm?" Ria asked, dismayed and wide-eyed at the shrieking gusts.

"I believe it is the same one," Puh told her. "I think we just saw a break in the clouds, as we sometimes see between bands of rain."

The noise caused the children to awaken from their naps. They were frightened at the cacophony of sound, so we tried to distract them with bits of food while Bror told more stories. Our day went on as before: waiting, waiting, and watching the waves roll in from the entrance of the cave, gaining ground with each sweeping cascade of water.

"I do not like this, Tris," Morning Star said, inclining her head to indicate the incoming water.

"I do not like it, either," I agreed quietly.

I noticed that Raena and Ochs were now on their feet and pacing, looking around the cave as though seeking something. Then, Raena took a running leap at the ledge and scrambled up on top of it.

"Oh, Tris! Get her down from there!" Morning Star implored me. "She will lie on top of our stores and they will be squashed."

But before I could react, Ochs had jumped up and joined her.

"Now both of the dogs are up on the ledge," Morning Star spoke unhappily.

"Get the children up there," Puh said suddenly.

"What is happening?" I asked Puh.

"I do not know," Puh answered, "but I trust the dogs. *They* know."

We quickly picked up the mats and, shoving the dogs and our supplies back, placed the mats on the ledge, then topped with the blankets so the children would be up off the rough stone.

"Come, Twie," Black Wolf said, beckoning her to him. "I will lift you up."

Twie looked to Puh for his approval, with a fearful look on her face.

Puh nodded to Twie, "Go ahead. Black Wolf will set you up on the ledge, then we will hand the smaller children up to you."

Twie nodded and approached Black Wolf, who easily placed her up on the rock shelf. One by one, Black Wolf, Puh, and I handed the other children up to her. Saree and Mi would not leave their dolls behind, so the dolls went up, too. Finally, my youngest sisters, Twie, Saree, and Mi were comfortably situated on their perch, trying to keep Mror, Fox, and Pony entertained and reasonably still. For now, Ru and Morning Star continued to hold their infants.

I had been so preoccupied with moving the children that I had not noticed the increased rate of incoming sea until I felt the first wave come in and lap at my heels. I turned around and watched in horror as more water poured into our sanctuary, each of the waves higher and more forceful than the last.

"The ocean!" Morning Star cried out and grasped my arm.

I looked at the rock shelf once more. It was now crowded with as many beings as it could hold. Where Raena and Ochs were hiding, I could not tell, but they must have squeezed themselves tightly against the back wall of the ledge, or perhaps they were in the deep shadows, lying on our stores, just as Morning Star had feared.

"The tide will start to go out soon," Puh said. "Just stay together. I will move our lamps up a little so they are not doused by the waves."

"I will get this one, Puh," I volunteered, moving to shift the lamp to a higher outcrop.

The water continued to rise. Morning Star's eyes were wide with fright, but there was not much I could do to provide reassurance, other than to grasp her tightly. When the waves began to slosh around our waists, I realized that we would have to lift the babies up onto the shelf, as well.

Hona and Raven began to cry, as though they sensed that some change was imminent.

"Morning Star," I began, "we must move the babies up to the ledge."

Morning Star's mouth dropped open at this idea. I heard Ru gasp as she came to the same realization.

"I do not want to let her go," Morning Star told me. "She is only a baby."

"I know," I said gently. "But Raven will be safer up on the ledge."

"I will take good care of her," Twie called to us.

"Me, too," Saree chimed in.

"Me, too," Mi added.

Morning Star still did not want to give up the child. Bror, too, was having to persuade Ru to release her grip on her infant, but finally, Ru relented and little Hona, still crying, was passed to Twie.

"Let me take Raven," I said, putting my hands on our baby. "I will give her to Twie. It is best. She will be better off up there. Dryer."

Morning Star began to weep silently as I took Raven from her embrace; reaching up, I placed my daughter in Twie's waiting arms. Poor Twie was already holding one squirming and crying infant, but she gamely took Raven from me, grimly resolute in her determination to care for her charges.

"Twie," I said, "I am entrusting my children to you. Do not let them go — hold them tightly!" By now I had to shout to be heard over the wind.

"I will do all I can," she promised, shouting back.

"Many thanks," I said to her, patting her hand.

I now turned to Morning Star, who was still in tears. But as the depth of the water crept ever higher and the waves slammed into us even more forcefully, she knew that she would need both hands to hold on, just to keep from being washed away.

The water was soon deep enough so that only Black Wolf and I could stand on the floor of the cave and still keep our heads above the surface of the highest waves. The others were forced to hold onto the shelf and bob up and down with each incoming salvo. I held onto Morning Star with one arm wrapped around her, keeping her pinned to my chest.

"Tris," Morning Star shouted to be heard of the rushing water, the booming waves at the entrance to the cave, and the winds that now screamed down the passageways, "The water cannot get much deeper!"

"The tide should start to go down," Puh said, having overheard her. "The tide should have turned long ago. It will recede."

"But when?" Black Wolf hollered over the storm.

Just then Twie cried out and I saw Fox lunge past her, reaching for me.

"Puh-Puh!" Fox whimpered. "*Puh-Puh!*"

"No, Fox, *stay put!*" I commanded.

But Fox was already falling off the ledge. Morning Star shrieked in alarm. Fox had almost hit the water when Raena's head appeared out of the dark recesses of the shelf and she grabbed his leg in her mouth. As we all held our collective breath, Fox hung in midair, suspended by his extremity. I let go of Morning Star long enough to take Fox from Raena.

"Good girl," I said to her. "Let go of Fox now. Good girl."

Raena released Fox obediently and I pushed Fox, unscathed, back onto the ledge.

"Stay put!" I ordered. "Stay with Twie!"

"A huge wave is coming in," Bror warned us.

I turned just in time to be smacked in the face by a comber that almost knocked me down. After it passed, I saw that our lamps had guttered out in the spray, and now we were in darkness.

"Tris!" Morning Star called to me, and I felt her hands clutch at me.

"I am here!" I replied, reaching for her.

I had just wrapped an arm around her, to hold her to me again, when another wave slammed into us, ripping Morning Star from my embrace.

"*No!*" I cried, flailing in the pitch black, reaching for her once more.

In the confusion of voices and sounds, my hand touched something warm, a slender limb. One hand gripping the ledge, I held on tightly to this limb, but the wave was outgoing now, and pulling it away from me, pulling it from my grasp. I held . . . and held . . . and yet, it slipped and slipped until a hard joint came up against my hand. Was it a wrist, maybe? I drew it to me and a moment later, I heard Morning Star's choking gasp. She was sobbing, sputtering, and coughing, but she was still with me, at least for as long as I could hold on.

"Morning Star, are you all right?" her father asked, panicked.

Morning Star could not seem to speak.

"I have her," I told him.

I kissed Morning Star repeatedly.

"I have you," I whispered to her. "I have you. I have you. I will not let you go."

She could only nod mutely, still choking on sea water, as she held onto me.

The storm raged. The entire cave seemed to tremble under its wrath. Now that we were blinded by darkness, we could only hold onto the rocky shelf and listen to the terrible winds and thundering seas while trying to keep the bitter salt water out of our mouths and its burning sting from our eyes.

* * *

How long it lasted I could not say. When the waves finally withdrew, we were thoroughly chilled and exhausted. Our muscles were cramping and our hands bleeding from holding on for dear life to the rough stone for what seemed like an eternity. We relit our lamps and took stock of our situation. Other than being cold and wet, and slightly battered by the waves knocking us against the inside of the cave, we were otherwise unharmed. Best of all, the children were fine. They had stayed warm and mostly dry on the shelf. As soon as we were certain that all was well, we discussed exiting the cave.

"Tris and I will take a lamp to the front of the cave and make sure it is safe to leave," Puh said. "There will be a lot debris — we will need to make sure we can return to our cache of building materials so we can set up a shelter for the night."

And, make sure that our cache is still there, I thought to myself. But it would do no good to further upset the others, so I kept that to myself, but I knew that Puh was thinking the same thing.

As Puh and I waded to the cave we saw much debris floating on the water. Near the mouth of the cavern the storm had deposited whole trees, piles of seaweed, lumpy mounds of dirty sea foam, and assorted sea creatures, now dead.

Upon exiting the cave, we could see that the rain had stopped. A layer of clouds, fine and gray like wispy smoke from a dying fire, drifted across the moon. The waning orb lent an eerie glow to the destruction that surrounded us. We left the lamp near the cavern's opening to mark it and paused to take stock of the damage. Then we noted that the sea had cut a deep swath through the shore, leaving behind a rocky island where the cave was located.

"How lucky that we chose to shelter in the cave," Puh said. "The sand has all been washed away and only the rock remains. For now, we are stranded."

Then a bank of clouds swept in to blot out the moon.

Chapter Seven

Puh and I stumbled through the semi-darkness, past various piles of detritus left by the wind and waves. Sometimes we were forced to climb over enormous downed trees that must have been carried some distance from their original location. The wind still came in gusts, but it was nowhere near as powerful as it had been at the height of the storm. I felt a few drops of rain just as we were preparing to reenter the cave.

"The rain is returning," I remarked.

Puh looked up at the sky and then out to sea.

"We may still have a few heavy squalls to come through yet," Puh stated.

We picked up the lamp and sloshed through the water that still washed in and out the entrance of the cave, even though the tide must have been near dead-low by now. I wondered how long the sea would remain at higher levels. Now that the bulk of the storm had passed, would it continue to drop until it was back to normal?

"Is it raining again?" Morning Star asked when she saw me.

"Just a little," I said.

"What did you find out there?" Black Wolf questioned.

"Was it bad?" Ria followed. "I cannot imagine the wreckage the storm must have left in its wake."

"It is bad enough," Puh replied. "Debris is everywhere . . . entire trees, even. Plus, the beach between us and our campsite is eroded away down to bare rock."

"Do you mean there is no more dirt?" Bror asked incredulously.

"We did not want to venture too far from the cave with just the moonlight to guide us," Puh started to explain. "But as far as we could see to the south of the cave, there was no sand. The ocean has carved out a new inlet. We can get a better look at it tomorrow."

"So we will not be reopening our stash of building supplies to erect a shelter for the night?" Ru surmised.

"No, not tonight," Puh answered.

"Well, let us settle in, then," Black Wolf suggested. "The cave is plenty spacious for all of us, although it will be a tad damp after the ocean invaded our little sanctuary."

"But Da," Morning Star began, "what if the ocean comes back while we are asleep when the tide rises up again?"

"The tide will make the water come up higher, but I do not think it will be anywhere near as high as it was before," Puh assured her.

"Can we be positive that the cave will not flood again?" Morning Star was understandably concerned. I drew her close to comfort her while we all awaited Puh's reply.

"We cannot be absolutely sure," Puh said, pausing a moment, "but the force of the storm was what drove the sea toward shore, and now it has passed. It may take a short time to level out. However, I do not think the next tide will be much higher than usual."

Black Wolf, too, approached Morning Star and touched her shoulder, smiling down upon her, "I will stay awake and watch the water so we will not be caught unawares. Although I doubt the dogs would allow that to happen. And speaking of the dogs, they are much calmer now. I believe they know that the worst has gone by."

The nook that formerly housed the toilet holes, which were swept into oblivion by the maelstrom's waves, was not one of the many available that was chosen for occupation. Instead, we excavated new holes and then each settled with our families into several small alcoves, covering the damp sand with mats and whatever tarpaulin hides and blankets we had brought to keep us reasonably comfortable throughout the rest of the night.

I lay with Morning Star in my arms as our children dozed nearby. We were awake, talking quietly. Morning Star still seemed rattled by her near-drowning, and I could hardly blame her. I had once come close to meeting a similar fate myself, and I knew it was a distinc-

-tly unsettling feeling.

"I have never in my whole life been as frightened as I was today," Morning Star whispered to me.

"I was afraid, too," I admitted. "So afraid to lose you . . . so afraid the children were in danger. Raena, what a good dog." I reached out to touch her and felt her cold nose on my hand. "You saved our little Fox; you are such a good girl," I told her, stroking her head.

Raena's warm tongue licked my hand.

"She is a good dog," Morning Star agreed. "Those waves were so strong . . . if she had not caught Fox . . ." Morning Star broke off and I could feel her shuddering sobs.

My heart pained me, both at her grief and at the anxiety that revisited me from the awful events of the day. I kissed Morning Star fervently and murmured, "I would not let anything happen to you or the children." But as I said those words I was still disconcerted by the incredible force of the storm. The powerful waves had ripped Morning Star from my grasp with terrifying ease. It had taken every ounce of strength I had to keep her from being washed away.

Morning Star sniffled a moment but then seemed to calm herself.

"I know," she said, holding me tighter. "I know you will always take care of us, and for that, I am grateful." Morning Star then returned my kisses. Sleep did not come for some time.

* * *

The next morning we found Black Wolf snoozing

near the mouth of the cave, as bright sunny skies shone outside. He had made of a fire from various pieces of driftwood that the storm had flung up on the beach, and it was now just a pile of smoking ashes and bits of wood that were too wet to burn. He had been snoring heartily, but he awoke at the sounds of our muted chatter.

"I really did stay awake all night," Black Wolf said self-consciously when he saw us. "I stayed awake until I saw the tide begin to recede again, and also, I saw the sun rise."

"No one could doubt you, old friend," Puh said to Black Wolf, helping him stand. "I could see the high-water mark in the cave from last night's tide. It may have been a bit higher than normal, but it appears you stayed dry."

"Yes," Black Wolf answered, nodding in agreement. "I watched the water creep up the low-lying section of the first chamber and I watched the water creep out. And I kept my fire burning most of the night to give me something to do. Much of the wood did not care to burn. It smoked quite a lot, but fortunately, the outward slope of the ceiling took it outside. However, the resident spiders did not care for the smoke and they rained down all around the cave's entryway. *Ack!* I stayed back to keep them out of my hair. It was lucky that I was not attempting to cook anything over that fire, as it surely would have ended up with a crunchy coating of toasted spiders."

"Thank you for staying up all night. It must not have been very comfortable," Morning Star said to her father, giving him a hug. "All the same, I am so grateful; I slept much better knowing you were out here."

"That is reward enough for me," Black Wolf said as he embraced her, too. "You all had little ones to care for, so I was the logical choice to stand guard. And I was glad to do it. But now I am hungry! What do we have to eat?"

"Did the thought of toasted spiders pique your appetite?" Ria asked, grinning up at Black Wolf. "Well, let us then break our fast."

It turned out we were all quite hungry. After a good meal, we were ready to discuss our plans for the day. It was easy to see that the storm had cut new inlets into the beach, including one that now flowed into a swampy area where the water was diffused amongst the muck and bulrushes. We just needed to find a way around the swamp to relocate our cache of stored foods and, hopefully, find our sleds still intact, or at least repairable. Then we could begin the trek homeward.

"The beach on the other side of the cave has not been eroded as badly. We could walk up the shore a way until we have bypassed the marsh and then cut across land to our former campsite," I proposed.

"I was thinking the same thing," Puh said. "With luck, we could be there by midday and construct a shelter just big enough to sleep in for one night while we prepare the sleds for travel. Assuming the sleds are still in one piece."

We all agreed that this was the best course of action. Once our belongings were packed we were ready to begin our hike up the beach. The children were excited at the prospect of this adventure, but as we walked in the soft sand they gradually tired of the excursion. Especially Saree, who juggled her dolls from hand to hand and found that three dolls in two hands were awkward to carry. Twie valiantly offered to tote one of the dolls for her little sister, and Saree gratefully accepted, although she was somewhat aghast to see Twie carrying her cherished baby in such a nonchalant fashion. Saree may have had an expectation of her doll being lovingly cradled, but instead it was handled indifferently, sometimes held upside down, sometimes dangled by the hair.

We had walked for some time when suddenly Raena and Ochs stopped in their tracks. They held their noses high up in the air, and their ears were pitched forward. Then they abruptly spun and looked behind us; we were startled to see several large seals haul themselves out of the ocean. The dogs began to bark wildly, and positioned themselves between us and the seals.

The seals burped a few barks at the dogs and hissed with displeasure, but otherwise ignored them and soon found places to flop contentedly onto the sand. Another seal pulled itself out of the waves and joined them.

We decided to keep going, but it was not long before more seals came up out of the water and their numbers only increased.

"These seals must have been at sea during the storm and are just now returning to land," Puh said to us as he watched five more seals emerge from the waves.

Not only were they returning from the ocean, but they were evidently rejoining their seal family members and friends on a stretch of shore where great numbers of them were amassed. As we neared, we could hear that they were an unruly congregation. Most of the seals seemed content to watch us go by them, scratching at themselves like dogs at the hearth. Others were placidly soaking up the sun and napping peacefully. Some, particularly the big males, took umbrage at our presence. They charged us, flopping up the beach and spraying sand as they went, their mouths opened wide with noisy aggression and displaying formidable sets of teeth.

"Halloo!" A voice called. "*Halloo!*"

"Who do you suppose they are?" Black Wolf asked, pointing at the newcomers.

We looked out across the wide expanse of swamp and saw three figures in the distance, waving at us and calling out to get our attention. The dogs immediately turned their focus to the source of the voices. They barked a warning but soon concentrated on the seals, as they were much closer and potentially more threatening to us.

"There are people out here!" Bror seemed surprised. "Have you ever met others out here, before?"

"No, I have not," I answered.

"I have never seen any signs of other people," Puh began. "But it does not surprise me to know that some clans come to the coast to stock up on food for the winter."

Puh waved back to the people and we started to walk toward them. Likewise, the men also began to approach us.

I noted that the strangers walked with a peculiar gait as they strode through the marsh. Even at that range, I could tell that their feet seemed very large. It was only as they drew closer that I saw the reason.

"They are wearing snowshoes!" Black Wolf exclaimed.

"How very clever," Bror murmured. "I would never have thought to use snowshoes when walking across a swamp."

"Halloo!" one of the men said again, now that they were almost upon us. "I see you have dogs! Are they friendly?"

"Pleasant day to you," Puh returned. "Yes, the dogs are friendly. How did you fare during the storm?"

The men were smiling broadly, but all the same, they somehow seemed defeated. Their shoulders were slumped as though they had borne a great weight, and despite their agreeable smiles, their eyes looked aggrieved. They were Old Ones, about my age or perhaps a bit older, but they did not share the red hair and pale skin of my clan. They had dark brown hair, dark eyes, and well-tanned flesh. They were dressed in loincloths much the same as we men were, but they differed in their footwear. They wore an odd sort of woven fiber boot lashed to the soles of their feet, which were then tied onto snowshoes. The men seemed a little surprised to see our dogs, but they accepted them calmly.

"It is good that you have dogs. We hear that they can be very useful, but we have never actually seen any before," a man said. "The storm was very bad. *Very bad.* We lost eleven of our group. And you? Did you lose anyone?"

"We were very fortunate," Black Wolf told them. "We sheltered in a cave on the beach and it protected us from the worst of the weather."

"Cave?" Another man piped up. "Do you mean the Cave of Spirits?"

"I do not know if it has a name," Puh admitted. "But it is a half morning's walk down the coast," Puh indicated in the direction whence we had come.

We had to yell to be heard over the loud squawks and barks of nearby seals, some of which were still quite agitated at our unwelcome intrusion.

"Let us leave the beach," one of the three men said. "Those seals will soon lose their patience. We only came out to see if any of our traps survived the storm, but we have not seen any evidence of them. They must have been washed away."

Fox had been standing quietly at my side, but now he touched my hand to get my attention.

"Puh-Puh," Fox said. "Look at baby seals! Look like puppies! Fox have one?"

"*No,*" Morning Star said firmly before I could answer.

"But, Muh-Muh!" Fox protested.

"No," Morning Star said again. "They may look like puppies but they are not tame animals like our dogs. They will bite if you try to pick them up."

Fox's face fell with disappointment.

"Even if no make them mad?"

"Yes. Even if you do not do anything to make them mad," I said to Fox. "That is how they protect themselves. And besides, they may look like little puppies from here, but when you come up close, you can see that they are in fact large creatures."

We followed the men as they led us to a place beyond the seals' colony where the ground beyond the beach was less swampy. The men took off their snowshoes, as they were no longer needed, and slung them over their shoulders as they walked.

"I am Mok," said one of the men. Mok was shorter than average, but he had a lean, powerful build. "And this is my brother, Harin, and this is our cousin, Tuk."

Introductions were swiftly made. Mok, Harin, and Tuk seemed friendly indeed, and also very concerned that we had been displaced and were in need of a food and shelter.

"Our homes have been badly damaged," Tuk stated grimly. Tuk was a bit taller and perhaps a bit younger than Mok. "Some were completely destroyed. But we are setting up temporary housing until we can rebuild something more substantial that will hold up against winter weather. Please feel free to come with us; you can stay until you decide what to do next."

"Yes," Harin agreed. Harin appeared to be the younger brother. He was taller and more slender than both Mok and Tuk. All the men wore their hair and beards long, but Harin's dark braid was by far the longest. Harin's single plait started at the nape of his neck and he wore it tossed casually across his chest and over his shoulder like a garment. "You have so many little ones with you. You will need to keep them safe and fed. Our families will be glad to have your company."

"That they will," Mok said with a nod. "We have had other strangers with us for over a year now and we have so enjoyed their presence. They are men of your people," Mok said to Black Wolf.

Black Wolf brightened at this news.

"I wonder if they are anyone I know," Black Wolf pondered. "Do they speak of going to the annual fall Gatherings of The People?"

"No, but then, one is injured in his head and he does not speak," Tuk said, shaking his head. "The other, his brother, only speaks of returning home to the mountains when they are able to travel again. For now, they live among our little clan and assist us in bringing in food and firewood."

"I believe they hoped to go home later this summer," Mok added.

We were now walking singly or in pairs down a narrow path that bisected the marsh.

"You are building homes to stay the winter?" Puh questioned the men.

"Oh, yes," Mok said as though it should have been

obvious. "How would we survive without good shelters? Although, I must say, we are in a bit of a quandary. Our homes just flew apart in the storm. We must devise a way to construct something much stronger."

"That was the most violent weather anyone has ever seen," Tuk agreed.

"It was," Harin nodded vigorously. "My aunt is the oldest person in our clan, and even she said that she had never seen the like."

"It was certainly the most severe tempest we have ever experienced, as well," Black Wolf agreed.

We continued to talk about the storm as we trekked, our hosts pointing out various things to us: the evaporating puddles of seawater left behind by the wind-driven high tides in low spots on the land, piles of seaweed and dead sea life, and even some deceased birds — all of which by now had attracted the attention of an assortment of undiscriminating corvids and gulls.

As we neared the tree line, it became apparent that we had been wise to take shelter in the cave. Trees lay strewn about, twisted and broken. We had to clamber over and through numerous downed trees before we finally reached the little collection of hastily erected tarpaulin huts.

"Where are the men of The People you spoke of?" Black Wolf inquired, looking around eagerly.

I cast a glance about as well. Those residents I saw were all Old Ones.

"They are assisting with the burials," Harin replied. "They will soon return."

"Burials?" Bror repeated. "Did you say you lost eleven members of your families?"

"Yes," Mok nodded gravely, his eyes tearing. "A most terrible loss. We were forty-four in number; we thought our clan was doing so well. Then the storm came and took so many lives with it."

"We grieve for your losses," Puh said earnestly. "How can we help you?"

"That is kind, but we invited you here in hopes of helping you," Harin exclaimed. "We will soon have our camp rebuilt, and we have plenty of food for the time being."

"Perhaps we can help one another," Black Wolf suggested.

"Black Wolf!" someone called out.

Black Wolf spun around, and we all turned with him.

"Running Buck!" Black Wolf responded. "How did you come to find yourself here? Where is Sky Fire? Do you know your families think you both dead?"

Running Buck quickly closed the span between himself and Black Wolf and grasped his forearms in greeting, and then embraced him heartily. Running Buck's father, Gray Elk, was Black Wolf's first cousin, and Black Wolf had not seen Running Buck in some years.

"Sky Fire will soon be here," Running Buck hesitated before resuming. "He moves a little slowly these days, and he is resting in the shade with the others. He will return with them before long." Running Buck shook his head, "Poor Ma and Da; we never meant to worry them or our mates and children. We came down the river to see the salmon run and catch some fish to bring home with us after we delivered two dogs for Da, but then we were charged by a bear. It was not a big bear; it was a sow with a cub. But we caught her unawares and she caught us unawares, as well. The bear slapped Sky Fire in the head and he has not been the same ever since. The sow took off a big piece of his scalp; the skin has grown back but there is no hair there. His mind seems a bit . . . simple now."

"*Simple?*" Black Wolf questioned.

"Yes. It is hard to describe. He seems to be slowly regaining strength, and he moves well enough, but he tires easily and his mind does not work as it used to. It is as though it moves slowly, too," Running Buck told Black Wolf. "We were lucky that Tuk and his clan took us in. I do not know where we would be if they had not found us and cared for Sky Fire while he was so severely injured." Running Buck paused and clapped a hand on Tuk's shoulder. "These are fine people. We owe them much."

Just then a woman sauntered over. She was tall for a woman of the Old Ones, and like Mok, Tuk, and Harin, she had dark hair, eyes, and skin. She seemed weary and sad, but she had a quiet dignity. Suddenly, she showed a spark of interest as she looked Black Wolf up and down, her eyes lingering with curiosity at the tattoos on his forearms.

"We have guests," she said, also turning to scan

the rest of us with a smile. "I am Terah. Welcome to our clan. I am afraid you find us with everything a bit ahoo just now. But we will soon set everything to rights."

Introductions were made yet again, but I still had the distinct feeling that, even though she was polite to everyone, she had more than a passing interest in Black Wolf.

"Terah is my aunt," Harin said to me in an aside.

"The same aunt who is the oldest person in your clan?" I said, surprised.

"Yes," Harin nodded.

I had envisioned someone much older. I was not always good at guessing the ages of people; I found animals were easier to judge. Some people managed to acquire more signs of aging than others, and Terah did not appear to be exceedingly old. She was perhaps the same age as my Puh. She may have seen thirty-five or - six winters, but not many more. She was a well-made woman, and despite being a bit muddy, with her hair slightly mussed after all the turmoil from the storm and work to restore order in their small village, she was still an attractive person. Like some of the other women we saw here, she wore a scallop-shell pendant, stained in a ruddy hue and suspended from a cord around her neck, and she had small shells decorating her clothing.

I then noticed that Morning Star was watching Terah closely. She too had seen Terah's reaction to her father, and she gaped at the woman as though shocked to find a predator in our midst. Black Wolf seemed oblivious to the attention he had garnered. He was bus-

-ily engaged in conversation with Running Buck.

"Did you escape harm during the bear's attack?" Black Wolf asked.

"Almost," Running Buck replied. "My injuries were very slight. The bear bit my hand — her teeth just grazed it — but it was no concern at all at the time. Later, it swelled up like a wisent that failed to complete a river crossing." Running Buck blew out his cheeks to illustrate a drowned and bloated animal. "But our new friends knew just what to do and now my hand is just fine."

Running Buck held out his extremity for our inspection. It was scarred, but seemed perfectly functional.

Terah seemed determined to insert herself into the conversation again.

"Let us break for our midday meal," she suggested. "Grief has dulled our appetites, but our new guests must be hungry. Come and eat and tell me how you survived the storm."

Terah led us to an area where the debris had been moved aside and we could find seating atop various downed tree trunks that had been dragged near the outdoor hearth, which was currently unused. The fallen tree trunks still appeared to be a little damp from yesterday's rain, but they were more comfortable than the moist soil at our feet.

We brought out some of our own stores to share, and our hosts also produced generous quantities of foodstuffs.

"Do not use up your food just now," Harin said gently, when he saw us opening our sacks of dried fish. "We have plenty. Truly. The one thing we never lack here near the ocean is food. Potable water may become scarce, but we have lots to eat."

Terah sat next to Black Wolf and quietly plied him with questions as we ate.

"How is it you came to be so near the coast?" she asked. "Other than Sky Fire and Running Buck, I have never seen any People from the East here."

"For that matter, seldom do we see any Old Ones, either," Tuk piped up. "This is a rather lonely location. We almost never hear news from the outside."

"Yes, therefore guests are always a welcome sight," Terah added.

"We were living down the coast, south of here," Black Wolf explained. "We had spent the last moon or so catching fish and hunting seals, and we were just preparing to go home when the storm struck."

"They sheltered in the Cave of Spirits!" Mok told Terah.

Terah's eyes widened. "That must have been an unearthly experience! Did you see any spirits? They rage and howl and cry out whenever a storm hits."

"We saw no spirits," Puh began, "but we certainly heard a lot of eerie sounds. I thought it was the wind blowing amongst all the rocky columns and stone formations."

Our hosts looked doubtful. They evidently preferred to cherish the idea of those mournful spirits rather than to consider the notion that the wind might have been responsible for the noises in the cave.

"Have you not heard the stories about the spirits who live in that cave?" Tuk asked.

We shook our heads. The cave had been filled with rocky protuberances, and it tended to be wet in many places, but we had seen remarkably little sign of life inside it.

"The cave has voices," Tuk went on, "They are all that is left behind of the many people who have tried to shelter there during past storms."

Morning Star and I exchanged uneasy glances.

"Do you mean to say that people have sheltered there in the past?" I questioned.

"Oh, yes," Harin informed us. "And as bad as this storm was, our stories tell us that others were far worse; — more powerful, and of far longer duration! Those who attempted to gain sanctuary within the cave were overcome and then washed out to sea."

I shuddered inwardly at this news.

"There were certainly a number of spiders in that cave," Black Wolf pointed out. "The storms do not seem to bother them."

"We do not go in that cave. Not ever," Terah told us. And then, seeing our discomfort at this topic, she politely changed the subject. "You all seem to have young families . . . except for you, Black Wolf. Have you a family?" Terah inquired demurely.

Black Wolf hesitated a moment. He quickly glanced at Running Buck, who in all likelihood did not know about his relationship with Willow Woman.

"Actually," Black Wolf started, "I have two. Morning Star, Tris's mate, is my oldest daughter with my mate. We also have five younger children. Then I have a second family, as well." Black Wolf seemed ready to continue, but he broke off his sentence abruptly. Apparently, he had decided that it was enough information to divulge to a stranger.

"Two families, that is quite an accomplishment," Terah said. "Alas, I no longer have a family, such as you speak of. My mate lost his life six years ago while netting salmon, and my children are grown with families of their own. I have much missed their company."

"Your children did not settle near here?" I asked.

"No," Terah responded. "I had four daughters. One died as an infant, another when she was still young girl. My other daughters were paired with men who live far to the north. I have not seen them since they left us. My parents passed when I was hardly more than a child, and my siblings are all gone, too. I am quite alone."

"I am sorry to hear this," I said to Terah. My sister Ru had nearly left us for a distant pairing, as well. We were all grateful that she did not choose to leave. "You have had to endure all that and plus your recent losses as well."

Terah made an effort to smile bravely.

"I do not often let myself dwell on sad things. And, I am thankful to still have my nephews and their families," she said. "I would rather think to the future. I am ever hopeful that better days are ahead."

Terah looked at Black Wolf long and searchingly, but again, Black Wolf seemed not to notice. I felt Morning Star shift on her seat next to me, causing the tree trunk on which we were perched to roll slightly. I hazarded a glance at her and saw her consternation.

Moments later, however, our meal was interrupted when the remainder of their group returned, bringing Sky Fire with them. I had not met Sky Fire before, but he was easily identifiable as he stood amongst the Old Ones in his company. While not as tall as Black Wolf, he was at least a head taller than his friends. Sky Fire wore his hair parted to one side, seemingly to cover the bald spot left by his wound. His countenance lit up as soon as he saw Black Wolf, and Sky Fire immediately quickened his pace as he approached him. Black Wolf arose from his seat just in time to have his cousin fling his arms around him.

"Sky Fire!" Black Wolf cried out. "How good to see you!"

Sky Fire said nothing, but he clung to Black Wolf as tears appeared at his eyes and rolled down his cheeks. Black Wolf tenderly wiped away his cousin's tears.

"Do you cry out of happiness?" he asked Sky Fire.

Sky Fire only grinned at him in response.

"Does he understand me?" Black Wolf questioned Running Buck.

"I think so," Running Buck said with a nod. "He seems to hear, but he does not speak."

"Sky Fire, I am so surprised to find you and your brother here," Black Wolf said a trifle loudly to his cousin. "I am told you hope to go home soon?"

Sky Fire still only looked at Black Wolf with an elated grin.

"*Go home?*" Black Wolf repeated. "Do you think you can make the journey?"

Sky Fire nodded slightly, barely perceptibly. Black Wolf turned to Running Buck, unsure that Sky Fire had truly responded to his question. Running Buck rose from his seat and peeled Sky Fire's arms from around Black Wolf and gently led him back to where he had been sitting. Running Buck brought his brother a few pieces of smoked fish. Black Wolf and Running Buck then resumed their seats.

"He does seem to want to go home," Running Buck told Black Wolf. "And I believe he is strong enough to make the trek. The problem is that he is nearly defenseless. And I cannot be sure I can defend us both if we run into another situation as we did with that sow."

"But we have told you that we could escort you home," Mok reminded Running Buck.

"I know," Running Buck said gratefully to Mok, "but now that the storm has wreaked such devastation on your homes and you have lost so many loved ones, we cannot take you away from here. You already have much work to tend to. We will help you rebuild, but then we must find our way home."

Mok and some of the others started to protest, but Black Wolf spoke up, "Did you follow the River of the Bears here?"

"Yes, we did. We were delivering some of Da's pups to a clan who lived four days' travel down the river," Running Buck replied. "After we left the dogs, it was too much temptation not to come farther down the river until we found salmon. The run was almost over, but we caught several fine fish and feasted for many days. We were going to smoke a few more fish and bring them home when we met with the sow and her cub."

"How many days' walk from here were you at that time?" Black Wolf inquired.

Running Buck pondered this question, "Perhaps less than two days. Not far."

I could guess that Black Wolf was considering making the trip with his cousins. Not only could he restore the long-lost brothers to their parents and their own families, but he then would be but a short journey from his own second family. Black Wolf looked to Puh. As a friend from boyhood, he knew that Puh would be reading his mind.

But as it turned out, it was Ria who spoke up. "Why could we not take them up to Gray Elk's? Afterward, you could visit with Willow Woman and your son as well. They will still be at the Fen of Falls — at least until they must leave for the Gathering."

Black Wolf seemed relieved that he did not have to propose this excursion.

Our meal continued quite pleasantly, with much excited chatter. It was only later when the food was cleared away and we broke into groups to help our hosts continue to clear away debris and set up temporary lodgings that Morning Star managed to get in a few words with her father.

Black Wolf was holding Fox, showing him the tortured grain of a large fallen tree limb and explaining how the wind had caught in its leaves and had cracked the big branch right off the trunk.

"And see here?" Black Wolf indicated another tree whose roots were ripped from the ground. "The ground under this tree was saturated by all the rain until it was so soft that the storm was able to push the whole thing over."

Fox was suitably awed. Morning Star was less impressed and had other things on her mind. Carrying Raven, she stood by her father.

"Da," Morning Star started, "we will not stay here long, will we?"

Black Wolf seemed taken aback by her question.

"I do not suppose so. Why do you ask?" Black Wolf then pointed to the tree again, "Look Fox! A squirrel's nest! They will need to build another home in a new tree, now."

"Da," Morning Star tried again, "I believe that woman has designs on you."

"Woman?" Black Wolf repeated. "I have not noted a great number of women here. The only one I have even spoken to is what-is-his-name's aunt."

"Harin and Mok's aunt," I supplied. "Terah."

"Nice little woman," Black Wolf commented. "They all seem like nice people. I did not get the feeling that any one of them had designs on me."

Morning Star seemed to relax. She traded glances with me, smiling wryly. In past years her father had had quite a roving eye, and I wondered if she was concerned that he might resume his old habits once again.

That night, as we put our children to bed in the small hut we had built for our stay, Morning Star once again broached the subject.

"I am glad that Da is not inclined to cozy up to that woman," she said.

"I am glad that you are glad." That seemed like the safest thing to say.

"Da is a grown man and he can do want he wants," Morning Star began. "But I want to go home. I do not want to be stuck here while he makes himself yet another attachment, only later to finally take Running Buck and poor Sky Fire home, probably visit with Willow Woman and Oak at the Fen of Falls before we can at last return to our own homes! We will be lucky not to have consumed all the food stores we worked so hard to accumulate by then!" Morning Star shook her head. "Da . . . it is his good looks and his height that draw women to him. He has always attracted a great number of feminine admirers."

It was true that Black Wolf had always enjoyed the attention of women, but despite my initial impression I was not sure that Morning Star had anything with which to concern herself. Terah appeared to like Black Wolf and to be rather curious about him, but I did not sense any kind of serious romantic fervor from her. On the contrary, she seemed devoid of emotion most of the time.

Chapter Eight

The weather remained mercifully sunny for most of the next day. A few bands of dark clouds occasionally wandered through, sometimes weeping a few drops of gentle rain that kissed our faces and passed harmlessly before allowing the sun to come out again. This, and a steady breeze, helped to dry everything that had been so saturated by the storm. There had been much wreckage to be removed, but the clan's small compound was now nearly cleared of all the demolished homes and fallen trees and branches. It appeared that the dwellings had been constructed of a combination of wood, which formed the frames, and woven bark strips to create the walls, which were then coated with numerous layers of an earthen mixture which I was told consisted of dirt, pulverized dried grasses, and dried manure collected from the droppings of any local herbivores as could be found. The roofs were layers of hide tarpaulins, whose seams were painted with pine tar.

The new structures were erected over the footprints of the old ones, though our hosts were careful to reinforce the buildings' frames to prevent a repeat of the same disaster.

Puh shook his head at this.

"No work of man could have stood up to that tempest," Puh said to me quietly, out of hearing of the others.

"I agree," I told him. "Many of nature's creations failed to successfully endure the wrath of the storm, as well."

By the fourth day with our friends, they had settled into their new households and we spoke of taking time to celebrate this accomplishment.

"Why could we not cook a feast on the beach, as we did not long before we left our former camp?" Black Wolf suggested.

"That is a fine idea," Tuk said. "The fish are usually shy after a storm, but they may have resumed their old habits by now. And even though we have not yet replaced our crab and fish traps, we can still spear our prey."

"We will need to catch a number of fish and harvest what shellfish we can find to feed everyone," Harin joined in. "And also, we must dig a long trench and start a fire within it."

Terah nodded, too, but she did not seem to be as excited at the prospect of a feast as all the others.

"I believe you have finally worked up an appetite," she said. "Mok and Harin, why do you not begin to excavate the trench in the sand and tend to the fire? Tuk, you and your other cousin Rek can gather some more men to go after the fish and clams."

The men turned away to embark on their various missions. Morning Star, Ria, and Ru were all still involved in readying their little ones for the day, while Puh, Bror, Black Wolf, and I stood by with our dogs and Black Wolf's cousins, hoping for something to do.

"We picked up a lot of seaweed when we had our feast," Bror began. "Would you like us to gather some for today's beach bake?"

Terah smiled wanly.

"Why, yes; that is a fine idea, Bror," she said.

"I will help," I volunteered.

"Me, as well," Puh said. "Perhaps we can assist with digging clams, too."

"What about mussels?" Black Wolf inquired hopefully. "Do you have mussels around here? I understand that they prefer to grow on rocks."

Terah thought on this for a moment.

"We may be able to find some a bit farther to the north where there is a cluster of rocks," she said. "I do not know if there will be mussels upon them, but there are oysters."

"If someone is willing to guide me, I would be happy to go and see," Black Wolf said eagerly. "How far is this place?"

"It is a long walk, but I will take you," Terah responded. "We will need to wear snowshoes on our feet and carry a few baskets with us."

"I will just go and tell Morning Star that I will be on the beach for a while," I said, leaving my companions. Puh and Bror said as much, too, so that their mates would not worry about their unexplained absences, either.

I found Morning Star in our shelter, which she had extended slightly during our stay by adding another tarpaulin to the structure to give us a little more room. The door flap was tied open to let in fresh air and sunlight, and she was kneeling on the matting as she fussed with Fox's hair. Poor Fox was not enjoying having his curls untangled and rearranged. His sisters Pony and Raven both had smooth, straight hair that did not snarl as easily as did his.

"I will be with the other men at the shore for a while," I told her. "We have decided to have a fish bake on the beach, as we did not so long ago."

Morning Star smiled at this, absently rubbing her right shoulder as she sometimes did since the storm had nearly carried her away. She had not complained, but I cringed inwardly as I thought about the jarring her shoulder must have suffered while the outgoing water was trying to drag her out of the cave as I desperately clung to her arm. I took a moment to gently move her hand aside and massage the sore joint, prompting Morning Star to smile up at me and reach to momentarily lay a hand on my bearded cheek.

"Fresh food! That will be wonderful!" Morning Star said, seeming pleased at the idea. "The little ones will want to nap later this morning, but maybe after that we can look and see if there are any suitable greens and tubers in the area. So far, everything I have seen has been either crushed by falling trees or soggied by the torrential rains. But it could be that those who live here may know where we can find some edible plant life. Perhaps some onions, if they have not turned to mush."

"That would be pleasant," I said, stooping to kiss her farewell. "I will return as soon as we have harvested enough food. We have quite a crowd to feed."

"Yes, we do," Morning Star replied, smiling brightly and returning my kiss.

I left Raena with my family and went to rejoin Puh and Bror, without mentioning to Morning Star that Black Wolf would not be accompanying us. I saw no reason to potentially upset her by revealing that tidbit of information.

Puh, Bror, and I followed the narrow path through the forest until it came out at the marshy grasslands that separated it from the shore. The trail narrowed further once we reached the swamp, and at times we still had to walk though puddles of water left by the storm's higher tides. We each toted a large basket to fill with our harvests. The sun was nearing its peak when we reached the ocean. We usually tried to avoid the beach at this time of day, but if we were going to feast this evening, we had better catch our dinner before then.

The long ditch had already been dug, and driftwood was now being collected. The tide was going out, but it had a long way to progress before we could attempt to dig clams. However, we could drag more driftwood toward the ditch. There was wood aplenty all over the beach, and although some of it was still wet, especially on the underside, we collected any we thought could be persuaded to burn. The shore was also liberally strewn with seaweed that had been ripped loose by the storm and deposited on the beach. Numerous decaying sea creatures and birds also remained, but countless winged scavengers had by now nearly stripped the carcasses bare.

As the ocean gradually receded, Harin explained to us how his people caught fish without using traps. He showed us a spear made of wood, with the far end split into four sections, held apart by a wedge and lashed tightly to keep the four-pronged assembly rigid. These four tines were honed to sharp barbed points. It was easy to see how one might lance a fish with such a weapon, but I was curious as to how they managed to get close enough to do such a thing.

I was just noticing that I was sunburned yet again and pondering that the ebbing tide was perhaps low enough to allow us to begin to gather the makings of our dinner when I saw two boys come running toward us. Puh and Bror were already knee-deep in the water with their fish spears, but I was still on the beach, tightening the hafting of my newly constructed lance. I recognized the boys from our hosting clan.

"Tris," said one of the boys as he panted for breath, "come with us."

I was surprised that there were none of the usual polite greetings or even a request to join them. But I could see that they were alarmed, so I called to my companions, "I am going with these boys for a little while. I will soon return." Then I addressed the lads, "All right, where are we going? Has something happened?"

"Yes, they are stuck in the pond," a boy said, grasping my arm and beginning to pull me in the direction whence they had come.

"Who is stuck in a pond?" I questioned.

"Black Wolf and Terah," the child hastily answered.

"Let us go, then," I responded. Stuck in a pond? How bad could that be? I was sure this could be easily sorted out.

I quickly followed the boys at a trot. They led me to the trail that crossed the swamp, but then broke off that path to another that was even more tenuous than the first. The ground, if one could call it that, was quite wet. The brown muck squished up between my toes, and we had to be exceedingly careful about where we placed our feet because of the sharp spikes of the newly sprouting grasses that grew amid the established greens and the many broken shells the littered the area.

"You usually wear snowshoes on your feet when you cross the swamp, do you not?" I asked as we picked our way along.

"In the mushy areas, we do," one youngster replied.

If this was not among the areas that could be called mushy, I could not imagine what a truly mushy area would be like. It seemed as though we had gone quite some distance. I was ever aware of the scorching sun overhead and the heat, which made sweat run down my forehead and into my eyes. I tried to wipe away the dripping perspiration with a knuckle, knowing that my well-salted fingers would only further irritate my eyes. Flies flitted about, sometimes causing us to slap at them when their vicious bites drew blood from our tender flesh.

At last I saw what might have been called a pond. It was an inlet that was connected to the sea at high tide but was cut off from the open ocean as the tide receded. I could see a rocky shore not too distant up the coast, where Black Wolf and Terah must have gone in search of mussels. The boys motioned for me to continue to follow them. The swamp grass thinned out then, and we were walking in spongy mud that sucked at our feet with each step. Then the boys stopped and pointed ahead of us.

"What am I looking for?" I asked.

"They are there," one boy informed me.

"Where? Behind those clumps?" I questioned.

"Clumps?" the boy repeated, looking perplexed.

I stared harder. Then I realized: Those were not lumps of mud; they were people!

I started to run toward them, but a boy called after me, "Do not run! Walk carefully!"

"Find their footprints and walk in their steps," the other boy recommended.

I stopped immediately and looked about me for footprints. I soon found some. Obviously they belonged to Black Wolf. No one else had feet that size. Each track was now filled with water.

The boys did not attempt to accompany me. They stood back, watching with grim anticipation. I was almost upon Terah and Black Wolf before I could distinguish who was who and see what had happened. Both were almost entirely covered with the slimy muck that passed for mud. Black Wolf was visible only from the shoulders up. The rest of him was mired in the swampy earth. Terah was laid out full length across the ground, arm outstretched and holding determinedly onto Black Wolf's hand. Their eyes were closed with exhaustion, and the mud on the upper parts of their bodies had dried and even begun to crack in places.

"Black Wolf! Terah!" I said anxiously. "How long have you been like this?"

Black Wolf's eyes flew open.

"Tris!" he cried out. "I am ever so glad to see you!"

Terah's eyes opened as well.

"Oh, I am thankful that help has arrived," she said in her flat monotone, but she did indeed seem relieved.

"Let me take Black Wolf's hand," I said as I lay down on the mud beside her.

Terah waited until I had gripped Black Wolf by the wrist before she moved herself out of the way.

"Try to float on top of the mire," Terah advised Black Wolf.

"I do not even float well in the water!" Black Wolf retorted.

"Do not struggle!" she admonished him. Then to me she said, "Tris, just pull him slowly and steadily. I was not strong enough to pull Black Wolf out, but perhaps you can do it. When the boys came along Black Wolf told them to find you or your Puh, or Bror."

I nodded and pulled back on my arm to draw Black Wolf toward me. As I knew from past experience, he was a heavy man, and the drag created by the suction of the sludge that had ensnared him only made the task more difficult. I was also aware that the damp ground on which I lay was extremely odiferous.

"This mud has quite a smell," I observed.

"It is a rather piquant aroma," Black Wolf said. "I have been thinking on that. If we take some of this home with us, it will confuse our prey when we go hunting. They will never know that men are anywhere nearby." Then he complained, "My mussels will be ruined."

"I will be gentle, I will take care not to wrench your arm," I assured Black Wolf, still drawing him closer at a creeping pace, as I pulled him out of the mire.

"Not *my* muscles," Black Wolf clarified, "my mussels! The ones in the basket! Sitting out in the sun will surely have ruined them!"

"We will get more," Terah said, attempting to console him. She turned to the boys. "Go dump out the basket of old mussels and get fresh ones! And some oysters, too!"

The boys grasped the basket between them by the handles and took off at a swift pace, or at least as quickly as they dared on this treacherous landscape.

It seemed to take an eternity, but at last I had extricated Black Wolf and he tiredly slumped on the relatively solid ground nearby. He was still covered with the stinking muck from head to toe. Only parts of his upper face and the top of his head remained unsullied. As I joined him, I realized that I myself was now half-covered with a coating of putrid mud, as well. Even my hair, coiled and gathered into a long thick rope that hung down the length of my back, was slathered in slime.

"Let us walk down to the beach where we can wash off," Terah suggested. "The boys should have gathered a fresh load of shellfish by now."

Terah guided us through the marsh. She alone was wearing snowshoes. It turned out that Black Wolf's feet had been too big to enable him to wear any of the clan's snowshoes, so he had opted to go without, joking that surely his feet were large enough that he did not need them. Little did he know how important they were. The area by the pond, or inlet, as I would have called it, had soft spots that could swallow any being that happened into it. If Terah had not held onto Black Wolf, it was likely that he would have perished before help could arrive.

We found the boys, who had indeed collected a great quantity of both mussels and oysters and had bedded them in the basket with plenty of wet seaweed. The tide was still on its way out and the water was quite low here, so we opted to walk down the beach, as the water was somewhat deeper in the area where Tuk and his cousin Rek were showing Puh and Bror how to spear fish. Mok and Harin were nearby, digging clams as the tide receded.

The boys paused to set the basket down at the edge of the water where the contents would stay wet, and we came up behind them, eager to rid ourselves of our odiferous coatings. Black Wolf was so well disguised that he startled the brothers Harin and Mok, who turned upon hearing his footsteps scrunching in the sand.

"*Eeee!*" cried Mok as he sprung to his feet, and Harin's mouth dropped open in shock.

"It is I, Black Wolf," he said by way of identifying himself, only then aware that he looked less like himself than a giant grotesque creature that had crawled out of the swamp.

Poor Terah was not much better off than Black Wolf, and neither was I.

Mok and Harin began to laugh at themselves. Unlike those in my clan, these Old Ones did not laugh silently, but with a sound that was alien to my ears. Their laughter resembled the sharp barks of the seals.

"You gave me a fright!" Mok chuckled. "What happened to you three?"

"I found a soft spot in the marsh by an inlet, and before I knew it, I was sunk up to my waist and still sinking fast," Black Wolf told us.

"There are many of those places in the swamp," Harin said, nodding. "You were fortunate to escape."

"I only managed to get out because Terah held on to me so I would not sink into oblivion," Black Wolf said, smiling at Terah and patting her shoulder apprecia--tively, causing her to surrender a small smile. "And then those boys came along and we sent them to find help. They brought Tris back and he — for the second time in his life — pulled me out of a trap. Only this one was a bit more slimy. Terah has been too gracious to mention it, but she did warn me not to walk too near the pond."

Terah just stood by, looking down modestly at the sandy beach. Black Wolf grinned, looking at his begrimed physique.

"I surely am a mess," Black Wolf admitted as he began to wade into the water.

"A mess," Puh agreed, "But you are perfectly camouflaged. Hardly anyone would guess that you are in fact human."

"That is true," Black Wolf acknowledged with a hearty laugh. "I dare not stay still for too long or the gulls will try to pick my bones clean, just as they have everything else on the beach."

Terah and I followed, each of us continuing until we were approximately chest-deep in the ocean, scrubbing away at the mud as we proceeded. The mud, by then completely dried, came off in great silty clouds, so dirtying the surrounding water that soon I could no longer see my feet.

By the time the fish and shellfish had been harvested, we were ready to assist with the next step, which was removing the last remaining coals and ashes from the trench and placing layers of wet seaweed and seafood upon the hot stones at the bottom of the ditch. Finally, the whole thing was covered with spare tarpaulns, which were somewhat worn and tattered, but all the others had been used to create shelters for those of us who were visiting.

The sun was well into its decline by the time our evening meal was ready to be consumed. Another fire was set up on the beach to provide light for our sup, and also smoking torches to help drive away the many gnats and mosquitoes that had flown in to take part in the feast.

As Morning Star sat at my side, happily eating a variety of succulent fish, she suddenly turned to me. I half expected her to remark on the odor I now carried after lying in the muck. Her nose had wrinkled for just a moment when I first greeted her as she brought our children to the beach but she did not choose to remark on it just then.

"Tris," she said quietly.

"Yes?" I responded.

"I have a thought; that is, I have been thinking about Sky Fire," she said.

"His condition is most unfortunate," I said solemnly.

"It is," Morning Star acknowledged. "Do you suppose that Willow Woman's healer could help him?"

I pondered this. Willow Woman's healer was the most renowned in the lands. He had worked much magic on even the most seriously wounded patients. Even Black Wolf himself, after having received a most grievous head injury, was brought back to health under her healer's skillful ministrations.

"Are you saying we should take Sky Fire to Willow Woman's lodgings before we take him to his home?" I asked.

"Yes," Morning Star said with a nod. "I hate to prolong our journey, but I also hate to see Sky Fire like this. He has a family to go home to . . . his mate . . . his children. Will he even know them? Or know his parents? He is like a child in his current state. A very big child."

"I think it is a good idea," I told her. "He seemed to know Black Wolf on some level, so maybe there is hope. Let us bring it up with the others after we have finished eating."

Just then, our conversation was interrupted by Black Wolf's outburst.

"A pearl! I believe I have found another pearl!" Black Wolf shouted, leaping up from his seat to kneel by the fire. He held up his prize for closer inspection in the fading light. "I did not want to try an oyster at first — they do not look as appealing as the mussels and clams. They have a disconcerting appearance, rather like something that has come out of one's nose . . . but now I am glad I have, for at last I have found another pearl for Willow!"

We all clustered around Black Wolf to observe his find. This pearl was larger and lighter in color than the one he had discovered in the mussel.

"I must find a way to make the pearls into a gift for her," Black Wolf mused to himself.

* * *

We waited to return to the clan's compound be-
-fore we broached the subject of taking Sky Fire to Willow Woman's healer. We had now become used to the narrow trail that led from the forest to the beach, and it seemed almost mundane to make the crossing through the marsh, guided only by the light of the setting sun and a few carried torches.

Our hosts excused themselves to retire for the evening and put their children to bed, as we would soon be doing ourselves.

Our little huts, arranged in a circle, were near one another, and we paused to speak in the dwindling torchlight before settling in for the night.

"Tris and I have been discussing Sky Fire," Morning Star said to broach the subject. "It has occurred to me that Willow Woman's healer might be able to cure him, as he once cured Da."

Her idea produced some excited chatter from the others as everyone spoke at once, but Black Wolf looked doubtful.

"Sky Fire's injuries are more than a year old," Black Wolf said, shaking his head. "If he has not healed by now, I am not sure there is anything anyone can do — even a man as proficient in the healing arts as Gray

Owl. I am more than happy to go so I may at last spend time with my beloved Willow and our little son — who must have grown so much since I last set eyes upon him; I just do not want any of you to be too optimistic about Sky Fire's chances of being healed."

Morning Star seemed disappointed at her father's response.

"So you do not think it is worth a try?" she questioned.

"I would not go so far as to say that," Black Wolf shrugged. "Let us talk to Running Buck about it tomorrow and see if he has an opinion on the matter."

"Sky Fire might have an opinion of his own," Puh pointed out.

"That is true," Black Wolf agreed. "At least, we can try to ask him. I am never sure how much he understands, although Running Buck insists that he understands most things." Black Wolf then looked around at the darkening forest, "If we had not just taken our evening sup at the beach, it would be easy to forget how close it is to this little enclave of homes."

"That is true," Bror agreed. "Our hosts are a kindly people, but incredibly tough and resourceful. They manage to make a living from both the land and the sea."

"Indeed! Those nets I saw hanging up in the brush to dry after the storm — I would be interested to see how they are used in the river when the salmon run," Black Wolf said. "I was so tempted to think that we might be able to relocate to the coast, but now I see the various difficulties: the storms, the inhospitable swamps, and the constant need to conserve water because potable water is in short supply. Inasmuch as I would like to think that we will visit with these new friends again someday, I no longer desire to live here — although I am glad to have seen the ocean and experienced the novelty of life on the coast. There is a beauty to the col--ors of this place, a feeling of comfort in hearing the rhythm of the sea, and, of course, the bounteous fresh foods are not to be forgotten."

* * *

Later that night Morning Star and I were still pleasantly entangled as she lay in my embrace. I was nearly dozing when Morning Star softly spoke my name.

"Yes, my sweet?" I replied sleepily.

"I have been thinking."

"Yes?"

"I do not think that Terah has designs on my Da, after all."

"No?"

"No," Morning Star said firmly. "I think she likes Da and she thinks him a handsome man, but she has not shown anything but polite interest." Morning Star paused. "Terah reminds me of your Great Gran."

This revelation surprised me. I did not see any similarity — and besides, Terah was much younger than my Great Gran. If I guessed right, she was nearly half Gran's age.

"How so?" I asked.

"Like your Gran, Terah has lost almost everyone she knew. Her parents and older relatives are all long gone, friends from her youth, and her siblings as well. Her mate and all her children have passed, and many of her grandchildren and even great grandchildren, too. Do you not remember how sad your Gran was for so many years?"

I thought on this for a moment.

"Yes, I do," I said slowly. "She would not live in the house where she had spent most of her life and instead resided in the little house where you and I now live. It was not until you and I were paired that she gave up her house to us and was finally ready to take up residence in her old home again with Puh and his family."

"Now that I see Terah, still fresh in her grief, I can more clearly understand how your Gran must have felt," Morning Star told me. "It must have been such an all-consuming anguish. Poor Gran could not bear to be around others, especially those who still had their loved ones. It must have been too painful to be in the company of happy families when her own had perished."

I held Morning Star tighter and kissed her.

"You are so wise," I murmured to her, "I am sure you are right. Poor Gran lived with just her pet squirrels for company for years. It was only as I was leaving my boyhood behind that she finally came to terms with her grief and started to allow us back into her life again. Puh and I brought her food and hides, and made sure she had all she needed, but Gran scarcely acknowledged us. I am grateful to have her returned to the family again."

"I am, too," Morning Star agreed. "I cannot imagine enduring what either your Gran or Terah has had to cope with. To feel is both a blessing and a curse."

 **Chapter Nine** 

It would take at least six days to reach Willow Woman's summer lodgings at the Fen of Falls, but everyone in our group was willing to make the trek if it could help Sky Fire. In fact, Running Buck was willing to leave that same day. Our hosts seemed startled at our sudden departure plans. However, they generously offered their assistance: brothers Mok and Harin insisted that they would lead us through the forest until we reached our former camp. There, we could collect our sleds and the stores hidden in the cache. Afterward, we would go to the home of Bror's kin, where we had stopped in almost two moons past.

We hurried to pack and to make the quickest possible journey back to our old campsite. Fortunately, Harin and Mok knew the most direct route through the woods, and Sky Fire seemed to have no problem keeping pace with the rest of us. In fact, he gleefully carried Fox or Pony from time to time, which allowed us to move much faster, since toddlers on foot tended to dawdle.

The dogs trotted up and down the path, keeping watch on all sides. Their vigilance was appreciated as always, but we really did not expect to see predators here. Now that we were leaving the stunted woodlands near the beach, most of our difficulties were caused by the tangles of downed trees. These once-proud denizens of the now ravaged forest seemed to thwart our progress at every turn as we clambered over them, or found a route around them. Branches that had once reached for the sky now grasped at us as we passed by and often scratched our flesh. Finally, we found the path so familiar to us.

Our sleds were still inverted over the food cache, but we were dismayed to see that they were pinned in place by yet another uprooted tree.

"Well, it is good that the tree fell over the sleds in such a way that they were protected from the storm," Bror stated, pointing out the one positive thing that could be said about the situation.

"Yes, but now we have to remove it so we can access our belongings," Black Wolf groused. "And we have only our hatchets and one axe."

Our axe had been stowed under the sleds. I crawled under the tree's branches and felt around under those vehicles for its smooth wooden handle. My fingers came into contact with something and I drew it out. It was one of our shovels. I reached farther along the length of the sleds and finally touched the hafted axe head. I brought forth the axe and rose to my feet.

"How do you think we should proceed?" I asked.

"Right now, the roots and branches are holding the trunk of the tree up off the ground," Puh said. "Perhaps if we just cut away some of the limbs that are directly over the sleds and the cache, we can retrieve them and clear away just enough to get at our stores."

We all agreed that this was the most practical plan. I immediately began to hack at the few large branches that were blocking our way, while Puh, Bror, and Black Wolf chipped away at the smaller ones with their hatchets. In the meantime, the others foraged the nearby brush for berries; it would be midday before long, and we would need to eat before we hit the trail once more.

Harin and Mok, assisted by Running Buck and Sky Fire, pulled out the sleds and the remaining shovel as soon as they were free and gave us a quick assessment of their condition.

"The shovel is fine, but the bigger sled on top has a cracked frame," Mok told us. "Never fear, we will fix it while you continue to take away the limbs."

"We are almost done," I said. I had already removed the last of the large branches blocking our cache and was helping to drag away the smaller limbs and twigs that the others had lopped off.

When our summer's worth of dried and smoked foods was extracted and the empty cache was recovered with the layers of matting, tarpaulins, and all, our sleds were ready to go. This time, it was our stored goods that provided a meal for our former hosts. They had taken such good care of us that I was glad we could return the favor in some small way. Puh offered to leave some of our dried foods with them by way of thanking them for all they had done for us, but the men would not hear of it.

We bid Mok and Harin heartfelt farewells, embracing them and expressing our hopes that we would see them again one day. And then we set out.

The sleds were heaped with sacks and baskets and piles of the household items we had been using all summer. There had been discussion about bringing our accumulated stores home before going to Willow Woman's lodge, but Puh recalled Gray Elk's desperate situation when we were last there. Puh suggested that we carry as many supplies up to them as we could to alleviate at least some of their distress.

Our little ones had sometimes ridden on the sleds on our way to the coast while the sleds were relatively unencumbered, but now riders would not find their seats very comfortable. I was grateful that it was only a half-day's hike to the home of Bror's kin; it would be a grueling trek, at that. While the weight of a small child would not add significantly to our burden, I was glad for Sky Fire's willingness to continue to tote the children. Black Wolf and Running Buck pulled one sled while Puh, Bror, and I dragged the other larger vehicle. All those sturdy enough to wear a pack also carried a load.

When we came to a shady glade that was near the halfway mark, we stopped for a short break. I was quite thirsty and my stomach growled hungrily. As I looked up at a clear blue sky, I noted that the air was beginning to cool slightly. It felt wonderfully refreshing on my sweat-covered flesh. When we resumed our trip, Puh and I traded sides at the front of the sled, leaving Bror in his position between us.

It was nearly dark by the time we reached Aunt Vee's dwelling. Their three dogs set up barking vigorously as we entered their small compound. The family had just finished their evening meal and they looked up in surprise when they saw us. Our dogs were related to theirs, as all came from the breeding stock of Running Buck and Sky Fire's father, and there seemed to be some recognition amongst them.

Aunt Vee rushed forward and embraced Bror as he stepped out of the sled's harness.

"I am so glad to see that you are all safe!" Aunt Vee cried. "We had a terrible storm blow through six days ago. We knew it had come in from the coast and you must have been in the thick of it! Dor and Lor went to the shore to see if you needed help, but when they got there, they could not find any signs of life. We were so worried!"

"Are you all well?" Sere asked us anxiously. "We were safe, here. I worried that a lightning strike might cause a forest fire, like the one that happened a few years ago, but luckily, we were spared."

"The thunder did shake the ground, though," Dor told us. "It must have been absolutely wild on the coast."

"It was rather blustery," Bror said, smiling to set them at ease. "We were fine. We sheltered in a cave and we then met with another clan of Old Ones who had us stay with them for a few days."

"It was very pleasant to meet new friends," I added.

Aunt Vee gaped at us, but soon recovered herself and approached Ru, "May I hold the baby? I have not seen my sweet little Hona in far too long, and who knows how long it will be before I see her again."

"Of course," Ru said as she laid her baby in Vee's arms, "You will find her heavier! She has grown so these last few moons."

"Indeed, she is as plump as one could wish," Aunt Vee heartily agreed. But then she suddenly seemed to remember that we would not have had our evening sup yet.

"Oh, but you must be so hungry — you must eat!" Still holding the baby on her hip, she turned to her youngest son, Lor. "Bring out some of our smoked reindeer meat. And the leftover roasted tubers, mushrooms, and onions from our meal."

"Yes, Muh," Lor said obediently, and he promptly left us.

"Dor," she addressed her middle son.

"Yes, Muh?" he answered.

"Bring out our water bag; our guests must have an incredible thirst."

"Yes, Muh." And Lor also disappeared.

Sere was already adding more wood to the fire and inviting us to make ourselves comfortable. Puh, Bror, and I dragged the sled on one side of the compound and gratefully removed ourselves from the harness, rubbing our sore shoulders where the leather straps had bitten into our flesh. Black Wolf and Running Buck did the same. The smaller children were tired, and their empty bellies were beginning to strain their normally happy dispositions. However, I was amused to see that Sky Fire settled Fox and Pony on his lap and he silently mugged for them, conveniently distracting my tots until they could be fed. Morning Star smiled at this.

"Tris, please get some of our dried stores from the sled for the children," she requested. "Just some small strips of dried fish for them to chew on for now. The dogs would probably like to eat as well."

"I am sure the dogs would like to eat," I said, bending to give her a kiss before returning to the sled to retrieve the foodstuffs. I freed a sack of dried fish from the sled lashings and returned to the group, dispersing fish to both human and canine as I went. When I came to Sky Fire and my two youngest children, Fox and Pony immediately stuffed the fish into their mouths and began to gnaw on it. Sky Fire accepted at slab of the dried fish as well, and he continued to make funny faces for the children while he ate, greatly exaggerating his struggles with the tough flesh for their amusement.

The smoked reindeer was a great treat; we had not had any since our previous visit here. On our return trip home from the coast we usually traded goods with

Bror's family. They hunted the reindeer migrations so we were happy to barter our dried and smoked fish for their dried and smoked reindeer meat.

As we sat around the fire, we exchanged news about how we had spent our summer. We tried to downplay the severity of the storm so as not to upset them. It had been frightening at the time, but having fared so much better than had our new friends, we were quite aware of our good fortune.

Besides, especially after we had heard how much worse previous coastal storms had been, we hardly felt as though we had gone through anything in comparison. I was glad that Aunt Vee had baby Hona to occupy her attention so that she did not concern herself too much with our recent trials. It pleased me greatly to see that Aunt Vee and Sere still seemed to be extremely happy. Indeed, they had a pleasant household. They all worked together to keep themselves quite comfortable and well-supplied.

Then, as always, the talk eventually came around to discussing hunting.

"What do you think of the bright skies that have ushered in each dawn since last spring?" Sere questioned us. "And it seems to me that this summer was a little cooler than usual. I wonder if that means we will see an earlier rut and migration."

"We finally saw those odd creatures you spoke of, Black Wolf," Dor said. "They came around not long before the storm. I had never seen any such being before. They were sort of like an ugly wolf."

"A wolf with an absurd laugh," Sere added. "But these beasts do not seem to have a sense of humor. They seem to prefer to scavenge off the kills of others, but if they think they can do the job themselves, they have no qualms against taking down their own prey. They have been harassing us all summer."

"Have the creatures approached your home yet?" Puh inquired.

"Not yet," Sere responded, shaking his head. "But we came across them at an old kill site. They are wary of us, but curious at the same time. We see evidence of their presence frequently. I do not believe they are many in number, but I do not like to be sharing our hunting territory with these animals. It is my guess that they are the hyenas I had heard about in my youth, and at that time they were known to be intelligent and resourceful competitors for any available resources."

"I have heard the same," Puh agreed. "They are not as fleet of foot as wolves, but they have great size and strength in their favor. They are persistent and they are smart enough to wait for the best opportunity to seize prey."

"I worry that they might start stalking our home," Sere said grimly.

"We should take steps to eradicate them," Lor suggested.

"If these hyenas were known to our ancestors, then they must have been eradicated at some point in the past," Black Wolf spoke up.

"That is true," Bror said. "Perhaps this is the time to take action, while there are just a few in the area."

"Even if we succeed, the problem is," Puh began, "that when one type of animal is eliminated from its place on the landscape, it just creates the opportunity for another similar animal to slip into the vacancy."

"You do not think the hyenas can be killed off?" Running Buck asked Puh.

"Probably," Puh said with a shrug, "for a while, anyway. But they seem to have reasserted themselves in a location where they had been driven out for at least the past twenty or more years. I am sorry not to be more optimistic. We have kept them out for a short period, but they will keep testing the limits of their territories and expand as quickly as their breeding allows."

"So what is the answer?" Running Buck questioned.

"It would take a great many men to keep them at bay indefinitely," Black Wolf mused. "Let us speak with Willow about this when we take Sky Fire to her healer."

We all nodded in agreement. Willow Woman, as Head Elder, tended to see problems from a broader perspective than did we. Her father had raised her to eventually inherit his seat as Head Elder. I suspected that this, along with her innate wisdom, had endowed her with an ability to quickly assess and resolve issues.

* * *

Later that night, after Morning Star and I had settled our dozing children into the usual sleeping chamber that Aunt Vee set aside for us, Morning Star turned to me. "Tris, did you notice how Sky Fire behaved with Fox and Pony?"

"Yes, I did," I said, wondering where she was go--ing with this train of thought.

"He seems to interact with small children better than he does anyone else . . . except maybe our dogs."

I pondered this notion.

"He does not need to speak to small children or dogs to be understood," I said.

"Fox and Pony both speak," Morning Star countered.

"Yes, but not quite fluently." I cast about for reasons that might draw Sky Fire to our little ones and Raena and Ochs. "Perhaps he simply feels more at ease when he is with beings who do not have social expectations."

* * *

The skies were fair. A friendly sun hung high in the sky over a serene meadow of tall fragrant grasses and wildflowers. Dragonflies flitted here and there on gentle breezes. Fox bounded through the lea, an exultant smile lighting up his face. Suddenly, a harsh manic laughter disrupted the peaceful scene.

* * *

We left the home of Bror's family early the next day, as soon as we had breakfasted, made our trades, and repacked our sleds with the bartered reindeer meat. I was haunted by my Dream. It had started out so pleasant, but the demonic laugh shattered my sleep so badly that I lay awake for the rest of the night. Morning Star noted my sleep-deprived state, but when she questioned me I remained taciturn, as I knew she would be frightened, since Fox had figured largely in the Dream. I simply told her that I had not slept well — which was true, but I did not like to even dissemble. Morning Star knew me well enough to know when I was not being completely forthcoming, but she chose not to pursue it.

I made myself concentrate on following the path, keeping the sled centered as Puh, Bror, and I dragged our burden along the trail. As before, I saw that Sky Fire was eager to help tote the smaller children when they tired of trudging along. Even six-winters-old Saree and her three dolls rode on his back from time to time, although Sky Fire would end up carrying two of the dolls himself, since Saree could only manage one while she was holding on to her mount.

We stopped to rest at midday, but only briefly. When we halted our trek that evening, it occurred to me that if we had gone straight home, we would be there by now. But I had only to look at Sky Fire to strengthen my resolve to see our journey through. A few more days and we would be at the Fen of Falls, where we would find Willow Woman and her healer. I thought it likely that we would leave our sleds there when we finally continued the trip to Running Buck and Sky Fire's home in the mountains.

We had found a place by the trail where we could erect shelters, employing our traditional method of using saplings to form the frame and cladding the bent sap--lings with boughs of fir trees. This evening's huts were somewhat irregular in shape, but that did not matter. As long as we could find enough young trees spaced so we could bend them until they met with the tops of their neighboring trees and lash the tops together, they would make the skeleton of a fairly solid structure. By the time a good blaze was alight and our simple repast was ready to be consumed, we had built four small shelters, one for Puh's family, one for Black Wolf and his cousins, one for Ru, Bror, and their baby, and one for my family. These tiny abodes were just large enough to sleep in — even our spears were too long to bring completely indoors at night, so we slept with our spears pointing out the door opening, ready to take on any potential threat.

Raena also lay in the doorway, standing guard as always. The children were sound asleep and Morning Star was putting down folded tarpaulins topped by pelts to make a place for us to lie down. I peered past Raena at the darkening skies, taking note of the pink-stained clouds as the color slowly drained from them. It was a peaceful evening; crickets chirped and I could hear the eerie cries of lynxes as they yowled and screamed at one another somewhere in the distance.

"You were very quiet today," Morning Star said to me, speaking just above a whisper.

"I did not get as much rest as I would have liked last night," I admitted.

"Did you Dream?" she asked.

"I did," I hesitated before going on, but as ever, I could withhold nothing from Morning Star for long. "I Dreamt of Fox running through a meadow."

"Was he frightened?" I could hear the alarm in Morning Star's voice.

"No, he seemed happy. Joyful, even."

"But there was something that gave you unease?" Morning Star hardly needed to be told.

"Yes," I said, "I heard an awful laughter. It awakened me. And I have been thinking all day about Fox and his rash actions. He has great spirit, but he must learn to be more cautious. I must teach him to be more careful."

"Laughter? How odd. That does not sound so terrible. But he is only a little boy," Morning Star reminded me. "He will learn."

"His misbehavior is almost unheard-of in my clan," I said, perplexed.

It was on the tip of my tongue to mention my younger brother Dak, who had been the most adventurous of all of us. He had been killed by wolves after he had just turned fifteen winters old. But I did not want Morning Star to become any more frightened than she was already. And yet, Fox seemed to even outdo Dak when it came to his fearlessness and his penchant for risky behavior. Morning Star tried to soothed me.

"Do not forget that he is my son, too," Morning Star said gently. "He may look like you, but he has some of me in him as well. Do you not recall what an incorrigible child I was?"

Morning Star giggled a little, no doubt recalling some past mischief, but the idea that Fox might have inherited his mother's willfulness and disobedient nature did not ease my mind.   I stroked Raena's head a few times and she turned to lick my hand before putting her chin down on her paws.   I could just discern the glint from her open eyes and see her ears shift as she kept watch.

I crawled to Morning Star and took her in my arms, kissing her.

"I can only hope that Fox has inherited your intelligence as well," I told her lightly. "If he has a keen mind to go with his courage, he will be a formidable man."

* * *

The next several days were arduous as we struggled to bring our heavily laden sleds along the trails that brought us to the White River, which would lead us to the Fen of Falls. We did not travel along the river's bank, as those rocky shores were far too treacherous to traverse. I knew this only too well after having fallen in those roiling waters several years ago. As we made our way through this area, I found myself caught up in a deluge of vivid memories. The frothing waters of the White River were a short distance from our trail, but we could still hear the violent rush of the current and feel the weight of the thundering flow as it rumbled across the landscape.

The air surrounding the river was damp and chill. It was easy to be mentally transported back to the day that Bror and I had been walking along the river when I slipped on the slick rocks and toppled into the water. Old Ones are not typically good swimmers. We have heavy-boned, muscular bodies that want to sink rather than float. The strength of the river's current dragged me downstream at an alarming rate, hurtling me against boulders and numerous obstacles. I thought I would drown, until I was rescued from a soggy death by a cow mammoth. She had stepped into my path and then pulled me from the water. I was both amazed and startled by this inexplicable act of kindness. As a hunter who had once participated in a mammoth hunt, I did not anticipate that an animal such as a mammoth would feel compassion for another creature, especially one who was of a species that sometimes preyed upon them. But yet she had. She had stayed by my side for a short period before ambling off mysteriously; perhaps she had felt that with her good deed now completed, she could now return to the herd and go back to her endless grazing. But she had left me with an incredible sense of euphoria at my miraculous rescue.

Happenstance had brought us together several times after that. Each occasion had filled me with wonder and gratitude. There was something surreal about being in her presence. It had pained me deeply when she was killed by hunters. I sometimes relived that day in my dreams, each time running as fast as I could in an attempt to intervene, but I never made it in time.

Suddenly, it felt as though my grief were trying to choke me, and I tried to swallow it down.

"Are you all right?" Puh asked me, from his place in the harness beside me.

"I am just thinking of the cow mammoth," I replied. Then I quickly added to change the subject, "We have not seen many mammoths of late. They must be feeding elsewhere these days."

"That is true," Puh agreed, "we have not even seen signs of their passage. No huge patches of churned-up earth where they have been foraging for young shoots and roots, no piles of dung, no trees stripped of bark and foliage. Perhaps they have spent the summer up by the lakes. It was a dry season until the storm came. There would be plenty of water for them up there."

"Puh, would hyenas be worrisome to the mammoths? Is it possible that they might have driven them off?"

"I would not think so. Not to the adults," Puh said shaking his head, "not the healthy adults, anyway. Infants and the infirm mammoths might be fair game for hyenas."

* * *

Sometimes there were not enough trees, even the small saplings we used to make our shelters at the end of each day, and we were forced to construct crude lean-tos from our tarpaulins and the few sticks of deadwood that we could spare from our nightly fire. Unlike the area by the beach, there were ample predators here. Whether we had the shelter of a hut or a lean-to, most of us took turns guarding our sleds during the night, packed as they were with foodstuffs. I volunteered to take the first shift, to be relieved by Puh, who would then be relieved by Bror, then Black Wolf, and finally Running Buck. We each only lost a little sleep, and the fire was tended continually. I was always glad to at last be able to crawl into a warm bed and wrap myself around my mate. Morning Star would be awake, awaiting my arrival, ready to rub my aching shoulders, legs, and back. It was worth it to stay up a little later to come in to such wonderful comforts.

Not only were we on constant alert, but the dogs were tense, as well. We had come across numerous tracks from bears, wolves, and the enigmatic hyenas. From what we could gather at kill sites, the hyenas' tracks usually obliterated most of the paw prints of those that had actually brought down the animal. They made a thorough job of scavenging anything that was left, leaving little for latecomers to pick at.

We were still one day's walk from the Fen of Falls, puttering around our camp as we took down our lean-tos and stowed our gear, readying our sleds and packs for the trail. Early-morning mists still hung over the land, and a rosy dawn held promise for a pleasant day. Raena and I took Morning Star and the children to empty their bladders, as everyone was doing in various locations not far from our camp. As always, we left the site in shifts so that the sleds were constantly under guard. I was just about to escort my family back though the grasses and brush when suddenly I heard an odd cry.

It was like a high-pitched, sharp bark, almost bird-like in tone. Our heads swiveled as we looked for the source of this sound. Then a whoop followed.

"To the camp, quickly," I said, herding them in that direction.

I could see that the others were also gathering at the camp in the distance.

"Tris, what was that?" Morning Star asked me in a tremulous voice.

"I do not know," I answered. "I have never heard that kind of noise before now."

"Puh-Puh, was that a fox?" Fox inquired. Sometimes foxes made high yips and yaps that resembled the vocalizations we had heard, but I did not think so.

"No, Fox," I started, "those cries were somewhat deeper than a fox's cries. And definitely louder. I believe they were made by a larger animal."

Morning Star carried Raven, but Pony and Fox were on foot. Recalling my Dream of Fox capering though that sunlit meadow, I put Fox on my shoulders.

"Hold on," I said to him, and I lifted Pony onto my left arm, leaving my right arm free to wield my spear. Raena stuck close to us, her hackles bristling as her lips curled from her teeth.

Within moments, we were amongst our companions once again. Black Wolf, as the tallest of us, scanned the landscape for any signs of the creatures, but it was Running Buck who spotted movement in the foliage.

"I see animals out there," he said, pointing to the brush.

We all turned to view the beasts as they cried out and whooped a few more times. Then loud laughter rent the air. It was unlike anything most of us had ever heard, but it was exactly the demented cackle I had heard in my Dream. The hyenas seemed curious about us and paced back and forth, each pass bringing them slightly closer. There were perhaps eight of them. They appeared to be bigger than the average wolf, and certainly built much more heavily. Their heads were large and blocky, with rounded ears and powerfully built shoulders and chests. Their fur was a rusty brown, spotted with black, and it was longer along their bellies and spines. Their muzzles, tails and legs were solid black in color.

Raena and Ochs positioned themselves between us and the hyenas. I wanted to call Raena back and make her stand closer to us, but I realized that if the hyenas were to charge, we were safer to have the dogs engage them first. I hated the thought that Raena and Ochs might be overwhelmed and torn apart by these creatures, but I had to put the safety of my loved ones first.

I then noticed Ria edging forward as well, her bow poised and a handful of arrows tucked in her fingers. She had not yet drawn back on her bow, but I knew she could arm it in an instant.

"Ria, my love, that is far enough," Puh said to her.

Ria spared him only the barest glance, her gaze fixed on the hyenas.

"Yes, my love," she responded.

All at once, Sky Fire ran forward, waving his arms and barking like a maddened dog. He had an impressively deep and forceful voice.

"Sky Fire! Come back!" Running Buck shouted, running in pursuit him, Black Wolf following at his heels.

The rest of us stayed to protect our families and the sleds, but Sky Fire's actions had unexpected results. The hyenas scattered, accompanied by their chorus of shrill laughter as they sped away from the crazed barking human.

Sky Fire was grinning broadly when he returned to us. He did not speak, but it was now apparent that he could indeed make sounds.

Chapter Ten

When I first heard the thunderous cascade for which the Fen of Falls was named, I looked to Puh and Bror, and we smiled at one another. We had nearly reached our destination. I silently mused that our sleds weighed less now than they had at our outset. Not only had we consumed a considerable amount of food from the loads, but some items had been discarded at the trailside or burned in our nightly fire after having determined that they were not worth the effort of continuing to haul them across the countryside.

Sky Fire had not uttered another sound since his explosive outburst at the hyenas. All the same, we were encouraged that he had made noise of any kind despite that he had not outwardly changed in any way.

While we marched through the glades of huge fir trees that bordered the falls, I noted that humidity saturated the fragrant pine-scented air. Sometime later, lovely aroma of the trees was joined by the welcoming smell of wood smoke.

Willow Woman's grand summer lodge soon came into view. The huge structure was oblong in shape, probably twenty-five of thirty paces in length and eight or nine paces wide. It was made of bent trees, much like our trailside huts, but on a much larger scale. The lodge was walled with various twigs and grasses, and mudded over until it was impervious to wind and rain.

Black Wolf dropped his hold on his sled and slipped out of the harness at the first opportunity, running to the open doorway of the lodge, calling, *"Halloo? Willow? Willow?"* leaving Running Buck standing alone by the abandoned sled, looking slightly puzzled.

Bror, Puh, and I also left our sled as the rest of our group caught up with us.

"I am so glad we are here," Morning Star said wearily, holding a napping Raven on her shoulder.

I slipped an arm around Morning Star's waist and drew her to me, kissing the top of her head. We then heard a delighted squeal come from inside the lodge and we gathered that Black Wolf had found Willow Woman.

"I am glad to be here as well," I began. "It has been a long journey. Had we known how far we would be dragging these sleds, we could have brought some of your Da's dogs with us."

Moring Star grinned at this. Her father's dogs were used not only for hunting, but for pulling sleds as well.

"Since this was my idea, I guess I am to blame for your sore body at the end of every day," she said softly, rubbing my back briefly with her spare hand.

"As long as I keep getting those wonderful massages each night, I will not complain," I responded lightly.

Moments later, Slow Bear came out to greet us, smiling broadly.

"Welcome," he said, grasping my forearms in the way of The People. "Black Wolf came dashing in so quickly that I hardly had time to say *pleasant day* to him! He ran past me looking for Willow Woman, so I came out to see who had accompanied him."

Slow Bear oversaw Willow Woman's household and also took on any other duties she may require, as well. At The People's fall Gatherings, he was called upon to arrange who saw her and when, and he also acted as a second pair of ears, soaking up much information, which he later relayed back to her. Slow Bear already knew my family, Puh, Ria, and little Mror, and also Bror, but he needed to be introduced to Running Buck and Sky Fire, and my sister Ru and the other children. I could see that Slow Bear was confused by Sky Fire's manner. Sky Fire just nodded to him shyly, grinning sappily all the while.

"My brother does not speak," Running Buck explained to Slow Bear. "He is the reason we have come here; I am told that you have the best healer ever known. I am desperate to find help my brother. I will do anything to pay for the services of this healer."

Slow Bear listened solemnly to Running Buck's earnest plea.

"We do not exact payment for Gray Owl's skills,"

Slow Bear assured him, laying a hand on Running Buck's shoulder to soothe him. "Gray Owl has been bored of late. He will be pleased to have a new patient. Come!" Slow Bear waved us to follow him.

Slow Bear led us to an outdoor seating area by their huge fire pit, where he motioned for us to sit down.

"I will just go inside and have White Cloud make ready to have food and drink brought out," he said. "He was just rousing himself from a bit of a snooze when I last saw him, and he was telling me that he was going to check his latest batch of dried herbs. White Cloud should have returned by now."

"*White Cloud?*" Ru questioned as Slow Bear walked out of hearing.

"White Cloud prepares most of the food for the household," I informed her.

"By himself?" Ru was incredulous. "There must be a great number of people living in a dwelling this size. No wonder he was napping; he must be exhausted!"

"He does have some assistance, but he does most of the work," I told Ru.

It turned out that White Cloud did indeed have assistance, at least while we were staying at the Fen of Falls. Ru insisted that she would help him in his labors. Ru was accustomed to cooking for large groups of people; she had learned this at our Muh's side from the time she was a small child.

In the past, I had lent a hand or two, mostly out of boredom and a wish to be useful, but now White Cloud had several volunteers who were eager to assist. He took these proffered hands with good-natured ease, although he seemed a little flustered by the presence of so many young women. Most times Willow Woman was the only female in residence.

Refreshments were served, and our families were absorbed with the goings-on at the fire pit, leaving Bror, Puh, Running Buck, Sky Fire, and me to our own devices. Puh and I were soon tasked with keeping our small sons entertained, but we were free to talk quietly amongst ourselves. Slow Bear soon joined us.

"Come with me for a moment," Slow Bear requested, indicating that we should accompany him.

I was intrigued, as I am sure we all were. We followed Slow Bear a short distance from the lodge, where we were shocked to see an enormous hyena suspended by a hind leg from a tree limb. The stench emanating from the creature was not just due to death; this was one of the ranker animals I have ever smelled.

"We killed this one earlier today," Slow Bear told us. "Well, I cannot really say *we*, I took no part in it. Some of the men were on a hunt, but they brought this creature back in addition to their buck."

"Do you know what this is?" Puh asked him.

"Oh, yes," Slow Bear replied, "it is a hyena, a female. The females are the larger of the species, you know. As you can see, it can be difficult to tell the sexes apart, but she was lactating. She must have had young ones."

We exchanged glances. Of course the hyenas would be breeding. But this meant that their numbers were increasing.

"How many do you suppose are living in this area?" Puh then inquired.

Slow Bear shrugged and pondered his question a moment.

"Perhaps ten or twelve, perhaps more," he said, looking up at the hyena, "but there is one less now. Our hunters do not like these beasts. They have lost a number of their kills because the hyenas will harry them until they are driven away, and there are not enough men to fend off the creatures. So now they have no alternative but to take every spare man in the household each time they go out to ensure that they hyenas will not succeed at bullying their way in."

"Is this the first one you have killed?" I queried, standing near enough to touch it. Some of the fur was quite course. Fox reached out as well.

"Doggy," Fox said, petting the animal's foreleg. "It smell, Puh-Puh."

I was unnerved to see the huge canines exposed in the hyena's massive maw. I did not think I had ever seen such a heavy jaw or such large teeth as these. Lions, bears, wolves — they all had dentition that commanded respect, but these were truly awe-inspiring.

"This is not a dog," I corrected, "it is a hyena, Fox."

Sky Fire approached the dead animal warily, sniffing as he came closer. Running Buck came up to stand at his side while they both observed the hyena closely.

"We saw a whole pack of hyenas yesterday," Bror told Slow Bear. "They were very curious about us. What odd sounds they make."

"Did they come near?" Slow Bear asked.

"They tried, but Sky Fire scared them away," I said with a grin.

"How so?" Slow Bear inquired. "The hyenas do not frighten easily. They are apt to be very tenacious when they think there may be a meal in the offing. They have come to learn they just need to watch us when we are hunting and then, after the kill has been made, they come in and hound the men until they abandon their kill. There is no telling how much meat we have lost to them, and worse, we have not been able to figure out how to discourage them. "

"Sky Fire ran at them," Running Buck explained with pride. "He waved his arms like a goose taking flight and barked so fiercely that the hyenas did not tarry. They promptly turned tail and ran, whooping and cackling all the way."

"As I have yet to hear or see a live hyena," Slow Bear said, "I cannot say what sounds they make. But if their voices are as unorthodox as their looks, I can imagine that they must be indeed unique. Sky Fire ran at them you say? What a brave fellow!"

"Has there been discussion on how to deal with the hyena problem?" Puh inquired of Slow Bear.

"They arrived only this summer," Slow Bear said. "But, not only do they try to rob us of our kills, they also bring down horses, deer, elk . . . anything they think they can tackle. We are concerned about both the competition for game and the threat they pose to anyone they discover away from the lodge. They tend to stay away if it is a big group of men, and we do not often leave except in parties of two or three."

"What will you do with this one?" I asked.

"For now, we will see what hyena tastes like," Slow Bear said with a smile. "And we will save its pelt. The black on russet is most unusual."

Fox was still closely examining the carcass, touching the rough foot pads, prodding the limp limbs.

"*Eena*," Fox said, attempting to say hyena, and then he crowed out their odd sounds. Though he could not quite say hyena, his imitation of their cries was eerily accurate. "Fox sound like *eena?*"

"You do sound like a hyena," I told him.

At that moment, Gray Owl appeared at my elbow.

"Pleasant day to you," Gray Owl said, looking up at me. He was a small, slender, rather grim man, but he smiled in his understated way.

"Pleasant day, Gray Owl," I responded, then introduced him to the men he did not know: Running Buck and Sky Fire.

Gray Owl greeted each man in turn.

"I understand that someone is in need of healing," Gray Owl said, without appearing to address anyone in particular; but he then looked at Sky Fire as though he immediately understood that he was his patient.

"Yes," Running Buck said eagerly. "My brother Sky Fire was injured over a year ago. A bear cuffed him in the head . . . see this bald spot?" Running Buck lifted the long hair from one side of Sky Fire's head to expose a healed but naked scalp.

"Sky Fire, would you sit, please?" Gray Owl prompted him.

Sky Fire immediately sat down cross-legged, with his arms lying across his knees.

"Thank you," Gray Owl nodded. "You are too tall for me to examine your head when you are standing. May I look?"

Sky Fire did not reply or change expression.

Gray Owl looked to us. "He seems to hear. He follows instruction, or at least obeys requests; how much do you think he understands?"

"I believe he understands most things," Running Buck supplied. "But he does not speak since his injury. I had not heard him utter a sound until he barked yesterday."

"*Barked?*" Gray Owl repeated. "How unusual."

"Well, he was chasing away a pack of hyenas that was interested in us," Running Buck hastily explained.

"Sky Fire ran directly at them, barking like a dog on a boar," Bror added.

"It was a courageous thing to do," I chimed in.

"Quite," Gray Owl concurred, and then he turned to Sky Fire once again, "Sky Fire, if you have no objections, I will begin to examine you."

As before, Sky Fire's countenance gave no indication that he had heard Gray Owl, so Gray Owl plunged ahead with his task.

"A nasty wound," Gray Owl said, probing Sky Fire's skull. "But it has healed well. Was he unconscious for a period?"

"Yes," Running Buck nodded. "Several days."

"Was there obvious cranial swelling?" Gray Owl persisted.

"Oh, yes, his head was quite swollen. Like this," Running Buck put up his hands on either side of his own head, to demonstrate that his brother's had almost doubled in size.

Gray Owl winced at the thought, "He must have incurred quite an infection."

"And the blows were severe," Running Buck added.

"*Blows?*" Puh piped up.

"Oh, yes," Running Buck said. "After the bear swiped at Sky Fire, she knocked him against a large boulder, and next into a stand of trees. He collapsed then. Fortunately, a group of hunters were nearby and their sudden presence persuaded the sow and her cub to move off, averting further damage to either of us. I will be forever grateful to those men. They took us to their home and took care of us until my cousin Black Wolf and his friends came upon us and helped us to make this trek."

"Well, that explains the grievous head injury. Where is your home?" Gray Owl questioned.

"Do you know of Gray Elk, the dog breeder and trader who makes his home in the mountains?" Running Buck asked.

Gray Owl nodded.

"He is our father."

"That could explain why Sky Fire communicated by barking. If he was raised and has lived around dogs all his life, he must be as familiar with them as he is with people." Gray Owl seemed to be speculating out loud. "His speaking mind may have been damaged, but the part of his mind that remembers dogs has remained intact." Gray Owl paused in thought. "Your home is in the mountains to the northeast?" he presumed.

"Yes, that is where we are from," Running Buck confirmed. "I am most eager to get home. My mate, my children, my parents, I am told they all think us dead! But first, if there is anything at all you could do to help my brother . . . ."

"I will do what I can," Gray Owl started, "but for now, I just need to spend time with him. I will need to see if I can determine whether he can be made to speak again and how much he actually comprehends. The mind is a curious thing. Sky Fire sat when I asked him, so he obeys, and he has demonstrated that he can make noise when he so chooses."

Running Buck's shoulders slumped. "When you say it that way, it sounds as though he is a dog. He walks and sits on command, and he barks, but does not interact like a human."

"That is not what I meant and I am sure that is not the case," Gray Owl said, patting Running Buck's arm sympathetically. "Let us see. Be patient."

* * *

Later when we were all gathering for our evening meal, Black Wolf and Willow Woman at last appeared from the lodge and joined us. I was glad to see that Willow Woman was looking well after she had suffered a bout of ill health last year. Her black hair, braided and wrapped around her head, was now threaded with white, but her eyes sparkled with vigor and her skin glowed from under the head-to-toe tattoos. And although Willow Woman had not yet regained any of the weight she had lost, she nevertheless still appeared quite robust.

Willow Woman was wearing the pendant that Black Wolf had created for her. He had taken a leg bone from a deer carcass, split it into segments and then cut one of those slender slices of bone into a piece not much longer than the first joint of my finger. Next, he had cut holes into the bit of bone into which he glued the pearls he had found. Lastly, one more hole was made from which to suspend the pendant on a length of twine. The glue was black and one pearl was lumpy and tan in color while the other was roundish and off-white, but it looked quite nice and Willow Woman wore the gift proudly. After so much worry about how he would work the pearls into something for her, Black Wolf could not have been more pleased with her reaction.

Willow Woman greeted us warmly, hugging Morning Star and me with great feeling. Embracing Willow Woman was a unique experience. She was quite tall for a woman; in fact, Willow Woman and I were probably equal in height, and she had the well-fed physique of a bear readying for hibernation. Bror had once compared the act of hugging her to wrapping one's arms around a very large, warm water bag. I returned her exuberant squeeze and then grinned to see my petite mate almost disappear in Willow Woman's embrace.

Black Wolf and Willow Woman's son Oak, now nearly two winters old, took part in our meal as well. He was a large child, about the same age as my daughter Pony, but nearly twice her size. Oak and Fox, in spite of their difference in age, were too distracted by the presence of a new playmate to have any interest in their dinners.

"Tris, make him sit and eat!" Morning Star implored, worried that her little boy would not consume enough food.

"Let them play," I said to her gently. "They do not get to see other boys their age very often. Look, even Mror wants to play, too, although both Fox and Oak dwarf him."

"Poor Mror," Morning Star began, "he is a tough little fellow. The bigger boys bowl him over in play and Mror just gets up grinning and chases after them."

My little sister Twie was kept busy trying to herd the boys lest their rough play take them too far from the safety of the fire on this dark night. Torches helped to light the gathering, but beyond their glow, darkness crowded in on all sides. Soon, thick clouds began to scud across the sky, and at last the moon was obscured and every star was blotted out. We suspected that rain was coming and we were invited to bring our sleds inside the lodge for the duration of the coming shower.

Fortunately, the rain held off until after we had finished our meal, allowing us time to socialize with our hosts. It was late when we were finally shown to our chambers within the dwelling.

Morning Star and I were allotted the same space we used during our previous visit. Someone had kindly set up enough sleeping platforms for the children to all have snug little nests where they could cuddle up together. I had become accustomed to the lodge's sliding door coverings, which could be adjusted to expose entryways to each room and let in fresh air and light from the outdoors as well, but Morning Star still found them to be a novelty. She moved the smaller wall panels back and forth until she was satisfied that they were open just enough to permit a little air to enter, but none of the gently falling rain.

Fox and Pony were already sound asleep, exhausted by our long journey and an evening of frolic. Morning Star nursed Raven one last time before laying her down for sleep as well. I watched, relishing the sight of my lovely mate feeding our baby as the rain pelted the roof. Raven occasionally looked over at me and smiled, but soon returned to suckling at her mother's breast. Before long, her eyes began to close and she too was dozing.

When the baby was swaddled and placed between her brother and sister, Morning Star then faced me and looked at me in the dim lamp light. She placed her hands on my shoulders, observing how the sled harness straps had worn red grooves in my skin.

"Let me put more salve on these wear marks," Morning Star said, moving to retrieve a small bag of ointment.

I only nodded in response, and sat down to make the application easier for her, since the top of her head only reached my chest. I remained quietly seated as she painted the salve on my shoulders and chest, on the bridge of my nose where repeated sunburns had left the skin raw, and on the various insect bites I was sporting. Lastly, she looked at my feet, placing them awkwardly in her lap, one at a time. My feet looked so huge and ungainly in her small hands.

"Tris, after we arrive at home you must let me use a honing stone on your feet," she said. "You have calluses on top of calluses."

"Yes, my sweet," I replied.

"For now, I will just rub the salve into the calluses. It will help to soften them." Morning Star sighed. "While we were at the coast, your feet with clean and the constant wear of walking in the sand kept the calluses worn down. It has not taken long for your feet to become hardened and dirt-stained once again."

"Yes," I said again, but I was not really thinking much about the condition of my feet. I was thinking on how lovely she looked in the soft light.

Morning Star abruptly gazed up at me.

"You are staring," she said.

"Indeed I am," I agreed, pulling her up onto my lap.

Morning Star tried to mute her giggles.

"Oh, Tris! My hands are all greasy," she said in mock protest, holding her hands for my inspection.

"So I see." I bent to kiss her neck. "Just wipe your hands on my skin. It is parched enough to benefit from it."

Morning Star obligingly rubbed the salve into my skin as I continued to kiss her. I then removed our clothing, and carried her to our bed.

* * *

The rain had stopped sometime during the night and we awoke to feeble sunshine. I ventured outside with my family to take them to a safe place to relieve their bladders, Raena accompanying us for the same purpose. On our way back to the lodge, Fox found a piece of deadwood.

"Puh-Puh, Fox have this?" he asked.

"I do not see why not," I answered. "What do you want it for?"

"Fox make spear!" he announced with great determination.

"You will not poke other children or the dogs with it," Morning Star said to him sternly.

"Yes, Muh-Muh," Fox replied a bit dejectedly, as though he might have been hoping to do just that.

We found most of the household at the fire pit, where the morning meal was being served. Ru was directing everyone on where to line up to get their food as White Cloud stood by helplessly. I wondered if she had let him participate in any way. I guessed it was likely he had simply been too polite to insist upon doing his usual chores.

Gray Owl was at Sky Fire's side, observing him casually, and speaking to him quietly now and then. Sometimes Sky Fire actually acknowledged Gray Owl's gently persistent attempts at conversation with a nod of his head.

"Let us speak of the hyenas," Willow Woman said as we consumed a breakfast of berries, smoked salmon, and eggs cooked in their shells.

The pattering chatter stopped and all turned to face her.

"We should bring up the hyena problem at the Gathering this fall," Willow Woman resumed. "We can offer a reward to each hunter who brings a hyena tail as proof of the kill."

"*A tail?*" Slow Bear repeated, "But an animal can live without a tail. Why not the head? No creature can live without that."

Willow Woman nodded with understanding.

"That is true," she agreed. "Thank you for bringing that up, Slow Bear. The head, then."

"What will the reward be?" Running Buck asked.

"It will have to be a good one to give a man incentive to trek any distance to turn in heads as big and heavy as a hyena's," Bror pointed out.

Willow Woman appeared to be thinking on this.

"Perhaps it could be a nose instead of the whole head. And you might let each man choose his own reward," Puh suggested. "Since each man is apt to value different things."

"That is also true," Willow Woman agreed. "I think that would be best. Thank you, Tor."

"Remember when my brothers insisted on a mammoth as payment before they would allow us to be paired?" Ria reminded us.

"Well, it would have to be within reason," Black Wolf said, shuddering at the memory. He had participated in that mammoth hunt, during which, in the behemoth's last moments of life, it had let go a blast of manure on the unfortunate Black Wolf.

I was half following the flow of talk, half supervising Fox as he was attempting to fire-harden and sharpen his toy spear. He had seen me fire-harden spear shafts and tools many times. Fox had briefly tried to attach a broken piece of flint to the spear's end, but soon gave up as hafting was currently beyond him. Now he was gradually wearing his stick to a point with a stone. I was impressed with his tenacity and the amount of forethought he was putting into this project.

But in a moment of lapsed attention while he held his stick over the flames, it suddenly caught fire.

"Fox, look to your spear," I said, nudging him slightly.

Fox jumped at the sight of his spear aflame. I had been trying to let him do as much of the work as possible on his own, but he seemed frozen with inaction. I took the stick from his hands and quenched the fire by poking it into the loose dirt at the base of the fire pit.

"It is all right, see?" I showed him his spear, just slightly blackened at the tip. "It will be a fine spear." I spoke quietly so as not to disrupt the ongoing discussion.

Tears had sprouted at the corners of Fox's eyes at the potential loss of all his hard work, but now he instantly brightened.

"Many thanks, Puh-Puh," he said to me. "Fox go hunting!"

As the conversation continued, some suggested that we could save choice pieces of stone for knapping as a reward, or even finished spearheads, knives, and axes. But who was going to manufacture these things? Most of us could barely keep up with making and maintaining our own things. Others suggested that unpaired hunters might be lured by the idea of a match with a nubile woman, but I thought that proposal had the potential to be even more problematic than trying to come up with spears and axes.

Oak, Fox, and Mror were becoming bored with sitting still and began to tussle with one another, bumping into other children and adults in the process. Willow Woman held up a hand to halt the discussion.

"I think our little ones have had enough serious talk for now," she said with a smile. "Let us take this up again at our evening sup and just enjoy our visit for the time being."

"We could take the children out to stretch their legs," Slow Bear offered. "That will help them run off some energy."

"But not near the river or the falls," Morning Star said, her voice rising as it always did when she was somewhat anxious. "That fast water is far too dangerous!"

"No, not near the water," Slow Bear agreed. "The sun is well risen now, and it is a most pleasant day. We could just go a short way down the path. Tris, I took you, Bror, and Karno down there before when we went to the pond. Do you recall?"

"Yes, I do," I replied. "I think that would be fine." I looked to Morning Star for her reaction.

"I will stay here with our girls," Morning Star told me. "Raven will need another feeding and a nap soon, and Pony is tired enough that she may sleep a little as well."

"All right, my sweet," I said, kissing her cheek. "We will not be away for long."

Morning Star returned my kiss, and then bent to kiss Fox, who promptly wiped it away. Finally, she admonished him to mind his Puh-Puh. Fox just nodded, waving his spear and stabbing it into imaginary foes.

"And do not poke anyone with your stick!" Morning Star instructed.

"Muh-Muh! It a *spear!*" Fox responded indignantly.

"Watch him!" Morning Star said to me.

"Yes," I responded, kissing her one last time before she left us, with Raven perched on one arm and Pony grasping her hand.

Without further ado, Puh, with little Mror, Slow Bear with Oak (Black Wolf and Willow Woman having disappeared once again), and I with Fox, set off down the trail, Raena and Ochs loping alongside us. Puh, Slow Bear, and I were armed with our spears, and Fox with his toy weapon. Oak and Mror wanted spears too, so they picked up random sticks, sometimes abandoning one stick for another when they came upon a better option.

The tall fir trees surrounding the lodge were full of birds that twittered and flitted about cheerfully. I looked up past the tall treetops at blue skies and puffy white clouds that boded well for fair weather. It felt good to be back in the shade of the trees after spending so much time on the sun-scorched sands of the shore. Even our coastal hosts' woodlands were not as dense and well canopied as were these. Raena and Ochs seemed more comfortable in the coolness of the deep forest, too.

After a short distance, Slow Bear led us down another trail, which brought us to an open expanse of meadow. It was a peaceful place, full of late-summer flowers and grasses with ripe and bursting seed heads. We could see a few deer munching happily at the far side of the lea, but they ran away as soon as they saw us. A nearby crow cawed at their departing forms.

I then took note of several rabbits also enjoying the copious fodder. About this time, Fox pointed a finger at the bunnies.

"Abbits!" Fox said, not quite able to pronounce rabbit.

Fox broke away from us, spear poised for an assault. The rabbits bolted, running pell-mell in zigzagging lines as Fox trotted in pursuit, his long curly hair flying in the breeze.

"No, Fox!" I called, running after him, Raena and Ochs at my side. "Come back to me!"

Fox just laughed. He appeared so elated and so in his element that I hated to spoil his fun, but he could not go out into the tall grasses by himself; not even a grown man would do such a thing. Suddenly, my Dream of Fox capering through a meadow came to mind and my blood ran cold.

"Come to me, Fox," I said again. "*Come to me, now!*" This time I said it more forcefully.

Then a maniacal laughter broke the stillness of the day. Fox stopped in place. I was almost upon him and his eyes were wide as he looked up at me.

"Come to me, Fox," I said once more, but he stood stone still.

I finally reached him and picked him up in my arms, and then immediately scanned the vicinity for the producer of that cackle, just as another laugh, followed by a *whoop-whoop* met our ears. The dogs' hackles bristled and they looked about for the unseen threat, growling.

I hastily began to walk back to the path, where I could see that Puh and Slow Bear were also making their way toward me, spears at the ready. Oak and Mror were not in sight.

I heard rustling in the grass behind us and I turned just in time to meet a charging hyena. Fox gasped out, "*Puh-Puh!*" and he clung to me tighter. I jabbed my spear at the beast, just catching its upper lip with the tip of my spear. The animal cried out in pain and backed off, but it lingered, drooling blood, just out of the reach of my spear. Its companions came up to investigate us as well. The hyenas chortled, and whooped, and made sharp little barks, and each one darted in, feigning an attack. I knew this technique. We sometimes employed it as well: Harry your prey until you can catch it off guard, preferably from the rear, where it is less able to defend itself. The dogs barked fiercely, wheeling to meet the hyenas on all sides and nipping at them with audible snaps of their jaws. Neither dogs nor hyenas had successfully wounded their antagonists yet, but it was not for lack of trying.

Holding Fox as I was, I could wield my spear only one-handed, and Fox's grip around my neck was so tight he was almost chocking me. Suddenly, the hyenas scattered and retreated a short distance away, still vocalizing in their discordant way. Puh and Slow Bear now joined Fox and me and we backed our way to the trail, keeping an eye on all sides in case of another charge.

"This is not good," Slow Bear uttered quietly. "They may have backed off, but they could continue to follow us and harass us all the way back to the lodge."

Puh shook his head.

"They like better odds than this. I think they will leave us alone and seek easier prey," Puh said. "Let us collect Mror and Oak and go back to the Fen of Falls."

Mror and Oak had been placed high up on sturdy tree branches, where they waited uneasily for our return. When they retrieved their sticks at the base of the tree, Fox then realized that he had dropped his spear some--where and he began to cry.

"Puh-Puh, spear *gone!*" he sobbed.

Knowing that Fox had devoted so much effort into making his spear, I felt bad that we could not go back to look for it. I hugged him and kissed the top of his head to console him.

"I will help you make another," I promised.

Fox continued to cling to me for most of the trek back to the lodge.

When we returned, I went to find Morning Star. The little girls were still dozing, but Fox immediately threw himself at his mother, again in tears.

"Muh-Muh, bad doggies in grass!" Fox told Morning Star as she knelt on the matting to comfort him.

"What?" Morning Star could not quite understand his words, muffled as they were against her shoulder.

"*Bad doggies!*" Fox repeated.

"We came upon some hyenas," I said to Morning Star. "The dogs kept them off us. We came back right away."

Morning Star gaped at this news.

"Tris, was anyone injured? Any of the dogs?" she asked.

"No, we are all fine. The dogs too. But Fox was a little shaken up and he was upset that he lost his spear."

"Puh-Puh make new spear," Fox said, wiping his eyes.

"I will help you make one," I clarified, sitting down on the matting next to Morning Star.

Morning Star looked worried.

"These are animals we have never had to defend ourselves against before," she said. "They scare me!"

"They are animals like any other," I told her. "Some beasts are much worse than hyenas. These just seem frightening because they look and sound so different."

Morning Star smiled a little.

"My brave mate. I know you face many things that are far larger and even more dangerous; those *bad doggies* do not scare you," she said, leaning over and craning up to kiss my cheek.

"All the same, it may be best for you and the children to stay here when we go up to Gray Elk's," I said solemnly. "I would not like to expose you and the children to any unnecessary danger."

Morning Star pondered this.

"Yes, I suppose it would be best if we women and children stayed with Willow Woman while you make the journey," Morning Star acknowledged. "If you have to fight off hyenas and who knows what else, it will be easier without being encumbered by us."

 **Chapter Eleven** 

The others were in agreement. When we eventually set out for Gray Elk's mountain aerie, we would leave our families at Willow Woman's enclave at the Fen of Falls. In the meantime, we settled into a routine, occasionally hunting to bring in fresh meat, ever watchful for the hyenas.

Gray Owl spent every day with Sky Fire, feeding him magical preparations that were designed to cure any number of potential ailments. Sky Fire choked down these remedies willingly, but I could not see that there was any difference in him. However, I trusted Gray Owl to know what he was prescribing. Gray Owl also tried to prompt Sky Fire to talk by speaking about things he could relate to. He asked him about his family, his boyhood, anything to get a response from him. I wondered if it was my imagination, or whether Sky Fire actually seemed to show some interest in these conversations, even if he did not yet reply.

After a period of this treatment, it at last seemed to

have some effect. One afternoon Raena barked happily in play with Ochs, and Sky Fire barked back. Gray Owl sat up straight and turned to Sky Fire, barking at him with enthusiasm. He finished his string of barks by saying Sky Fire's name several times. We all looked at Gray Owl in shock. This was rather unexpected behavior, considering his normally staid nature.

Sky Fire looked at Gray Owl curiously, head cocked to one side, and he made a soft woof. Then after silently working his mouth for a few moments, brow furrowed in concentration, he said in a husky voice, *"Not dog. Sky Fire."* He pointed to himself.

His words were hard to distinguish, but there was no doubt that he had at last spoken.

* * *

We had been at Willow Woman's lodge for nearly a moon when it was decided that we would now escort Running Buck and Sky Fire to their home. Sky Fire still said only a few words, but Gray Owl believed he would gradually improve. He admitted that it was only a guess, since the head held many mysteries even for a healer as skilled as he, but Gray Owl suspected an infection or swelling of some sort had persisted in Sky Fire's head that had affected his ability to produce sounds. For some unknown reason, his ability to bark had returned before he could speak. Sky Fire was as difficult to understand as a toddler who was just learning to talk — much to his frustration. As he continued to improve, Sky Fire often seemed to know what he wanted to convey, but was sometimes at a loss to do so.

The journey to Gray Elk's home would only take two days, so we packed light. Willow Woman offered to provide warmer clothing for the trip, as the temperatures would be colder up in the mountains. We gratefully accepted a cloak each. We then loaded our packs with extra dried provisions to leave with Gray Elk. The last we knew, he and his family were in a very bad way after the loss of Running Buck and Sky Fire to help procure food, so we were determined to bring as many supplies as we could carry.

I did not relish the thought of leaving my family behind, but we expected to return in about five days; we could not afford to tarry. It was by then late summer, and fall would be upon us shortly. We desperately needed to get back home and prepare for another long winter. As it was, at least half of the stores we had acquired at the shore had been eaten or traded or were being carried up to Gray Elk's. It would require much rigorous hunting and foraging to make sure we would have enough to see us through until spring.

Willow Woman also did not like to relinquish her time with Black Wolf. As we prepared to depart, she held him tightly.

"You will take care, will you not?" Willow Woman pleaded. "This time you came back to me looking so healthy; absolutely aglow with vigor! You must take good care to avoid injury."

"Of course I will," Black Wolf said, smiling down at her. "Do not worry. I have thought on how to deal with the hyena problem. I will kill enough to make a coat from their pelts and everyone who sees it will want one just like it." Black Wolf was being facetious, and he grinned at this own quip. "We will turn all the hyenas into garments."

Willow Woman appeared to be too concerned for his well-being to catch on to his jest.

"I think that is a fine idea," she nodded. "But do take care to eat enough while you are away. I would not like to see you grow as thin as you were before."

Now Black Wolf laughed heartily.

"We will be gone for only five days; I will not wither away in such a short span of time!" Black Wolf became serious again when he saw her crestfallen visage. "I will take good care," he vowed. "Give me a kiss now."

We all took leave of our families and strode away from the lodge, taking Raena and Ochs with us. I turned briefly to wave to Morning Star and my children one last time before they would be lost from sight; like Willow Woman, I hated to be parted from my loved ones for even a few days. Morning Star smiled wanly in return and Fox waved and called out, "Puh-Puh, see soon! See soon!" My little girls waved as well. Then they were gone, obscured by the foliage along the trail.

My pack was heavy, but it rode comfortably on my back. It would feel heavier yet when we reached the foothills of the mountains. The higher we climbed, the more onerous our burdens would be.

Black Wolf began to sing, as he often did when we were on a trek, as always at a lung-bursting volume. He had many favorite tunes; however, he often took liberties with the lyrics.

> *The mighty hunter is bold and strong*
> *His aim is sure and his spear is long*
> *He hunts daily so he will not be leaner*
> *And when he needs a coat he kills hyena . . .*

"That will ensure that mighty hunter will be living alone," Puh said quietly.

Black Wolf broke off his song, "I wonder if there is any way to get the smell out of the creature's fur."

"If so, the fur would make a very striking pelt," Bror noted. "And, after all, minks are stinky little beasts, and yet their cured pelts do not smell."

"I will have to think on that," Black Wolf said, then resuming his song.

> *The mighty hunter is a persistent man*
> *He will succeed where no one can . . .*

Sky Fire barked in accompaniment. Unruffled, Black Wolf continued to sing until we came to a burbling stream. It was midday, and the weather was quite pleasant.

"Shall we break here?" Puh questioned.

We all nodded in agreement and found places to sit while we dug into our packs for water bags and both dried and fresh foods. I was glad to rest in the shade and to flex my back and shoulders while free of my pack. We ate quickly, sipping at water frequently. Now that Sky Fire was saying a few words, Running Buck was speaking to him often.

"We are going home, Sky Fire," Running Buck told him. "Soon we will see Mama and Da, and you will see Sweet Rain and all your little ones."

Sky Fire nodded vigorously and smiled, but he did not reply. I still could not tell how much he actually comprehended. When we recommenced our journey, Black Wolf almost immediately recommenced his song.

The very best hunters always know their trail
They know not to strike a mammoth's tail
It may just turn and knock you down with a swoop
And if it does not turn, it might hit you with poop . . .

Sky Fire began to bark once again. Raena and Ochs joined in this time. Black Wolf just sang louder. Running Buck attempted to convince Sky Fire that he could sing, too, but Sky Fire just looked at him and barked once more. Perhaps he had decided he was a dog, after all.

I wondered how Black Wolf could keep this up without straining his voice, but I was glad to see him looking so well and so happy. As Willow Woman had said, he appeared to be in fine fettle. He had continued to fill out, his powerful physique finally gaining in proportion to his great height. Considering how painfully thin he had become during his convalescence after his head injury, this was an accomplishment indeed. Black Wolf's skin had become deeply tanned during our summer on the coast, and unlike Puh, Bror, and me with our sun-blistered peeling skin, his — what was not obscured by his copious body hair — had a wonderfully healthy sheen. At this moment, however, one of his lower legs had been shaved to the skin to allow new tattoos to be applied. The dark lines and patterns matched those on his forearms, which also closely resembled those covering Willow Woman's person.

But perhaps best of all from Black Wolf's point of view, his hair had at long last grown enough to reach his shoulders and could once again be plaited into the many braids he usually wore. The tight plaits stuck out from the top of his skull; in the past the hair had been so long that the braids gave him the appearance of wearing a large spider on the top of his head. The shorter version had quite another effect — unless the spider had met with a disastrous accident and had lost the tips of its extremities. However, since Black Wolf could not see himself, he was oblivious to this shortfall, and he was insistent on resuming his former hairstyle at the first possible moment.

We saw occasional signs of the hyenas' presence, but so too did we see ample sign of other animals. Black Wolf's only slightly varying repertoire of songs kept most creatures at a distance, so we did not actually view them in the flesh; but we saw their tracks, their droppings, areas where they had rolled in the dust, trees that had been raked with claws or perhaps stripped of their bark by a buck scraping the velvet from his antlers. Sometimes all we saw were the remains of a beast that had been killed, after the site had been thoroughly scavenged.

Now that we were not accompanied by our families we were able to travel much faster, and we did not need to be as concerned about the proximity of predators. As six hunters more or less in our prime, there was not much we need fear. We were still required to be vigilant, but between Black Wolf's never-ending torrent of noise and our dogs' continuous scouting, there was little likelihood that we would be surprised by a stealth attack. We were pleased at the distance we had covered by the time the sun had dropped low in the sky and we had found a large rock overhang under which we could shelter for the night.

The space beneath the overhang took the form of a rough bowl shape; a charred area just outside showed that it had probably been used by men in the past. We set down our packs within the shelter and began to forage for deadwood. We had each collected several heaping armloads by the time the sun had nearly set.

I quickly gathered dried grass and mosses and some small twigs for tinder and took my flint and an iron oxide rock from my pack. Several strikes later, I finally had produced enough sparks to ignite the tinder, and I gently blew on it to encourage the flames. As soon as they were well established, I set the burning tinder in the middle of the charred patch and gingerly arranged the twigs over it, taking care not to smother the fledgling flames.

The six of us had to huddle close to fit under the overhang. We did not attempt to spread out and lay full length but slept half sitting up, leaning against our packs. The dogs tried to find spots where they could curl up without being too close to the fire. They wanted to keep watch by the opening, but they could not take the heat from the flames. It was not comfortable enough to truly rest, and one of us would rise often enough to keep the fire well fueled. Black Wolf was the only one who seemed to sleep soundly, and he snored vociferously straight on through 'til morning.

My eyes cracked open as the first rays of the sun crested the horizon. I could only just see the brightening sky though the limbs of the trees. I noted that the dogs were alert and rising to their feet.

A shrill laugh split the air. Suddenly, all my companions were coming awake.

"What is so funny?" Black Wolf said drowsily, raising himself up on an elbow.

More raucous laughter followed, and then we heard an odd grunting. Raena and Ochs barked a warning and their hackles stiffened.

Black Wolf was soon standing with us, looking out into the early-morning gloom, each of us grasping our spears.

"It is them again. Definitely not funny," Black Wolf muttered. "I dare them to come closer. I will size them up for my new coat."

Puh was adding more wood to our fire.

"I do not like to worsen our vision in these dim conditions, but the fire will likely keep them at bay," Puh explained.

As Puh had said, the bright flames made us almost blind to anything beyond the circle of light it provided. All we could see of the hyenas were their eyes, glowing from the darkness of the surrounding woodland.   A couple of hyenas tentatively crept forward, ears swiveling and noses twitching as they sniffed the air cautiously.

Running Buck moved to meet them, but Puh put out his arm to stop him.

"They are just getting a feel for how many of us are here," Puh said quietly. "They will not like what they find. We are all mature men and there are too many of us for them. Besides that, they will not like the presence of the dogs. They will move off as soon as they realize this."

As Puh had predicted, the hyenas melted away into the forest with barely a cackle. We exchanged glances and settled by the fire to consume a quick breakfast as the sun continued its ascent. Today we hoped to connect with a trail that was known to us; there would be some comfort in being on familiar ground.

Slow Bear had told us that this path would take us to the grasslands near the foot of the mountains. I had only seen this area from afar. Mammoths liked this place during summer, since it had plenty of water even when dry conditions prevailed most everywhere, and plenty of fodder, too. Although one mammoth cow had acted kindly toward me and in fact had saved my life several times, the empathy shown by this animal was not the behavior we typically expected of these beasts. We usually avoided mammoths if we could. As animals sometimes hunted by men, they were rightfully wary of our presence and could be outright hostile if confronted.

A large mammoth could be twice as high at the shoulder as a man was tall and could easily weigh as much as fifty or sixty men. They were powerful almost beyond belief, and intelligent as well. Therefore, we tried to skirt the mammoths' favorite haunts by the widest margins possible.

When we did see them in the distance, we usually tried not to attract the mammoths' attention. But today the watchful behemoths saw us first and trumpeted the news of our arrival across the open landscape. They then moved away to increase the span between us and themselves.

Seeing the hairy creatures brought a fresh wave of sadness over me, so sorrowful was I that my mammoth friend had met such a terrible end at the hands of hunters. I knew I could not begrudge them the kill — after all, that was what we did: we killed animals to provide for our families. Hunters cannot afford to become unduly attached to any creature that might someday become their dinner.

We crossed the grasslands, staying far from the mammoths, but noting where they had plowed up the grasses to access the roots and tender shoots. The grasses were well grazed here, and the roots and shoots contained what little nutrition that was available.

It was still morning when we came to the lower reaches of the mountains. The woodlands were sparse here and the higher we ascended, the more stunted the trees became. Running Buck grinned broadly to be so close to home — finally back on this well-loved turf after being absent for more than a year.

"Sky Fire, we are almost home," Running Buck said happily. "But I have not climbed like this in many moons! *Ack!*"

I shared Running Buck's sentiment. We could walk and even run almost tirelessly, but climbing these steep slopes was quite another matter. The trail weaved back and forth and wound around rock formations, making our progress torturously slow. Black Wolf was now forced to leave off his singing, as it took most of his breath just to tackle this path. Once we rose above the tree line we did not have much shade, and the temperatures rose quickly. This was a stark contrast from the snow-covered mountain we had left last spring. I could feel sweat trickling down my body, especially under my pack and where my cloak rode across my left shoulder. I found myself putting my fingers under the pack straps to hold them off my raw skin where they abraded my flesh.

We stopped often to sip from our water bags and rest our taxed leg muscles. At one point we surprised a small herd of ibex, and they darted away, their springing steps clearing the great chasms in the rocks with each bound. The ibex looked as though they had spent a fruitful season on the foothills of the mountain and on the prairie, grazing all through the long summer days, gaining fat and bearing their young. Seeing all this bounty on the hoof made me regretful that we could not take the time to hunt some of these animals. However, even if we chose to try out luck, we were all so heavily burdened that we would not have been able to carry the meat up to Gray Elk's cave.

When Raena and Ochs began to call out with happy barks, I knew we must be getting close. Soon, we could hear the deep woofs of Gray Elk's dogs, and Gray Elk himself was waiting for us with his pups. He smiled to see us, but when he realized that we were accompanied by his long-lost sons, he startled us as he began to laugh and cry at the same time.

Gray Elk rushed forward while Running Buck ran the last few steps and met him, arms outstretched. Sky Fire shouted *"Da!"* and he too, ran up to meet his father. Then Sky Fire seemed either too emotionally overwhelmed to speak further, or perhaps, considering his recent difficulties, he was simply unable to articulate words.

Gray Elk stood for a moment, weeping joyously with arms wrapped around his sons, but then he was eager to bring us all to the cave's living quarters so that the rest of the family could enjoy the reunion as well.

As we followed Gray Elk down the long passageway through his cavernous home, both his dogs and ours barked and panted with excitement. I then noted how thin Gray Elk had become. He was grinning excitedly and absolutely beaming with pleasure as he spoke, telling us about how pleased the family would be to see Sky Fire and Running Buck. These hallways were normally lighted with many lamps, but as on our last visit when we had learned about their impoverished living conditions, only a few lamps illuminated the way. They provided just enough of a glow for us to find our footing and to highlight the many antlered skulls of giant deer, elk, and red deer that silently peered down at us from the shadows above us.

If I had been surprised to see how thin Gray Elk had grown, I was shocked to see his mate, Buttercup, appear, her cheeks drawn and her clothing hanging loosely off her shoulders. Her hair was limp and a bit scraggly. A few short years ago she had been quite a handsome woman, well groomed and exuding good health.

The rest of the family soon came out to welcome the lost brothers. Only their sisters' mates were not in residence, as the constant need to provide the necessities of life for the household was now their sole responsibility, and they were away from the cave most times.

Running Buck swept his mate off her feet as he greeted her, swinging her around and kissing her enthusiastically.

Sky Fire, in contrast, met his mate shyly. He grasped one of her hands with both of his, rubbing it gently, smiling softly. She seemed to be in a state of disbelief. She was a small woman, no bigger than my Morning Star, but she soon reached up and put both arms around his neck and held him tightly.

"Sweet Rain," Sky Fire said, uttering his mate's name.

He had spoken so quietly that I was not sure if I had actually heard him correctly, but when I saw her ans-

-wering smile, I knew I had.

All in all, it was a delightful homecoming for the two men. And it was all the better for us because we could now unload the supplies we had carried up the mountainside in our packs. Buttercup made sympathetic noises regarding the chafe marks on our chests and shoulders where the weight of our packs had caused the straps to dig into our skin. But then the sight of all the food was enough to send Gray Elk's family into a frenzy of activity as they sorted through the various foodstuffs. Buttercup had been on her knees examining this windfall, but she abruptly broke off and approached Black Wolf, hugging him as she tiptoed to kiss his cheek.

"Thank you, Black Wolf," Buttercup said. "Thank you for bringing our sons home to us, and thank you for this food."

She smiled up at Black Wolf, wiping a few tears of gratitude from her eyes. She then moved to Puh, who also received a long hug and a kiss and words of appreciation. Bror and I had our turns next. Buttercup then asked after our families and smiled when Bror and I told her about our new daughters.

"But you men must be famished — and exhausted after your journey," Buttercup said. "Please make yourselves comfortable by the hearth while the girls and I put together a meal for you. I must say that all the food you have brought us will do much to improve the quality of our offerings."

I then saw Buttercup pause as she took a gander at Black Wolf's shaved lower leg and the new tattoos that embellished it. She might not have noticed the matching tattoos on his forearms, given that they were covered by a coat of thick black hair. Buttercup quickly recovered herself and moved on without comment, too polite to question Black Wolf about his decorations.

* * *

Black Wolf, Puh, Bror, and I stayed only the one night and then took our leave of Gray Elk's family early the next morning, making our descent down the mountain under a violet dawn splashed with clouds of deep pink. The day was mild, but occasional fat raindrops fell from the sky, splatting on our skin but not wetting us unduly. This part of the trip was much easier; it was downhill, our packs were light, and our spirits were buoyed at the memory of how happy we had left Gray Elk and his clan.

Best of all, Sky Fire seemed to have recalled everyone, all except his youngest child, who had been born after he was presumed lost. This infant, named Sky Fire in honor of his father, was now old enough to able to sit up and pull himself to standing upright. It was somewhat confusing to have two Sky Fires in one household, but no one seemed to mind. The only sad note was that Running Buck had learned that his youngest son had succumbed to illness during their absence.

As the brightening skies brought light to the mountainside, the wild creatures began to rouse themselves from the places where they had dwelt the previous night. Birds sang, insects buzzed and hummed, and several goats made a hasty retreat upon spying our party as we made our way down the twisting trail.

* * *

We made good time back to the Fen of Falls. We had barely time to greet our families and remove our packs when Slow Bear waved for us to join him. A short distance from the lodge, four hyenas hung suspended from trees, just as the earlier hyena had been strung up by a paw to let it bleed out. These animals were of a variety of sizes and ages, but they were all adults. Slow Bear proudly showed off the deceased animals.

"After we harvested the hide, meat, and organs off a deer carcass, we left it out in the woods as bait to attract hyenas," Slow Bear explained with a grin. "It was easy, if not terribly comfortable to lie in wait from the safety of some sturdy tree branches and then drop our spears amongst the brutes."

"What will you do with all the meat?" Puh asked.

"We sampled some that we took off the first hyena we killed," Slow Bear said, making a face. "It was rather strong. White Cloud can make almost anything palatable, but this beast was a bit much for me. But then, it may be that it is an acquired taste, and it could be I simply have not acquired it yet." Slow Bear then shrugged. "Perhaps he will devise a new method to prepare the hyenas that will improve upon their flavor."

"What did they taste like?" Bror inquired.

Slow Bear thought on this for a moment.

"Rather like they smell," Slow Bear finally replied.

"*Ack!*" Black Wolf said with revulsion. "I do hope White Cloud is not planning to serve hyena, whether a new recipe or not, at our nightly sup."

"You have no fear of that," Slow Bear assured Black Wolf. "Willow Woman told White Cloud to dry the hyena meat and see if the dogs will eat it. If so, we can put it aside for any visiting canines."

I looked up at the hyenas as they gently swayed in the breeze, wondering what our dogs would make of their dried flesh. So far, the dogs had had only violent reactions to meeting with live hyenas. What would they make of dead ones?

"In any case," Slow Bear went on, "we will continue to pursue these beasts. There are not many left in this area now."

"We saw some on our trek out to Gray Elk's," Black Wolf said, "but none on our return trip back."

"They may be becoming more wary of men," Puh pointed out. "They are intelligent animals. They may have learned to avoid sites that smell of men. Even baited sites."

"That could be true," Slow Bear said with a nod. "But we must carry on with our mission to eradicate the brutes. It is truly worrisome that they are absolutely fearless when they come up against only a few hunters. We have enough to contend with on our lands without worrying about being driven away from our kills by the hyenas."

* * *

Later that night, Morning Star and I lay contentedly in each other's arms. It had been so good to come back to her and share a bed together. I never slept as well on the trail as I did when in my mate's embrace. It did not matter if we were at home or elsewhere — anywhere I was with her was home to me. We had just made love several times, and even though a slight chill made me momentarily shiver as the sweat evaporated off my skin, I was completely at ease.

However, sleep did not yet come. Thoughts began to roam through my head. Particularly since taking Running Buck and Sky Fire back to their families, I was so very aware of how fragile life was and how precarious our existence in this world. I did not often ponder the fickleness of fate; but why did terrible tragedies visit some and not others? And why did I feel so guilty about my comparative good fortune?

Chapter Twelve

A biting wind blows, and the drifting snows have obliterated many of the familiar landmarks. A group of strangers approaches, bundled up against the cold so that only their eyes and frosted brows are exposed. They are six adults and one child, two of the men dragging a small sled behind them. Each step is hard won against the deep snow and the winter gusts that roar through stands of leafless trees.

The Dream was so vivid that I could still feel the burn of minuscule bits of ice that nipped at the exposed flesh on my face. I could smell the snow and the raw wind, and even the smoky aromas carried by the strangers. But it was not winter in the waking world. In fact, the mild night was disturbed only by the calls of nearby owls and chirps of the crickets. I could not tell who the mysterious people in the Dream were, but they were a tall people. Even though they were dressed in bulky clothing, I could tell that they were of a more slender build than we Old Ones; therefore they must be from one of The People from the East's tribes.

Amidst the backdrop of soft rhythmic breathing from my sleeping family, I listened to the deep hoots of the owls and soon heard a small shriek, most likely a victim of one of those great birds. I had seen evidence that various vermin visited the area around the lodge at night, and I speculated that the huge fir trees that surrounded the site provided excellent roosts from which the owls could survey the ground below for potential prey. I wrapped myself around Morning Star a little tighter and waited for either sleep or morning to come.

* * *

"I know we must leave soon," Black Wolf was saying as we broke our fast.

"The elk and giant deer are already starting to spar," Slow Bear pointed out.

This meant that the rut preliminaries had begun, at least for the larger species of deer.

Willow Woman was sitting very close to Black Wolf, so that their sides touched as they ate. She appeared grim, but she seemed to be trying to work up a smile.

"That means that fall will soon be upon us," Willow Woman stated. "We will have to begin preparations to leave for the Gathering in a moon or so. Little Oak and I will see you there, will we not, Black

Wolf?"

"Of course you will," Black Wolf said, pausing his eating for a moment to grasp her hand and give it a squeeze. "I will go home and help to take in as many deer as we can before I have to leave for the Gathering. Perhaps I can get Fish Hawk to go too — if I can tear him away from my daughter Petal long enough to attend. If not, some of the men from the Village will stop in for me and we will make our way there together."

"I hope the weather will be favorable at that time," Slow Bear remarked. "There will be many people traveling. I have seen signs of an early autumn; besides the rutting bulls and bucks, flocks of migrating birds have been passing overhead, and the leaves are changing color and beginning to drop."

"The ibex bucks were already starting to come down off the mountains when we were returning from Gray Elk's," Puh said. "But of course cold weather comes to the mountains sooner than it does in the valleys and flatlands."

"In that case, I believe we had best get out and harvest as much fruit and greens as soon as we can so we do not lose them to an early frost," Willow Woman suggested. "So many berries are ripe just now, and various mushrooms will be ready for reaping, as well."

"The apples are still as hard as a rock," White Cloud piped up.

These fruits were usually picked after they had ripened and were still rather firm; before then, apples were incredibly sour, and slicing them was almost like cutting into pulpy wood.   But they could still be harvested for a short period even after the weather had turned cold.   Most tubers and other root vegetables like leeks, onions, and parsnips could still be harvested even after the frost, as long as we dug them up before the ground froze.

This conversation was a poignant reminder that we needed to be on our way as soon as possible. I knew that Black Wolf wanted to extend his visit with Willow Woman and Oak for as long as he could, but the time to leave was upon us. We stayed only a few more days — just long enough for Fox to create yet another spear to add to his now growing collection — and then we began the long trek home.

I was grateful to be pulling a much lighter sled on this journey. Puh and I were paired up with our travois sled, and Black Wolf was dragging his much smaller one. Our loads were pared down to the seal hides, and a small number of sacks of dried smoked fish and seal meat, modest amounts of dried berries and rose hips, a few covered clay pots filled with rendered seal oil, and quite a few shell bowls. As before, Bror brought up the rear of our procession.

My sunburned skin had healed significantly while under the cover of the forest at the Fen of Falls, and the marks left on my chest and shoulders from both our treks from the coast and up to Gray Elk's had also faded, leaving me with new skin to be afflicted with wear on the way home. However, we were jubilant to be at last on our way to the family compound. We men would not be able to stay there long, as the fall hunts would soon occupy most of our time. But I was eager to arrive at home and reassure our families that we had not met with some terrible end. After all, we were supposed to be at the coast for only two moons at most, and we had been away for more than three moons. If, like Bror's clan, they had ventured to the shore in search of us, they would have found nothing but a beach swept clean of any evidence of our presence. I speculated that they were probably worried, and might even have supposed that we had perished in the storm.

Morning Star had made this trip from the Fen of Falls once before, and she was excited to recall various things we had seen when we had last passed this way. This time we did not detour to the place of The People's annual Gathering but went straight home. We also did not follow the White River with its rocky banks and violently frothing waters, but cut across the landscape, where our sleds would be easier to transport over the comparatively smoother ground.

Black Wolf sang, as always, but I thought he seemed somewhat downcast, likely due to leaving Willow Woman and Oak for the upcoming moons. But he did remark that he was glad we did not come across any more hyenas on our journey. The only animals we did see were generally viewed from great distances. As soon as they sensed our proximity, either due to Black Wolf's songs, our occasional chatter, or the sound of our footsteps and the rails of our sleds slicing across the soil and turf, they turned and ran away. Even a herd of mam-

-moths, looking small against a backdrop of vast grasslands, peered at us dolefully for only a moment before they too ambled off.

As before, each evening we stopped when we found a place to erect our little trailside huts. Then we would make a fire to fend off the chill of the late-summer nights and many biting mosquitoes at bay. The storm we had experienced on the coast had brought much rain as it swept inland, which in turn had caused a huge increase in the mosquito population. It was likely that these pests would continue to plague us until after the first frost.

Although traveling with family usually meant we were moving at a slower rate, especially since we had to accommodate the smaller steps of younger children, I was pleased with the progress we had made after several days. I thought we would be home in about two more days — possibly only a day and a half. The little ones had actually kept up a good pace, but then I realized that many of our young children were not as small as they once had been. Little Saree, at six winters old, hiked along determinedly, still shuffling her three dolls from hand to hand. Twie had again offered to help her with her dolls, but Saree did not feel that Twie attended to her babies with sufficient care.

"Saree, I will hold them nicely," Twie promised, hands extended to take a doll from her sister.

"I will carry them," Saree insisted. "I have seen how you mistreat them."

I grinned to see that Saree herself held one of her

precious babies tucked under one arm, but I had to admit that if a doll were to have an opinion, it was probably better than being dangled upside-down such as when toted by her older sister.

"Will we take our midday break when we reach the stream?" I asked Puh.

Puh paused before replying as we brought the sled around a bumpy curve in the trail.

"That would make sense," he said. "I believe we will all be ready to have something to eat and drink by then."

"Fox hungry!" Fox chimed in.

"Just like his father," Morning Star said with a laugh, "always hungry!"

"Fox and Puh-Puh hungry!" Fox went on. "Eat soon?"

"Yes, my little Fox," Morning Star said to soothe him, "we will eat soon."

A spectacular sight came into view as we rounded the bend. On one side of the trail the deep green forest sported occasional bursts of colorful autumn foliage, and on the other an expanse of golden grasses waved underneath bright blue skies. Not too far ahead, a sparkling river threaded its way across the landscape.

In the field, a number of giant deer does grazed peacefully, some accompanied by half-grown fawns. A giant deer stag stood at the edge of the harem, solemnly keeping watch over his herd. We would not go near these animals, primarily because the bucks could be extremely volatile during the rut. Granted, it was early in the season yet, but I had been charged by a giant deer stag once before, and it was not something I would care to go through again, especially with my family in close proximity.

The giant deer were some distance off, but I could still see them perk up their ears and look at us. No doubt they had heard Black Wolf's slightly breathless rendition of *The Mighty Hunter* even before they saw us, and they trotted away with their high-stepping gait, occasionally stopping to peer over their shoulders as they went.

The ground began a gradual descent here as the well-worn path worked its way toward the stream. Some creeks and rivers could be a bit murky and have an off taste, but this was a clear, fast-moving stream, and the water had a mercifully untainted flavor. This made it a favorite watering spot for all manner of creatures.

"I will be glad to sit for a little while," Black Wolf said. "My feet are hurting and, like Fox, I am hungry too."

"I think we all will be glad to rest for a while," Bror agreed. "Even the dogs seem to be anticipating a break."

I cast a glance at the dogs. They too were focused on the stream. It had been a warm day, and their panting must have made them excessively thirsty.

As we reached the running body of water, we found that the air was noticeably cooler there. We had to raise our voices somewhat to be heard over the cheerfully burbling creek. Puh and I set the sled to one side and then gratefully stepped out of the harness straps, rubbing the places where the harness had chafed our skin. Black Wolf did the same. Everyone else was also divesting themselves of their burdens. Those with packs promptly opened them to retrieve their water bags and passed them around so that we all could have a drink. I squatted on the bank of the stream and splashed water on my face and neck, thoroughly enjoying the relief it brought. The others followed suit. Even Ru and Morning Star stooped to dot a little cool water on the babies' cheeks.

After slaking our thirst, we left the muddy banks and found a spot on the sun-bleached grass where we could sit in comfort and consume a meal of dried foods. Raena had been relishing a roll in the fragrant grasses, but she suddenly rose to her feet and began to growl.

"What is it, Raena?" I questioned, but her only reply was to bark in alarm.

Ochs too, got up and joined her. They were looking at the edge of the nearby forest, which now erupted with the enormous hairy bodies of mammoths. I had only a moment to be surprised at their presence in that treed place, as mammoths prefer open prairies. They would occasionally eat leaves and bark from trees, but that was not their usual diet.

This was a herd of mammoths, led by a matriarch who was followed by other cows with their infant and juvenile offspring. The mammoths were walking quickly and heading straight for us.

We were trapped against the stream, which was too deep to be forded. Our only option was to withdraw either up- or downstream before they were upon us.

"Let us go," Puh said in a low voice. "No fast moves; do not bother to pack anything up. We must go. Now."

"All right, Puh," I nodded.

"Ochs, come," Puh called his pup, who obediently approached. "Shush," Puh commanded the barking dog, still speaking softly. "Tris, call to Raena. We must keep the dogs quiet."

"But Puh, where will we go?" Ru cried, clutching little Hona to her chest.

"Walk. Walk now, slowly," Puh reiterated, motioning to Ochs to stay with us.

We abandoned our belongings except our spears and backed away from the oncoming mammoths, staying in a tightly packed group. The mammoths kept striding our way, more and more of them. I was surprised that they did not seem as agitated by our presence as they usually were. We were unable to get out of their way quickly enough, and soon we were in their midst as they hurried by with heavy steps that shook the ground. I kept my arms around Morning Star and our children as Raena cowered by me, wild-eyed, with her tail between her legs. I could not blame Raena; we were scarcely less wild-eyed ourselves as the behemoths passed by us on all sides.

The mammoths entered the stream, hardly breaking their stride. Only the smaller ones balked slightly at the water's edge, but the current was not so strong that they could not swim across with their elders. The reason for their odd behavior soon became apparent. Three bull mammoths exited the forest on the heels of the last cows, and they proceeded to chase the herd across the stream, puffing with effort from the pursuit.

I could feel Morning Star trembling with fear as the earth quaked when the bulls thundered by, their eyes shifting only slightly to take us in as they passed, but otherwise they did not deign to acknowledge us. They had something far more urgent on their minds.

The great beasts had finally completed their passing, the last bull bringing up the rear as it endeavored to shake the wreckage of Black Wolf's sled loose from its left hind foot, which had become entangled in the sled's frame and harness. We stood transfixed in place amidst the clouds of swirling dust, stunned by what had happened.

I then realized that I had been holding my breath, and I exhaled with relief that we had survived unharmed. But the well-trampled site where we had been resting was now in shambles. As one, we all began to walk toward what remained of our belongings. Black Wolf had to recover what was left of his sled from the muck at the edge of the stream.

"Oh, the ill luck of it all!" Black Wolf fumed as he sought to salvage what he could. "The brute broke my sled, crushed half its contents and soggied the other half in the water!"

Puh shook his head with sympathy, helping Black Wolf retrieve his things.

"That is indeed unfortunate, old friend," Puh said. "Some of our stores have been ruined as well. Our sled is damaged, but I believe we can fix it without too much trouble."

"Put your things on our sled," I offered to Black Wolf. "There is plenty of space now."

"*Argh*," Bror said, also shaking his head, "we worked so hard to put so much food away for this coming winter, and it has all been for naught. At least the seal hides are still good."

"And much of the seal oil seems to be all right," Ria added. "Only one pot was broken, and even so, we can scoop up most of the fat and transfer it another container." Ria was already seeking something in which to put the spilled oil.

There was not much else to be done other than to locate our various packs, some of which were kicked about, some were trod flat, and see what was still worth keeping. My pack was one of the ones that had been knocked several paces from its original resting spot and then, by the looks of it, fell victim to the weight of a number of massive mammoth feet. My hatchet handle had snapped in two and my water bag was crushed to the point of bursting open, flooding all the nearby items. But luckily, the small leather bags that contained my knapping and hafting implements, fire-making flint and iron oxide stones, and a little dried food, managed to keep their contents dry.

We ate our midday meal as we worked, refilled any water bags that still held liquid, and finally, taking care to step around the numerous piles of mammoth excrement, loaded our repaired travois sled.

"This is indeed a sad vehicle," Puh observed as we lashed the last of our belongings to its much-repaired frame. The sled had appeared a bit battered after the first post-storm fix; after a second repair, it looked downright wretched. Then he added to Black Wolf, "I am so sorry about your sled, my friend. I will help you to build a new one after our return home."

"At least none of us were hurt," Black Wolf said, waving Puh's comment aside. "And at least none of those brutes emptied its bowels on it." Black Wolf stepped back to take in the pitiful fruits of our summer's labors, and he suddenly grimaced. "*Ack! Ack! Ugh!*"

"Have a care where you place your feet, old friend," Puh said quietly to Black Wolf, who had just then extricated his foot from a still-warm pile of mammoth dung.

"The brutes! The *brutes!*" Black Wolf grumbled as he waded into the stream to clean his soiled extremity.

Ria, feeling pity for Black Wolf, brought a stick to him that he could use to loosen the manure from his skin.

"Take this, Black Wolf, dear," Ria said. "It has a nice flat end that will help scrub away the — um — *dirt*."

"Thank you, Ria," Black Wolf said. He smiled down at her, pausing to touch her shoulder in appreciation for her thoughtfulness.

"Sand will help to scrub it off, as well," Morning Star called out to her father.

"Thank you, daughter," Black Wolf said, his voice now tinged with irritation, since the sand was an obvious suggestion. "I can manage from here on in," he muttered. "I may have lost my sense of humor, but I have not lost my wits."

As soon as Black Wolf's feet were cleansed, we were ready to recommence our hike. It was discouraging to know that we were returning with a mere fraction of the goods we had set out with, but I knew we were fortunate to be coming home with our lives.

* * *

The next day, it was late morning when we heard Black Wolf's barking dogs come bounding up the trail to meet us, tails wagging so furiously that their whole bodies swayed with pleasure. Black Wolf greeted each one with enthusiasm, scratching them behind the ears just the way they liked it, and ruffling the fur on their heads. The dogs were quickly followed by Ty and Fish Hawk, who appeared astounded to see us.

"What has happened?" Ty asked as they accompanied us to the family compound. "We feared we might never see you all again! There was a great storm and we were much afraid that it had been worse at the coast."

Great Gran also approached. I noted that her hands were shaking and she had tears in her eyes. I stepped out of the sled's harness and took Gran's small thin, dry hands in my own large meaty ones to steady them. But Gran slipped free of my grasp, and put her arms around me and held me tight.

"Tris," Great Gran began. "I saw a terrible storm in my Dreams and oh, I was so frightened that those red skies portended awful tidings! I am so glad to see you all returned and looking so well. You are all well, are you not?"

Puh was explaining about the storm, attempting to speak of it in a way that would not unduly alarm anyone — if that was possible. Black Wolf then eagerly welcomed his children. I just hugged Gran. She felt so small and brittle in my embrace, tinier even than my petite mate.

"Everything is all right," I assured Gran, patting her back. "The storm was bad, but we were able to shelter in a cave, and afterward, there were some Old Ones who came to our aid. And they had previously found Black Wolf's missing cousins and had restored them to health, so we had to bring them home before we could return. I am so sorry that you all were worried."

Gran wiped her eyes and then looked up at me. She took my hand and squeezed it affectionately while a smile broke across her face.

"It is so good to lay eyes upon you once again!" Gran said. "And to see you looking so big and strong and handsome."

I felt tired and dirty, but my heart melted at her words.

"It is so good to see you as well, Gran," I responded. "I have missed you."

"There was a time," Gran started, "when I thought I had lived too long. I did not want to care for anyone ever again. Almost everyone I had ever known and loved was gone. Everyone who was left was young. They were busy raising their families, and they were so happy. I was old and alone and so consumed by my grief. It was just too much to see all the happiness that I had once experienced with my own cherished mate and children. I knew that there was no cure for what ailed me, and that nothing would ever bring my loved ones back. Every new day just brought more pain when I awoke, and my parents, siblings, my dear Garish, and my sweet children would still be dead. Do you remember those days, when I lived in the house where you and your family now dwell?"

I nodded mutely, feeling tears sting my eyes at Gran's melancholy words.

"I could not live in the only home I had ever known, so your father created that little house for me and then saw to it that I was kept supplied," Gran told me. "Your Puh, one of my many grandsons, he somehow understood. He was there for me whenever I needed him, but neither did he impose himself on me. Your Puh is a man of great wisdom."

"Yes," I agreed. I had often accompanied Puh on his journeys up the hill to bring Great Gran food, refill her water bag, tote armloads of wood, or bring a selection of cured hides to be made into clothing. Most times Gran had barely acknowledged our presence, at least until after I became somewhat older.

"You," Gran reached up and touched my face. "I then began to see you in my Dreams, and I knew that you would grow to be a Dreamer, like me. Then I knew I had to leave my grief behind and help you to learn about your gift. I soon saw that you, like your father, carried within you a great heart, both in spirit and love. I no longer feel as though I have lived too long. Now I am glad that I am still here to behold the fine man you have become."

"I think that I benefit from your being with us more than you do from following my progress from a boy to a man," I said in an attempt to lighten Gran's mood. "You have taught and continue to teach me much that could not be learned elsewhere."

My brother Ty then approached Puh. Ty and Aessa were hand in hand. I noted that Ty seemed rather ill at ease.

"Puh," Ty said, breaking away from Aessa long enough to touch Puh's arm. "We had almost lost hope that everyone would return. You have been away far longer than you ever were when you went to the coast for the summer. And, after the storm, well, I . . . we . . . well, Aessa and I . . . we asked Gran if she thought it would be all right if we were paired."

Ty paused long enough to wait for Puh's reaction. Puh smiled and drew both Ty and Aessa to him, wrapping his arms around them.

"And you are concerned that you should have waited for our return?" Puh asked, still smiling. "If we had not returned, you would have waited for nothing.

And, to be frank, I am not surprised. I have wondered when you and Aessa would ask to be paired. It pleases me greatly to see you both so happy. "

Ty visibly swallowed and his shoulders slumped with relief. Aessa grinned broadly.

"We have made a home for ourselves," Aessa said brightly. "It is small, but we do not need much."

"And it was becoming rather crowded in the main house when everyone was in residence," Ty stated.

I suddenly saw Ty in a new light. He was no longer the little brother who was shyly trying to find his way in life. He was a man. Like Muh's side of the family, Ty was tall for an Old One, and he also had Muh's deep red hair. He was still somewhat slender for his age, but his serious demeanor and full beard gave him an air of maturity that was far beyond his years. Seeing him with Aessa at his side, her fingers entwined with his, gave me a warm feeling. Like Puh, I was so pleased for them.

"I have news as well," Petal said, wearing a smile as she came up to her father.

"Let me guess," Black Wolf grinned. "You and Fish Hawk have decided to get a dog."

"Oh, Da!" Petal exclaimed, her laugh coming out in soft peals, "I will be having a baby this winter."

"I know, I am teasing you," Black Wolf stepped forward to embrace Petal and then, in turn, Fish Hawk. "This is just the first of many. I am sure of it."

Fish Hawk smiled at this. I hoped he was heartened to hear Black Wolf's words after having lost his first mate and child to a miscarriage. But I felt he had little to fear. Petal was not only well suited for creating and maintaining a happy household, but for bearing children.

Little Fawn now joined us, flanked by her small girls; Swift River and Hawk ran up panting behind them. Little Fawn seemed to purposely ignore Black Wolf, but she immediately went to Morning Star and placed her arms around her.

"I have hardly slept of late," Little Fawn said with tears running freely down her face. "I have been so worried for you all."

Little Fawn reached for little Raven and took her from Morning Star, kissing the baby's cheek. Raven seemed unsure about this interaction with a person she scarcely remembered, if at all, but she bore up good-naturedly. Little Fawn had hugs and kisses for me, Fox, and Pony, as well. Fox and Pony were both excited to see their grandmother and were happy to jabber at her about our adventures.

The full story of our journey came out as we all settled around the hearth, eating from our hard-won stores and sipping water from gourd cups. The unpacking would keep until later. There was much news to impart. Black Wolf may have felt Little Fawn's snub, but he seemed gratified to receive the adoring attentions of his sons, who had grown noticeably taller and filled out a bit more over the summer. Both boys sat on either side of him and listened to their father's descriptions of our trials with rapt attention. No one seemed to mind that we had returned from the shore with so little to show for our time away from home.

* * *

The air had a definite chill to it that evening, and the wind began to grow in strength until it shook the trees. I stood at the entrance of our little hillside home with Raena at my side. We looked out at the setting sun, a deep blazing red against a purple sky. I blew out a breath and saw that it created a frosty little cloud. A few yellowed leaves fluttered to the ground nearby, settling into place with little rustling piffs. Fall was here. The first stars were just beginning to sparkle in the nighttime sky as I withdrew into our home, securing the door flap behind me.

It was good to be back. Morning Star had coaxed flames to life within the fireplace and lighted a lamp to help chase away the shadows. The children were tired from the long trek and had already been put to bed. I peeked at them as they dozed contentedly, three snug little bodies in a row. Morning Star and I would soon be in our bed as well.

This was my favorite time of day. The children were safe and warm, our cozy abode was closed up for the night with Raena curled up by the doorway, and Morning Star and I finally had time to ourselves. Even after our years together, I still had not gotten over the novelty of watching her undress. She then began to loosen her braids and comb through her hair with her fingers. I knelt by Morning Star's side, running my hands through her smooth black hair. Her silky tresses slipped through my fingers as easily as trickling water. Morning Star looked up and smiled at me.

"I love you, my sweet," I told her, pausing to tenderly stroke her cheek.

"As I love you," Morning Star returned.

She was and had always been the only woman to dwell in my heart. I drew Morning Star to me and kissed her as we lay down together.

Later that night, just as I was drifting off to sleep, I had a moment in which to reflect that even though our attempts to renew our depleted stores had been nearly futile, I still had much for which to be grateful.

* * *

It is evening and we are gathered around a large fire, watching the flames reach up toward the starry nighttime sky, glowing embers floating up on the hot smoke. The firelight reveals that we are not standing by our outdoor hearth, but rather on a snow-covered meadow. The darkness hides the visages of my companions, but I feel that everyone is solemn. Not Gran, though. I feel that Gran is smiling . . . she is light!

Author's Note

As always, I include the obligatory disclaimer that all characters depicted in this novel are completely fictional. Any resemblance to persons either living or dead is coincidental.

The title of this installment *The Blood-Red Skies* is taken from an actual event in history. Approximately 40,000 years ago, the Campanian Ignimbrite super eruption occurred in what is now Italy. This was one of the most cataclysmic events known to have taken place in Europe in the last 200,000 years. It was thought to have lasted several days and caused great destruction. Immense amounts of sulfur-dioxide were spewed into the stratosphere and it is believed to have created an ash plume that could have been more than 40 miles high. Life may have been completely wiped out in a 60+ mile radius of the eruption and ash deposits are found more than 1500 miles away from point of origin.

There has been much discussion on how human life was affected and how long it may have taken for both the climate and the natural world to recover. It has been speculated that the eruption may have contributed to the demise of the Neanderthal. However, it was unlikely that the Neanderthal and Cro-Magnon in Western Europe would have been significantly affected. Due to the ash content in the atmosphere, skies would have been stained in particularly dramatic colors at sunrise and sunset. Additionally, the temperatures would have dropped by a few degrees for a period of years, but they would not have suffered the dire fates of those who lived in close proximity or those who lived downwind to the Campanian Ignimbrite eruption.

Other aspects of this tale are also taken from real life. Many years ago, I found myself in much the same predicament as Tris when he rescued Black Wolf from the mire. I was raised in a place not so different from where my characters summered at the coast, and there was a brackish pond near my home that was connected to a large bay at high tide. However, during one low tide, I was walking with a relative near the banks of this pond, when my companion saw something lying in the muck he deemed worth investigating. Like Black Wolf, within seconds, he was up to his waist. Fortunately, I could stand on comparatively solid ground and pull him out. The suction was so great that it sucked his boots off his feet. It was only after that I found out that it was a "bottomless pond" and historically, farmers had been losing cows to it for hundreds of years. That interesting bit of information was seemingly proved out later, when we found a bovine vertebra washed up on those same muddy flats.

Hurricanes have also impacted my life over the years. The storm in this novel may have seemed extreme, but potentially, hurricanes can be far worse. The storm described is meant to portray a moderate, fast-moving hurricane.

Additionally, based on finds from archaeological digs, we now know that Neanderthals who lived by the coast or seasonally foraged for food near the ocean were found to have harvested various shellfish, fish, seals, and even porpoises, and decorated themselves with the shells they found there, as described in the novel.

In this volume, Cave hyenas are introduced to the story for the first time. I have depicted them (left) to be shaggier than their contemporaries, with the idea that many Ice Age era animals (such as the Woolly Rhinoceros and the Woolly Mammoth) had a lot more fur than similar modern species. Cave hyenas were big animals; females were the largest of their species and are thought to have weighed as much as 225 pounds. They had powerful jaws and digestive juices, and were capable of consuming and digesting entire animals. If they were like the hyenas which we are familiar with, they would have lived in large matriarchal packs and would be extremely intelligent, impressively versatile predators and scavengers.

This book is dedicated to my father, who – more than anyone else – has made me the person I am today. He has always been my mentor. Words cannot express the depth of my gratitude for his careful tutoring throughout my childhood and the moral support and teachings that continue to present day.

The next book in this saga *The Dreamer VI ~ The Outsiders* is due to be published in the summer of 2021. Thank you for your readership!

With warmest regards;
E. A. Meigs

Index of European Ice Age Animals

Antelope (Saiga Antelope) These small antelope (24 to 36 inches tall at the shoulder weighing approximately 80 to 140 pounds) ranged over a good part of the northern hemisphere. They are exceptional in appearance due to their unusual muzzles, which feature a long, flexible snout that looks much like a truncated elephant's nose.

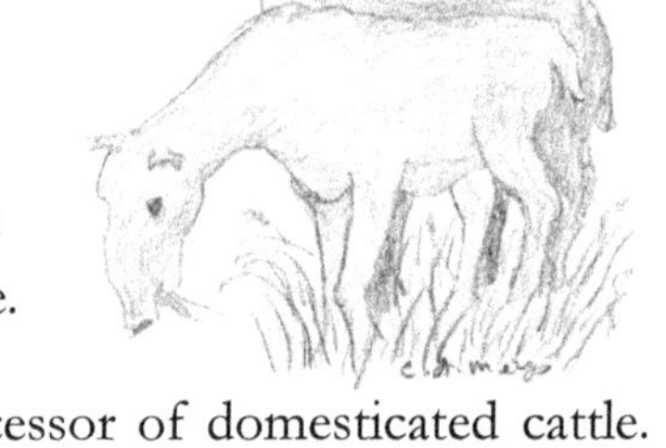

Aurochs (Extinct) Predecessor of domesticated cattle. Size varied between 61 to 71 inches at the shoulder, with weights of 1500 to 3300 pounds. Their horns could reach up to 31 inches in length. Sometimes aurochs is spelled "auroch", but from

my readings, I am lead to believe that but the "s" is often included even when the animal is referred to in singular form because it is an alternative form of spelling "ox" and isn't intended to indicate plurality.

Boar Wild boars are the plows of the animal world. They are built for digging. Their heads and massive

shoulders make up a good part of their bodies and their large, sharp tusks, which continue to grow throughout the life of the animal, are very effective at turning over soil. The largest adult male boars can reach weights of nearly 800 pounds and attain a shoulder height of 49 inches. Sows (females) are much smaller and they lack the mane and thick shoulder/back "shield" of the boars. Their tusks are also of a more modest size. The coloring of their coats varies from anything between white and black, but most tend to run towards darker shades.

Brown Bear
(Eurasian Brown Bear) Although this bear is called a "brown bear" its color can range from black to a tawny light brown. Males average 550 to 650 pounds but very large specimens can exceed

1000 pounds. Females weigh 330 to 550 pounds. During pre-history, the brown bear did consume some plant matter, but it was generally carnivorous.

Cave Bear (Extinct) This was a very large, stout bear. The average male weighed in at 880 to 1100 pounds. Females averaged a little over half that (495 to 550 pounds). Despite their size, bone analysis and other indicators suggest that cave bears were primarily herbivores.

Cave Lion (Extinct) (European Cave Lion) These efficient feline predators were some of the largest known cats in animal history. Based on skeletal

remains, it is speculated that the males may have reached 11 ½ feet in length from nose to tip of the tail, and weighed over 880 pounds.

Chamois A medium-sized goat/antelope. They are 28-31 inches tall at the shoulder and range in weight from 55-132 pounds. Besides being a fine source of meat, their hides were used to make garments.

Crow (Carrion Crow) A large black bird, approximately 18 to 21 inches in length with a large, heavy beak that is well adapted to catching and eating small prey such as mice, frogs, insects, etc., and scavenging off the kills of other animals.

Elk (Eurasian Elk) ("moose" in North America) A medium-sized elk/moose, now extinct in many parts of Europe. They average from just over 600 to just over 1000 pounds, with shoulder heights at 5.6 - 6.9 feet.

Fallow Deer A medium-sized deer, about 30 to 37 inches at shoulder height and weighing 66 pounds (small doe) to 220 pounds (large buck), although unusually large bucks may tip the scales at 330 pounds. Their winter coats are brown, but they are

freckled with white dots on their backs and sides during the summer.

Giant Deer (extinct) (Irish Elk) The giant deer was one of the largest deer ever to walk the earth. Commonly, it has mistakenly been called an Irish elk, although it was neither exclusive to Ireland nor an elk.

This huge deer averaged nearly 7 feet in height at the shoulder and carried antlers with a spread that could span 12 feet. They are estimated to have weighed nearly 1200 to just over 1300 pounds but larger individuals could have reached upwards of 1500 pounds.

Horse The Eurasian Ice Age horse came in many different varieties.

They were more than likely the size of modern ponies and appeared in all colors, spots and stripes. They may have resembled the Przewalski's horse that still exist today or the now-extinct Tarpan horse.

Ibex (Alpine Ibex) A moderate-sized, dun-colored mountain goat. The bucks' horns sometimes reach 39 inches in length. The does' horns may grow to a length of nearly 14 inches. Similarly, bucks achieve a much larger body size (35 to 40 inches at the withers and weighing from 150 to over 250 pounds) than the does (29 to 33 inches at the withers and 37 to just over 70 pounds).

Lynx (Eurasian Lynx) The biggest of all species of lynx. Approximately 24 to 30 inches at the shoulder, and including its short tail, it may be 31 to 51 inches in body length.   The largest males weighed nearly 100 pounds, but the typical lynx will run between 18 (very small female)  and 66 pounds (good-sized male).

Marten   (European Pine Marten) A small, weasel-like animal with dark brown fur, often with blond markings or a blond bib on its chest.  At a little less than 3 ½ pounds and about 21 inches in length, the marten was hunted for its beautiful, silky fur.

Mink (European Mink) A small mink,

even the largest is just under 20 inches in length and only about 1¾ pounds. They have been prized for their dense, luxurious winter coats.

Porcupine (Old World Porcupine) This rodent wears an impressive coat of quills, some of which may be up to 14 inches in length (Crested Porcupine). These species of porcupines come in a variety of sizes: the smallest adults run from 11inches to 34 inches long, and may weigh between 3.3 to 60 pounds.

Red Deer (European Red Deer) Another very large species of deer. The buck weighs in at 350 to 550 pounds (48 inches at the shoulder) and does run 260 to 370 pounds (45 inches at the shoulder). These deer, unsurprisingly, are known for their

reddish coats. During autumn, the males often have a short mane on the backs of their necks.

Red Fox The biggest of the fox species, the adult ranges from 14 to 20 inches tall at the shoulder and weigh from 5 to nearly 40 pounds. These animals were often harvested for their fine fur.

Reindeer (Also known as caribou) This important game animal consists of several different subspecies and varied in size from 120 to 550 pounds. Color varied as well, but all subspecies shared many of the same basic characteristics, such as a fairly

impressive set of antlers (in most reindeer, both the bucks and the does grow antlers) and a two-layered coat of fur, featuring a woolly undercoat that thickens dramatically each winter and an overcoat of longer, coarse, hollow hairs.

Roe Deer (Western Roe Deer) This small deer averages just over two feet to two feet, 6 inches at the withers, and a mere 33 to 77 pounds. Nonetheless, they were an important source of meat for prehistoric humans.

Sheep The actual breed(s) of ancient sheep that roamed Ice-Age Europe are unknown, but it is recognized that sheep were hunted and eaten by early man. It is possible that the Mouflon (shown in image) is the modern day link to prehistoric sheep. The Mouflon have a shoulder height of less than 3 feet and weigh from 75 to 110 pounds.

Snow Leopard This beautiful cat is well adapted to life in a cold, mountainous habitat. It has a stout build and long, dense fur that varies in color from white to pale gray, with dark gray to black spotted markings. It is about 24 inches at the shoulder with a weight of 60 to 120  pounds, although larger males have been noted at 165 pounds. Their fur was considered to be very desirable and they have long been hunted for their pelts.

Vulture (Eurasian Griffin Vulture) This large scavenging bird may have a wingspan of over 9 feet and weigh as much as 33 pounds, although most individuals range from 14 to 25 pounds. It is known that early men consumed the meat of vultures.

Wisent (European Bison) An impressive animal, the wisent is the heaviest land animal that still resides in modern day Europe. Fully grown specimens range from 5 to 6 ½ feet at the shoulder and weigh 660 (small female) to

more than 2000 pounds (large male). The wisent was an important source of food and hides for prehistoric humans.

Wolf (Eurasian Wolf) These are the largest of the European or Asian wolves. Their sizes vary greatly from 70 to 212 pounds. Although their coats could be black, white, or even reddish, by far the

most common color was a grey/buff and white combination of medium length, dense fur.

Wood Grouse (Western Capercaillie) This Eurasian bird is the largest of the grouse species, weighing as much as 15 pounds. The cocks have an average weight of 9 pounds and a wingspan of 36 to 48 inches. The hen is considerably more modest in size, with a weight of

approximately 4 pounds and a wingspan of 28 inches.

 Woolly Mammoth (Extinct) This large mammal lived in Eurasia and North America, and was similar in size to today's African Elephants, but with considerably longer tusks, a shorter tail, and much smaller

ears. The males of this huge species could attain heights of up to 11 feet at the withers and weigh over 12,000 pounds. Females were somewhat smaller, although still impressive in size at up to 9½ feet at the shoulder and weights up to nearly 9000 pounds. Their hairy hides came in a wide range of colors that could be anything from blond to quite dark. They were protected from the extreme Ice Age weather conditions by a double fur coat that consisted of a short, dense, woolly undercoat and strands of long outer guard hairs.

Woolly Rhinoceros (Extinct) Looking much like a modern rhinoceros in  a heavy fur coat, the woolly rhinoceros sported two horns on its long snout and carried its thick body on short, stout legs. This animal averaged about 4000 to 6000 pounds, with a shoulder height of about 6½ feet. The larger front horn that grew from the woolly rhinoceros' nose could reach lengths of 24 inches.

About the Author
E.A. Meigs

I was raised on Cape Cod (Brewster, Massachusetts, USA) at a time when the Cape was still a rural area made up of woodlands, marshes, beaches, streams, and ponds. There, my life was divided between the land and sea. My father was a commercial fisherman, backyard boat builder, and an outdoorsman; so I had an early introduction to boats, working in the commercial fishing industry and spending lots of time in the local fields and forests. When I wasn't on a boat or roaming the great outdoors, chances are I was reading or writing. I have been a compulsive writer literally since I could first put words on paper, producing my first full length novel at ten years old. Even at that age, my goal in life was to someday find a way to combine my love of nature, the outdoors, and writing.

After raising a family and embarking on a long and varied career that included many years working on and around boats and in the commercial fishing industry; a stint with Florida Fish & Wildlife in a small field office; and other jobs that actually allowed me to use my writing skills, I awoke one day with *The Dreamer* in my head. I began writing the novel with the intention of producing just one book, but as the story progressed it became apparent that the plot would require much more than one volume to tell the tale.

I have two wonderful adult daughters and nine delightful grandchildren. I am an avid camper and I strive to get out hiking as often as possible, daily, when my schedule allows.